MW01613049

The Road to Dendura

Book One of the Creed Griffon Series

Best Wishes

C. L. Lewis

C. L. Lewis

First published by Dog Ear Publishing
4010 W. 86th Street, Ste H
Indianapolis, IN 46268
www.dogearpublishing.net

dog ear
PUBLISHING

ISBN: 978-160844-787-9

This book is printed on acid-free paper.

Printed in the United States of America

Count Yourself Warned

In the shadows they lurk fueled by intentions most despicable. Shape shifting demons wandering to and fro seeking those children whom they may, in their terms, 'collect.' Fueled by the pinions of dark magic these remorseless henchmen relentlessly hunt for the missing Apprentice. For unbeknownst to that child, he or she holds the key to life and death...all that is, all that was... Will you be next? The question is not will, but when. No child is overlooked. How will you defend yourself against their evil onslaught...And who would believe you if you could? Don't bother to look around. Of course, they're watching you...even now as you read this. It's just a matter of time. And should you be selected, they most certainly will not renounce their claim upon you. More importantly, what happens to you if they discover you're not the one they so desperately hope to find?

The date is January 9th, nearby; Pemberton Boarding School has ended their class session for the day. The victim, 12-year-old Fiona Talbert, goes about her business completely unaware she has been chosen...and that shortly, she will enter into a realm seen only in her nightmares. Bypassing a friend's invitation to get a bite to eat, she grabs her backpack and heads for the dormitories. The walk across campus is a cold and lonely one. However, it is one she's made many times before. She must traverse a small wooded area prior to arriving at her destination. Her only warning is that of her gut instinct screaming something isn't quite right. She detects an unshakable atmosphere of death. And in broad daylight before she can cry for help she is swarmed by the most hair raising creatures unimaginable... There are no witnesses and Fiona is not seen or heard from thereafter.

It is March 15th, approximately three months after the disappearance of Ms. Talbert. Within an instant 12-year-old Timothy Holderman has disappeared from the Pemberton Boarding School recreational grounds. Eye witnesses say he hit a foul ball into the woods and went to find it. After fifteen minutes or so, his friends go in after him. They spend roughly the next ten minutes calling his name thinking he's playing some sort of joke. He is nowhere to be seen. Police were called in yet again. Reports read, "The only thing left of Mr. Holderman was his baseball. No signs of a struggle. No indications of foul play detected. School security cameras reveal absolutely nothing. No intruders were observed. We may be witnessing the hands of a serial killer at work." Timothy has not been seen or heard from since.

CHAPTER ONE

Apples are Food, Not Weapons

J f I'd only seen the apple, it wouldn't have been so bad. I mean, how bad can it be to get hit by a girl? And, of course, Isabelle Polanski was all girl. Not only that, she was all bully! Unfortunately for me, she was also very popular. "I didn't even know she was behind us!" I yelled in exasperation. "Someone called my name; I turned, flying fruit, and BAM!!!" My eye received the full brunt of the fatal fastpitch! I found myself sitting on the floor surrounded by the scattered contents of my backpack.

As Isabelle was leaving, she hollered, "Have a nice summer, losers!" Her voice echoed through the 400-year-old hallways. For my sake, I was glad they were deserted.

"Hey Creed, you okay?" asked Burton. Burton Woods had been my classmate, neighbor, and best friend since kindergarten. And, of course, he'd been with me through most of my humiliating encounters with Isabelle, and a few others that landed me in the headmaster's office. "C'mon," he said offering me his hand for help up.

"I swear that girl has a mean wind-up! She definitely doesn't throw like a girl!"

"I'd like to throw her!" I said rubbing my eye."

"No one understands that better than me, Creed. But that probably wouldn't be the best idea right now."

"I know I know! I can't fight with her or anyone else for that matter… If I get in trouble one more time… And of course it doesn't matter if it's my fault or not! Guess who gets blamed? Why does Polanski hate me so much?"

Burton's brow creased as though his mind was churning deep thoughts. "Maybe it's because you super-glued her locker shut? Or maybe it's because you set her cell phone alarm to go off in Ms. Stillwell's Latin class? Then there was that time we had the tornado drill and you...." He stopped mid sentence. "I still can't believe you and her went to the Sadie Hawkins dance together!"

"It was our punishment for playing pranks on each other as *'ordered'* by Coach Dixon! You know that!" I snapped. Like any best friend he just liked to rib me about such things. What he didn't know was that she'd ditched me that night. When we'd arrived at the dance it was pretty awkward. We talked a little bit about school and stuff. She seemed almost nice. Even I thought we were making progress. But somehow she ended up spending the rest of the evening with her friends clear on the other side of the building. The corsage my mother made me buy got closer to her than I did. We didn't even so much as drink punch together. The next day at school, she ignored me and went back to being her same ole stuck up self! Oh well. Good riddance! Regardless, I could never bring myself to tell him the embarrassing truth.

"Okay, okay," I roared, "whose side are you on anyway? I'm no innocent bystander. I get it! The point is she always starts stuff and you know that! You don't expect us to just keep taking it, do you?"

"No, I'm sure you'll find another creative way to get back at her. C'mon, it's our last day of school! Save it for next semester. At least that way she'll probably have forgotten all about it."

I had to admit, Isabelle and I did have a checkered past, in part because of our significantly different social standings. Unlike me, most of the students attending Devonshire came from elite families from all over the world. It was a highly accredited institution which resided in the middle of nowhere. Trust me, "nowhere" was far from paradise. As a matter of fact, the school was located on the outskirts of a small conservative coastal community. Whoever heard of Sweetwater, Massachusetts anyway?

Unfortunately, the local area remained unscathed by the wonders of modern technology. It was a place where attendants still pumped gas, milk was delivered to porches, and residents kept their front doors unlocked. "Quaint" per my mother's description, "a genuine slice of the good life." On the other hand, most students felt it was a fate worse than death, complete with lack of fast food, mall, or movie theater. Despite all the negative propaganda, it really wasn't all that bad. I suppose if you weren't born with a silver spoon in your mouth, you could find plenty of stuff to do. You just have to be a little creative.

Case and point; Burt and I conveniently discovered where our librarian, Mrs. Murtaugh, hid the teacher's computer pass codes. I've successfully logged in using Professor Stillwell's account quite a number of times. And I can proudly say she's been reprimanded for looking up everything from monster trucks, to over-forties dating web sites. Of course I couldn't resist putting her on the email and mailing lists, too. For extra added humiliation all advertisements, catalogs, and literature are sent directly to the school under *her* name. I know she's raised quite a few eyebrows particularly in Devonshire's postal department. I assume by now, she's received enough junk mail to fill a few hard drives and a dump truck! But before you jump to any conclusions, she was due a little embarrassment. It's a small price to pay for siding with Shelby Corrigan and telling me I'd never amount to anything in front of the entire class. At least this way I get a good laugh out of the deal.

As predicted Stillwell was questioned about her unusual web surfing activities. She emphatically denied everything. Not too many people believed her side of the story, especially Mrs. Murtaugh. Since the computer lab resides within her library domain, she's in charge of that, too. Word has it that sweet little old Mrs. Murtaugh publicly and enthusiastically vented her disgust for our Latin teacher's distasteful actions. According to eye witnesses, the two really had it out! Stillwell was told not to use the school's computers for personal gain or whimsical fancies. The solution? The pass codes were changed... So the next time we used her code, we looked up buck skinning, samba dancing, and midget wrestling. Now the two ladies can barely look at each other. Students and faculty have been buzzing about it all year. Anyway, Burt and me were planning on putting Stillwell in a lonely hearts ad in the local paper but decided to lay low until things cooled down a bit. It may be a while.

Setting aside mischievous pastimes, the school in and of itself is considered a beloved landmark discretely nestled among a forest of trees at the end of a long and winding dirt road. Due to its location, if you didn't know any better, you might accidentally drive right past it. The prestigious Devonshire Prepatory is certainly a curiosity amidst the backdrop of a sleepy little seaside village. The grandeur of the place is highly misleading filling accidental passersby with exciting thoughts of mystery and intrigue... When in reality, it is simply a boarding school. Trust me, not much excitement in that respect.

With that being said, Devonshire is a massive stone estate complete with multiple outbuildings that branch out from each side of the main house in semi-circle fashion. A 300-acre parcel accompanies the brick fortress. The school is also furnished with dirt streets, a post office, and private medical facility. It could certainly qualify as its own little township. The structures located farther away from the main edifices become less pretentious eventually dotting the grounds with authentic old-style English cottages. They add an air of friendliness and warmth to the over-exaggerated surroundings.

Originally, the property served as the home of Sir Wingate Devonshire, a wealthy aristocrat and respected doctor. He'd fashioned the house after an extravagant Elizabethan castle for his fiancé. No one quite knows the reason why, but they never married. There are rumors that he murdered her for unnamed indiscretions, but no facts or body ever surfaced to back it up. Eventually, he converted a small portion of the castle into medical offices and buried himself in his work. It is said that years later, he died somewhere within its walls. Sadly, he had no family. His will deemed that everything was to be donated for the purpose of higher education, i.e. Devonshire Preparatory. The school's history is a long and varied one. Yet it still continues to be just what Sir Wingate desired it to be, a private school. Call it what you like it's just another fancy place for rich parents to dump off their kids...And students like Isabelle knew I didn't fit into their upper-class world. I suspected that's why she resumed her role of 'arch nemesis' after the dance was over.

To make matters worse, everyone knows I'm attending because of charity. Not having a lot of money or things didn't bother me. From what I'd seen, stuff like that only served to cloud the values and common sense of those who did. But I would've rather everyone not know *my* financial status. It gets tiring always having people believe they're better than you because their bank accounts are bigger.

What respect I did earn was through influential connections. My mother is the school's psychologist and noteworthy in her own right. I know what you're thinking…but she's just a normal mom to me. When she's not counseling spoiled brats *that think they've got problems*…she teaches an introductory psychology course for college credits. Sorry to say, they don't pay professors enough to cover the cost of single parenting and boarding school. So if it weren't for the scholarship it wasn't likely I could afford to attend. Things could be worse, as in Burt's predicament. His mom works in the dining facility. He's been called everything from lunch lady to hairnet! It isn't pretty.

"Ding dong the witch is gone the wicked witch is gone…Well at least for a while that is…" Burt stood watching me pick up the strewn contents of my backpack. "I'm glad summer vacation is here!" I wholeheartedly agreed.

"I think we both need a break from this place. What are you going to do during the time off?"

"Not sure," he declared… The most exciting thing Burt had ever done was drive his mom's truck around the parking lot of Pack 'n Go. Sorry to say, my travels hadn't even led me that far.

"What about you? Any big yachting plans?" I restrained my laughter knowing full well what he meant. It was customary for wealthy students to have a posh international family vacation in store for them. Then there were those kids whose parents skillfully neglected to include them in their travels. They ended up staying in the dormitories or taking off on their own adventures until the start of the next school session. Burt and I weren't afforded such luxuries. But to tell the truth, it worked out in our favor. We did live on campus… all year round as a matter of fact. However, we didn't get to live in the dorms like normal students. Devonshire set aside a modest alcove of those English cottages for some of the more financially challenged families it employed. Guess who fell into that category? You guessed it! Aside from the economic stigma, our situation did have its perks. We lived so close to the school that it gave Burt and I full run of the place while everyone else was gone for the summer. We knew every nook, cranny, and loose floorboard by heart. There wasn't a hallway, wing, or maintenance closet we hadn't explored.

As a matter of fact, the maintenance closet was how we befriended the school custodian, Mr. O'Keefe. Although the grounds were invariably equipped with many storage facilities, we just happened to stumble across the very one he'd locked himself inside of. We tried stifling our laughter as we opened the door. "Okay lads," he'd said in embarrassment, "even Houdini had assistants." Burt and I broke out into such contagious laughter that he joined in! Before that time, he'd pretty much kept to himself. But following his little misfortune, he took quite a shine to us. Especially after we'd promised not to breathe a word about it to anyone.

O'Keefe is best described as a tall Irish man, of stout build, and friendly apple cheeks. His disposition is warm. But I must admit; he can be a little off at times... in a strange and quirky sort of way...as if something upstairs is blissfully and purposefully not coloring in the lines. He's not mean or cruel. He can be stern, but that's what it takes to work around a lot of kids. His smile is quite genuine. And in all honesty, it's usually hidden behind a big bushy mustache that swirls around in a precise curl at each end. Frankly, I don't want to give the wrong impression. He's kind hearted, however not one you'd want to cross if you get my drift.

Devonshire employs him as Chief Custodian, a job he inherited from his father and one he's very proud of. No one is quite sure of his age. Curiously though, at times he doesn't appear old enough to carry such a big responsibility. It's not that he can't handle his duties; on the contrary, he exceeds expectations. He makes sure the school and grounds are kept in tip-top shape. Even the shrubberies are cut and sculpted to perfection. (Well all except for that one year when he decided to prune the bushes in the shapes of various fruits.) Still, if there's a plumbing or structural emergency he can be counted on for solid solutions. I can't quite put my finger on what it is about him. I guess I would've expected someone who didn't ride a motorcycle, enjoy knitting, or chase ground squirrels for fun…Not that any of those things are bad…*And yeah, you read that last one correctly.* I never could understand his fascination with the little critters. You'd have to see it to believe it, but he actually catches them with his bare hands! Mind you he never hurts them. He always releases them unharmed, giggling and chuckling as they bolt for freedom. I haven't yet built up the courage to ask him why he does it…

In any case, the students have always given him a fearful sort of respect even more so than the teachers. I suspect the rumor going around didn't help his public image much either. One of the pupils claimed they saw him talking to a tree. Of course nothing could be farther from the truth! Sure he's a bit eccentric at times, maybe even a little untamed…But he's not crazy! Whatever the reason, kids parted like the Red Sea when Mr. O'Keefe walked on by. Had they only given him the time of day, they would've discovered he was very intelligent and knew a lot more about the world than just cleaning up and fixing things. At any rate, he was never seen without his suspenders or hounds-tooth scally cap. The hat only served to highlight the twinkle of mischief in his eyes, while the suspenders he said were to "accent me fancy work duds."

As for my summer plans? I didn't need anything grandiose. Nevertheless that didn't stop my mom's admirable intentions. Last year she tried surprising me with a trip to astronaut camp. I think she got a little tired of hearing about the exotic adventures embarked upon by my peers. She meant well, but our car ended up breaking down, and of course my camp money went toward repairing it. As usual, I spent that summer earning extra cash by fixing lawnmowers and doing odd jobs for Mr. O'Keefe. But mostly, I would tag along with Burt on one of his treasure hunt expeditions. Two years ago, he'd received a metal detector for his tenth birthday. He'd been hooked on finding treasure ever since. His room lay cluttered with prized odds and ends he'd unearthed. Everyone knew what Burton's summer agenda would consist of…and hopefully mine, too.

Burt handed me one of the last littered remnants of binder paper. "Maybe we can use the metal detector in Tulane Creek," he offered. "The water has gone down quite a bit. We can practically walk our way across…

"How 'bout I teach ya to swim this year?"

"Yeah right. First of all it's a '*riverrrr*' not a creek… And to answer your question, I'll dive into that water when our dear Professor Stillwell smiles!" Of course that was the equivalent to an ice cube's chance in a frying pan. Everyone knew that tight-haired bitty smiled for no one!

"C'mon Creed! We're sure to find something this time! I promise nothing bad is gonna happen!" To date, the banks of Tulane River had only given up twenty-nine cents and wasn't worth the trauma. The truth of the matter is I have a slight aversion to water. Okay, a somewhat intense anxiety where water is concerned… I suppose it's better to call things what they are. Only Burt and, of course, my mother know this embarrassing piece of trivia. I can do a lot of the basics when it involves water but I have to admit, the thought of actually submerging myself under the stuff gives me nightmares. You get the picture.

In all sincerity, I don't know what my problem is. Simply, that something happens when I'm in it. The water always seems to have more control than me. Mind you I'm no wuss or anything. I've tried learning how to swim on more than one occasion. But each time it ends the same way. And since I wasn't planning on becoming an Olympic swimmer, I'd resolved to spend the rest of my life without possessing that particular skill. Yep! Absolutely fine by me! My mom's professional diagnosis? …Hydrophobia, fear of water. She says, "Not to worry. Everyone has at least one fear, strange little quirks if you will, hidden within our psychological makeup. F.E.A.R. is False Evidence Appearing Real, Creed…" Regardless of the cause, or the scholarly words that define it; I wasn't about to step foot in that river or learn how to swim…EVER!

"Okay, so if you don't want to go to the '*creeeek*,' maybe we can treasure hunt in the woods? Fair?"

"Fair" I agreed.

I happened to be very thankful for such a loyal friend. They didn't come easy in a place like Devonshire, where money dictated popularity. And if the truth be known, we're stronger than friends and more like brothers. Probably because we have so much in common. For starters, neither of us have a dad. Burton's left when he was just three years old. I only knew bits and pieces, but I got the feeling that they were glad he was gone. Mine died before I ever got a chance to know him. He was Devonshire's prized history professor. His work and theories gained quite a bit of recognition for the school. According to my mother, he was one of the brightest and most innovative minds his field had ever seen. History was his passion. He was proud to be a part of Devonshire's deep-rooted traditions, and they were proud to have him on staff.

Like my father, the school instructors were the "who's who" in their respected fields. And although they never mentioned it, many of the professors had revered him. I knew they expected me to live up to his exceptional potential. Regardless, each year offered another opportunity to show just how mediocre I was. After he died, I was awarded a full scholarship in his honor. Beyond that, anytime I tried to ask more about him, my mom would simply get depressed. In fact, I knew very little of him. Except that they were deeply in love… and they loved me immensely. If I would press her for too much more, she would come to the point of tears. In time, it became easier to just not ask anymore.

I grabbed my backpack and brushed off my school uniform. Something small and shiny caught my eye. "Hey, what's that?" asked Burton crouching down beside me. I gave him a crooked grin.

"It looks like our summer won't be so boring after all." There, neatly resting on the marble flooring was Isabelle Polanski's cell phone. I casually tucked it in my pocket. "I think the first thing I'll do to start this summer is put some ice on my eye. Then, maybe we can make a few calls to China." We laughed all the way down the winding staircase. The clip clop of our footsteps echoed in unison. Eventually, we would hit the dirt road that led to Devonshire assisted housing. The mildly renovated cottages were reminiscent of an old world English style village with thatched roofs, timber flooring, and lofts. It wasn't a palatial mansion on the Riviera, but it was warm and cozy…and I liked it there.

CHAPTER TWO
She's Lying

J could tell by the darkening sky and scattered splashes of rain that we were in for a strong storm. Hurricanes, tornadoes, or thunderstorms were nothing uncommon for us. Two years ago, a violent storm destroyed part of Tremington Hall. Normally, I consider my home a safe place. But I can still remember that night and just how bad the winds rattled the windows in our humble cottage. I also recall looking through those very casements watching debris and sedentary items suddenly take flight! Every once in a while I hear them make that same foreboding sound…clitter, clatter, shake, shake, if I slam our door too hard or there's a sudden 'thud.' It's an unpleasant reminder of how helpless the human condition is in such matters. Ever since then, I've been leery when I see the clouds roll in or the wind and rain come alive.

"Hey isn't that Professor Loremont?" exclaimed Burton. "Yeah, I'm right. That is him! I recognize the tweed blazer with leather elbow patches from here! For a man, he's a bit of a clothes horse. What do you suppose he's up to?"

"I'm not sure," I said hesitantly. "But it does look pretty fishy." Our English teacher had covertly exited the science building, and was now briskly walking across campus in the drizzle; head darting from side to side carrying a bunch of wires and liquid filled beakers.

"I get the distinct impression we're witnessing the beginning of war," I added. "Besides, that doesn't look like English papers to me…That looks like science stuff! You don't think he's stolen any of Howelgood's contest supplies do you?" Burt's giggling answered my question. "He's up to his old tricks again!"

"And they call us children!" I mumbled.

"Shouldn't we tell someone?"

"I'm not sure that'd be such a good idea for a few reasons. One, I've got both of them for teachers next year. And two, they've been feuding forever! Why break Devonshire's most beloved tradition?" I rolled my eyes. "Come on. Let's go home."

As we made our way out of the courtyard and down the path, a strange feeling overtook me…like I'd forgotten something important. Maybe I'd forgotten to do something? But what? It began to gnaw at the pit of my stomach. Burton kept going on about Professor Loremont.

"You know he might as well go to Hollywood and get it over with. I mean, he always looks like he's just stepped out of a cologne ad. What's a guy like him doing in a place like this? He acts like teaching is beneath him or something…" Of course, I was quite distracted. On and on he went…and then I knew! I felt around my neck. It was gone! I began searching my pockets…nothing! I became so fidgety that he stopped and faced me.

"What's a matter with you?" He was obviously annoyed. "You haven't heard a thing I've said!"

"My dad's talisman…it's gone!"

An expression of alarm replaced the aggravated look he'd been giving me. He was highly versed in the history of that pendant. It was one of a matching set. My father had them specially made as a wedding gift. My mother painstakingly handed it down to me after he'd passed away. I made the most solemn promise to take care of it and NEVER lose it... let alone take it off! How could I tell her? What would she think of me? I panicked. "I have no idea how we'll ever find it!" I shouted!

It was the size and shape of a quarter. Its exterior was ornamented with detailed silver scrolling. This precious metal formed a housing which securely held a trove in its core. Internally, the encasement consisted of a rotating snake fashioned in the shape of an infinity knot. The serpent was made of black stone. A bright red apple hung from its mouth. My mother wore hers rain or shine. When my father was alive, he was never without his, and until today, neither was I! He used to call it his talisman, his good luck charm, and now it had vanished! In some small way, that keepsake made me feel close to him. Besides his history book collection, it was all I had left to remember him by!

"That stupid Isabelle!" I screamed. "She must've made me lose it during all the commotion!"

"Do you want to backtrack?" he offered. "I can get out the metal detector and we can sweep every place we've been. We're sure to find it!" The optimism in his voice had me convinced we'd actually discover where I'd lost it. We were in sight of our homes. One quick stop at his house and we'd be off...Until I happened to notice my mom's car parked out in front. Her schedule usually kept her at the school until late.

"Hey, Creed, why is your mom home so early?"

"Dunno," I muttered. "I hope she's not sick." Come to think of it, I couldn't remember a time she had been sick or even late for work.

We looked at each other then picked up the pace. "Do you think she'll notice you're not wearing the necklace?" "Not if I use my backpack and school uniform as a cover."

I half expected to find her on the couch with a thermometer in her mouth. But when we arrived the house was quiet and completely empty. On the kitchen table were her purse and keys. Neatly tucked underneath the purse was a big manila-style envelope. It was addressed to her and resembled the same type of mailer used to send out final grades. I was never in the habit of reading anyone's mail, but marks were being sent out late and I wanted to prepare my excuses just in case. I opened it carefully trying not to let the rainwater dripping from my hair smear the ink.

"What's that?" Burton asked. "Stillwell give you another C- in Latin? I predict that's why she's home early!"

The letter was in some sort of cryptic code. It had been written on stiff, unlined parchment and sealed with strange, purple wax. The writing was foreign consisting of a bunch of carefully executed scribbles, dots, and dashes. Oddly enough it looked to be penned with an old-fashioned quill and ink bottle. I took it over to the desk lamp for closer inspection. Nothing made sense. But what stirred my curiosity most was my name. It was written several times in plain English. It stood out like a beacon in the midst of meaningless gibberish. The longer I held it the more I felt an overwhelming sensation that something had gone terribly wrong. And it had.

"Creed!!! Fire!!!" Burt tried grabbing the letter from my hands.

The paper had instantaneously ignited! It singed my thumb and forefinger before dropping it to the floor. Without hesitation I quickly extinguished the flames.

"What was that about?" cried Burt. "You must've held it too close to the bulb!"

I had done no such thing, but as I started to protest, I spotted her through the front window. She was running in the rain. "She's coming! Quick…Burt, do as I say! Grab a packet of popcorn from the cabinet and put in the microwave now!"

"What?"

"Please!!! Just do as I say! It will cover the burnt smell!"

While he was busy fumbling with the popcorn packet, I surveyed the damage. Only the tip was charred so I folded it over and neatly tore it off. Maybe she wouldn't notice.

"Creed! She's getting closer!"

I put the paper back into its proper place and in doing so, spotted my grades card resting at the bottom of the envelope. Of course there was no time to look at it! I motioned for him to follow me. We raced down the hall and up the stairs to the background noise of popping popcorn. I heard the front door open and shut. I tried to unnoticeably speak louder than usual. "Well, maybe if we use your metal detector we can find some more stuff for your room."

From the hallway came a shuffling noise, followed by her bedroom door closing. "Creed? Burt? You guys home? I think your popcorn's ready…Way ready!" Her face peered around the door. She was looking at us questioningly, but she wasn't asking anything.

"Hi Mom!"

"Hi, Ms. Griffon," Burton said tentatively.

After a short scan of my room, she tried to break the awkward undercurrent. "Anyone want a snack...that's not burned?" I guess we'd passed "inspection."

When we got back to the kitchen table, the letter was gone. But that was only a small part of it. She exhibited mannerisms quite out of character, especially for her. She dropped the package of cookies all over the wood floor and when it came time to pour the milk, she missed the glass entirely. "Here, Ms. Griffon," offered Burt, "I'll help you clean it up."

"Thank you, Creed...I mean Burt! Burt! I'm so sorry. It's just been a crazy day for me!"

While she was wreaking domestic havoc, I discretely reached the microwave and disposed of the evidence. After that, I took advantage of a little chaos to ask a few questions of my own. "What are you doing home so early?"

She answered with great hesitation. It sounded as though she was making it up as she went. "Uh, well, I wasn't feeling too good, but I'm doing much better. Mrs. Hadley in the cottage park office had some medicine for an upset stomach. It must be working. If only they had a pill for clumsiness, huh?" She nervously glanced at her watch. (I knew for a fact Mrs. Hadley was on vacation.) "I'd better take off before someone else finishes my research study! My schedule's been pretty cramped with the ball and everything. By the way, what happened to your eye? It's looking a little red and puffy."

"I, I fell off my skateboard," I blurted out. Burt nodded for support. Of all the stupid things I could've said. My mom already hated that skateboard! She was afraid I'd break something important. After much pleading, I'd received one for my 11th birthday last year. She'd constantly condemned herself for buying it ever since.

"That's funny," she mused, "I thought boys who rode skateboards scarred up their knees or elbows, not their eyes." After a brief pause and quizzical stare, she changed the subject completely, passing up a good opportunity to lecture us on the evils of skateboarding! Now I knew something was definitely wrong! "By the way, boys, if you want to make some extra money we could really use your help setting up for the Andromeda Ball." Burton eyed me and silently shook his head no.

The Andromeda Masquerade Ball was designed to inspire prospective students to take an interest in Devonshire's educational curriculum as well as the school as a whole. Every department from History to Physical Education was expected to offer their participation in one form or another. My mother has been in charge of the festivities for as long as I could remember. It's a very extravagant social function which draws interest from potential students around the world. Such an event is said to bring in at least half of our new enrollees. Countless dignitaries and nobleman have decided their children's educational fate based on its outcome. Over the years, the ball has gained quite a bit of notoriety. So much, in fact, that even enrolled students cut vacation just to attend. And without fail, every year, Ella Travers, a society columnist for *Dazzle*, makes her grand appearance. She creates such a stir everywhere she goes!

My mom, on the other hand, isn't moved by the hype. For her, this event is more than just a big party. The Masquerade Ball is where she and my father first danced together. She says that's where they fell in love. I know she takes great pride in seeing that every last detail is completed without flaw. No expense is spared! The chandeliers and marble floors are polished to perfection. Tapestries and ceiling mosaics are readied for lingering gazers. A staff of notable chefs is flown in from various locations around the world. They prepare the appropriate cuisine for each guest. Unavoidably, this includes the famous Chef Francois DeBonairte, a 'real charmer'... Without the toque the man is barely five feet, with thick bushy eyebrows and tight curly hair. He's not much to look at but has a keen eye for the ladies, particularly my mother! Last year, he nipped a little bit too much wine while cooking. He ended up proclaiming his 'amore' for her in front of the entire kitchen staff! I know she was thoroughly embarrassed. And of course, DeBonairte had made a complete fool of himself. Confidentially speaking, she considers him harmless but ridiculously pompous and slightly creepy! Thank God!

One can't discuss the Andromeda Ball without talking about the glorious Great Hall. It is the essence of the entire event. Such an esteemed edifice is saturated with revered traditions and staunch formalities. The ancestry can be overpowering to those that walk across its marble floors or underneath its fresco ceilings. This vast cathedral style auditorium has been used for many important school functions. However on this particular occasion, we get a chance to break from ritualistic customs. The hall gets transformed from stuffy to fun! It's brilliantly decorated in a celestial flair and readied for dinner and ballroom dancing later that evening. The tables are always set with the finest silver, crystal and china. Ice carvings will be cut and shaped as guests arrive. Shortly thereafter, they are filled with drinks. Masks and costumes are a strict tradition and steadfast requirement. Everyone attending will dress in honor of the chosen theme. Guest goers can count on an array of magnificent attire to further brighten the atmosphere. In the past, time periods varied from Egypt to ancient China in recognition of their achievements. This year's official theme? 'The Renaissance.'

And then of course, there's the much coveted Ingenuity Award. Per whatever era is chosen, resident professors are allowed to compete against departments in opposing fields. It's quite a spirited contest! Competitors manufacture or duplicate exhibits pertaining to historical experiments, inventions, writings, or memorabilia of pioneers with regard to their area of expertise. Specially chosen students and faculty help create these masterpieces. Entries usually take all year to construct and are done so with the utmost secrecy! The night of the ball, each project is judged and the best efforts receive the prized trophy. The Science and English divisions have forever had a friendly, but fierce, contest to see who can build the best display. They've had an ongoing rift for years. The truth of the matter is, Professor Howelgood, our Science professor, caught Professor Loremont, our English professor, spying on his kinetic energy entry three years ago. Things were never the same between them. But from what we'd observed earlier, Loremont's activities had ensured the science department an inevitable defeat...

"Sure Mom. Why not? We'll help set up."

Burt stared at me utterly bewildered. She gave me a peck on the cheek and grabbed her purse. "Thanks guys. Mr. O'Keefe will have a list of jobs for you to choose from. I've got to head to school now. You boys stay out of trouble, okay?" And with that she was gone. We watched her scurry to the car in the heavy rain.

Burton spoke as if he couldn't contain his thoughts. "What was that about? She was tighter than the strings on my violin!"

"I know! And did you see how she was spilling everything? She was totally out of control!" He nodded. "She's hiding something," I muttered. "I know she is, and I think it might have something to do with that strange letter."

"Maybe she's just nervous about the ball?"

I disagreed. "She's been in charge of the festivities for years! No, there's something more to it. I can feel it. I know it..."

Burton broke my train of thought. "Hey! Why did you tell her we'd work at the party? I'd rather just go as a guest this year! I've had all the food service jokes I can take!"

"It won't be so bad! We'll earn more money from working at the ball than you'll find with your metal detector all summer!"

CHAPTER THREE
To Handcuff or Not to Handcuff

"**S**o, if you didn't hold it too close to the bulb, then maybe it was like a secret message or something and it spontaneously combusted because you weren't supposed to read it? Or maybe your mom is wanted by the FBI!"

"Whoa Burt! Be serious!"

"Then why don't you just ask her what the letter is about? It's probably a prank from a fellow professor."

If there was one thing I knew in reference to my mother, it was that she wasn't necessarily the joking type. Not that she was stern or lacking a sense of humor. In fact she is a very loving and kind person. However, she was more the sort to be fascinated with the "who and why" of the matter. And, of course, there was the minor detail of snooping. It's not like I could just walk up and ask her. "She'll tell me in her own time," I said.

"So that's it? You're gonna settle for waiting? Doesn't sound like the Creed Griffon I know!"

"I didn't say that."

"Then what do you plan to do?"

"We'll take a quick look in there. Then we can hunt for my talisman." I motioned toward her room.

Burt's eyes grew as wide as saucers. "Are you crazy? I'm not going in there! That's taboo! I am not going in there with you!! It so happens that I'm her teacher's aide next semester! She'll flunk me for sure! Besides, there's something weird about snooping in your own parent's room...let alone your friend's parent's room. Let's just look for your dad's charm!" he pleaded.

"It's still raining pretty hard. I just want to take a quick peek, okay? Pretend we're on one of those treasure hunts you always like to go on and..." I could see from the look on his face, he thought I was crossing the line. Of course, she wasn't *my* teacher...she was my mom, not that it made anything better.

"What if she finds out, Creed? Is it really worth that?"

I tried to sound convincing. "I just want to take a closer look at it! I think she hid it in her room before she came upstairs."

"You're on your own man; your mom likes me!"

"Suit yourself," I said in disbelief. "Just be the lookout. Go in there, turn on the television, and help me out that way. Maybe you can find out when the storm will let up." As I headed toward her door, I heard him switch the TV on. If I was crossing the line, then so be it. Something was wrong. There was a deep, deep, knowing that told me so. But how could I explain such an overpowering awareness to Burt? I wasn't really sure what I'd find, but I deserved to know what was happening. Anyway, it sounded good, I guess. Reasoning always makes something wrong sound better than what it really is.

I turned the knob. I could've sworn I heard a clicking sound coming from behind the door. I couldn't tell for sure because of all the screaming.

"Creed! Creed! Quick! Quick!"

I tried slamming the door shut, but the funny thing was it had never opened in the first place. I think it was locked, but I had no time to check it out. *When did she start locking her door?* I thought to myself. I raced back down the hall expecting to find my mom in the driveway. Instead, Burt was engrossed in a burger commercial. "You called me in for this?" I hollered.

"No, this is just a commercial break. Just wait…"

He didn't get a chance to finish speaking. The news commentator came back on with a "live" news alert. "News 3 thanks you for joining us this evening. There is currently an Amber Alert out for this little girl." Before our eyes flashed a picture of Isabelle Polanski! "She has been missing since approximately 12:00 P.M. She was last seen walking to the parent pick-up location located on the West Wing of Devonshire, the well-known, upscale boarding school for grades K – 12. The child's parents state that her suitcase and book bag were found by officers approximately one block from the site. Foul play is suspected." When the newsman finished describing what she was last seen wearing he stated, "On a final note, Ms. Polanski's parents believe that she is still in possession of her cell phone because it was not found with her other belongings. Unfortunately, she is not answering any of their calls."

They broke for an interview with Ms. Stillwell, my Latin professor. She looked the same as always, skinny, omnipotent, and tense. As usual her red hair was pulled taunt into a meticulously wound bun. It made her eyes looked pinched. She kept fidgeting with the chain on her horn-rimmed glasses. "Isabelle is a sweet, wonderful, girl. I saw her just before she walked to the pick-up area. She was carrying her suitcase through Trenton Hall. Prior to that, I heard what sounded almost like a scuffle. I remember because I was emptying a few bags of junk mail…I mean garbage, in the first floor refuse receptacle. As I emptied my third bag, I heard yelling. It was Isabelle's voice and some other students. I think they might have been picking on her. Well it was over before I could get there…"

The reporter cut in sharply, "Can you identify these bullies?"

Ms. Stillwell just shook her head. "I'm not sure; I was standing too far away. You see my hearing has always been better than my vision and…"

The newswoman faced the camera and said, "You heard it live here first! Back to you, Bob and Linda." In the background Stillwell gave an awkward smile for the cameras.

My thoughts went whirling. Distant chatter from the anchor and co-anchor referred to the possibility that Isabelle's disappearance might be connected to the other two children reported missing three and five months earlier. This resulted in further speculation as to the so-called "bullies'" role being associated with the other vanishing children. "Poor Isabelle" I muttered. Burton was breathing so fast he could barely talk.

"Poor Isabelle? I'm sorry. Did you say poor Isabelle????? What are WE going to do, Creed? Those bullies are us! They think we're some sort of sick child nappers! We'll be kicked out of school for sure! They're going to put us in jail! We'll have to finish high school as inmates in some reformatory facility! Congratulations number 9-2-9-0-4-2-4!!! Here's your certificate in license plate design! Won't our mother's be proud!!!"

"Calm down, Burt. We didn't do anything. Isabelle was the one who started the fight. You can back me up."

"Yes, I know," he said, "but we aren't the ones missing! I know how these things always turn out. Who do you think they'll believe? We were the last ones to see her! And not to be mean, Creed, but you and Isabelle are always going at it. Why is that?"

I'd experienced one cheap shot too many. I wasn't about to take one from my best friend! "Hello! Burt…" I said in the most sarcastic tone I could muster. "Are you in there? Come back to me, buddy! I mean really…I'm not sure what it's like in 'planet oblivious' but in case you haven't noticed, our mommies and daddies don't own Rolls Royce's or employ a chauffeur to drive them around in it! We don't vacation in Peru or have $600 labels stitched to our butts! We're not one of the chosen! We're throwbacks!" He scowled at me. I knew I'd struck a nerve. A throwback was an insult some of the other kids had invented for us. It meant reject. I continued to vent. "We don't pick on anyone! People like Isabelle feel it's their moral obligation to define our lack of social status! Or could it be that you've learned nothing in the jungles of Devonshire?"

Burt's eyes focused on the floor. "I didn't mean anything by it, Creed…it's just one more thing they have over us… *Lord of the Flies* is a skip in the park compared to prepatory prison! I'd like to make it through just one school year where we're anonymous!" His head bowed in defeat. "I have an awful feeling that we won't recover from this." he whispered.

I took a deep breath. "We'll be okay. Now's not the time for us to be fighting. Wouldn't they love that? Besides, I'm not disagreeing with you. I know you're right. This time we'll get more than a lecture from the headmaster."

He looked up. "I'd like to think we could tell them the truth, but they won't believe us. You don't have to convince me of that. They'll drag our names all over and then we'll probably get pinned for it! Neither one of us fit the school's cookie-cutter idea of the perfect pupil."

"Don't worry. I'm not coming forward!" I said defiantly. "We didn't start that fight! She did! As far as I'm concerned, we should keep our mouths shut! It won't hurt anything because we don't know anything… We didn't do anything! So what could we possibly have to offer the police in the hopes of finding her? But, if I mention what happened, they'll be all over us like white on rice!" I watched his posture relax a little.

"Then you might want to put some ice on that eye. Your mom's right. It's not only puffy, it's getting black. The last thing we need is someone asking questions."

"I fell off my skateboard, remember?"

"Yeah," he said shakily. The trees outside began to dip lower in the wind. We kept watching the news to see if there were any new updates. Nothing! It was just the same old report spun over and over again. Burton stood up and peered out the window. Looking back he asked, "What do you think happened to her?"

"I'm not sure, but if she hit the guy anything like she hit me, she should be home by now."

The lights flickered off and on as the storm began to gain strength. Flashes of lightening streaked across the sky. In the middle of switching TV stations, the phone rang. I picked it up expecting it to be my mother. It was not. "Hello, is this Creed?"

"Who is this?" I replied.

"This is Mr. Packwood." I motioned to Burton to turn down the sound.

It's Packwood, I silently mouthed. Quinn Packwood was in fact the headmaster of Devonshire. Burton began to nervously pace back and forth. "Yes?" I stammered.

"Creed, I don't know if you're aware of it or not, but Isabelle Polanski disappeared off campus today…and, well, the police are here asking questions. I was wondering if you might come down to my office to speak with them."

I froze, but only for a moment before I answered. From the sound of his tone, he was acting as if he knew nothing about Ms. Stillwell's claims. I decided to play along. "Sure, Mr. Packwood. I'll be there. I'll do whatever it takes to help find her, sir. Can I call my mother first?"

I heard his deep sigh. "I already have, son."

"Okay then, I'll be right there!"

After I hung up the phone, Burt's voice erupted in panic. "Creed, what are we going to do?"

"I think things just got extremely complicated," I mused. "Tell them the truth!" I said enthusiastically.

"We can't! Weren't you just listening to me? Besides, this will be a perfect excuse for them to permanently expel us...put us in jail!"

"Calm down, buddy. It's me, remember? I'm on your side. We're going to tell them...our version of the truth."

His breathing slowed. "We don't know anything." I whispered.

Burt and I formulated our plan as we walked back toward the faculty offices. The heavy rain turned into a light drizzle again. "What's your mom gonna think? She already noticed your eye!"

"Stick to our plan," I said adamantly! "I hurt my eye while trying to jump a curb. You were there and saw me do it. Okay?"

"Okay," he said nervously.

"And, we don't know anything about Isabelle or what happened to her! We didn't even see her today, okay?"

As we neared the buildings, the hallowed halls of Devonshire seemed to grow colder than ever. We had walked these corridors countless times before, but it never failed. I was always made to feel that I didn't belong in such a pristine place. We passed through hallways lined with historical artifacts and portraits. We walked through the marble archways and past plush Victorian couches neatly staged next to one of the many robust fireplaces. Stained glass windows and mosaic designs adorned a large portion of the ceiling and walls. All things set aside, Devonshire itself could make even the most illustrious person feel very small and insignificant.

We drew closer to Packwood's office, each step more ominous than the last. "I think we're dead," Burton whispered.

"Put on your game face, pal. We'll be just fine." He gave me a half-hearted smile as I opened the headmaster's door. Mr. Packwood sat at his enormous ornately-carved desk. Volumes of books lined the shelves from floor to ceiling. Behind him stood a police officer, my mother, Ms. Stillwell, and two people who I assumed were Isabelle's parents.

"Good afternoon, sir," we said in unison.

"Hello boys. Creed, I don't recall telling you to bring your friend, Burton."

My mother spoke up. "Honestly Quinn, this isn't an inquisition."

He immediately adjusted his position "Very well. We were going to ask Burton a few questions anyway; we just haven't been able to get a hold of his mother yet."

"She's probably at her second job," Burt offered nervously.

"Have a seat you two." He motioned us toward two chairs opposite his desk. The introductions began. "This is Officer Farnsworth. He has a few questions to ask you, and this is Mr. and Mrs. Polanski, Isabelle's parents. Of course you know Ms. Griffon and Ms. Stillwell."

"Good afternoon," I managed to say to everyone.

Mrs. Polanski's eyes blazed with hatred. "Please have a seat, boys," said the officer. He moved toward us, notepad in hand. I could smell the leather from the gun belt he wore. It made sounds as he moved. "Now boys, it seems that we have an eyewitness that places you in the area around the time Isabelle disappeared."

"That's impossible," I blurted out! "Who would say such a thing?"

Burt looked like he was ready to cry, but held in there with me. As I scanned the room, Ms. Stillwell refused to look at me. It made me wonder how her story changed so quickly from that of the news report. Oh well, time to put that ad in the newspaper.

"I'll be the one to ask the questions, son."

"Yes sir," I mumbled.

"I can't help but notice you have a black eye." You could hear the condemnation in his tone.

Burton interrupted. "We were riding skateboards by our house the other day. Creed tried to jump off a curb and face-planted it right then and there! On his way down the board flew right up and POW!...hit him in the eye!"

My mom breathed a sigh of relief. I heard Mrs. Polanski make a "phft" noise. Officer Farnsworth continued, "It is also my understanding that in the past, you and Isabelle have had a few issues. Am I right? Have you ever mischievously handled her cell phone before?" I stared blankly at his police badge. He calmly continued, "We have statements from other students that tell us you set her cell phone alarm to go off in class. It was a rather expensive one wasn't it?" I didn't answer. "Do you have a cell phone?" I knew what he was insinuating.

My response was cold. "No, why would I need one of those?"

"Not need, *want*," he said with a smile.

The officer paused to look at his pocket notebook. Flipping the pages he asked, "Do you know a Fiona Talbert or a Timothy Holderman?"

I looked at Burt. We both shook our heads. "No sir? Who are they?" Of course I knew full well who they were, but I wasn't about to tell him that. They were the two kids reported missing from a boarding school not far from Devonshire. It had been all over the news for months.

"Well, Mr. Griffon, those are the two children reported missing some months ago from Pemberton Academy. They haven't been heard from since. We've got a witness that says you and your buddy there were the last ones to see Isabelle before…"

From behind me came a subtle knock at the office door. A familiar voice interrupted the hearing. "Oh, excuse me, Mr. Packwood, sir," said Mr. O'Keefe. "These two lads were helping me tend to the grounds earlier this afternoon. T'was wondering if I could have them back when you're done? I came looking fer them because they left without getting their final assignments fer the ball." He offered up two sheets of folded paper. "When I saw them walking up here, I just followed them and they led me to you. I hope you pardon my interruption."

I tried to hide my look of astonishment. My mother gave me an awkward gritted-teeth smile, raised her eyebrows, and slowly nodded her head. The police officer closed his notebook and addressed O'Keefe. "So, you're saying these boys have been with you all afternoon?"

"Aye, ever since the school half-day let out. They usually help me tend the grounds over summer break. I was amazed at how eager they were to get started. Why, they both showed up promptly at noon chimes, ready to work…said something 'bout wanting to earn enough money fer a new skateboard and metal detector."

The policeman's snide grin slid right off his face. "What time did they leave?" he asked.

"They left 'round four o'clock once we were done discussing the fountain-cleaning schedule. I went looking fer them and wound up here. "

Mrs. Polanski began to sob. Mr. Polanski comforted her. They were directed toward the waiting area outside. Officer Farnsworth followed after them. "I am sorry to have had to bring you two in today," said Mr. Packwood. He turned his attention to Ms. Stillwell. "I know you boys are not the type to be involved in something like this."

"Are we excused, sir?" asked Burton.

"Yes, but one last thing." He slid a pink spiral notebook across his desk.

"What's this?" I asked. As I brought it closer, I saw my name doodled all over the front of it. *Creed Griffon, Mr. and Mrs. Griffon, Creed, I heart Creed…* "Whose book is this?" I stammered.

"You mean you don't know?"

"No sir!" He could tell by my deep eye contact that I really had no clue who it belonged to.

After some hesitation, Mr. Packwood answered, "It's Isabelle's, son. It was found in a book bag inside her suitcase."

There was no time to go into shock, because the cell phone in my pocket began to vibrate. Thank God it wasn't set for ring tone. "Sir, I know nothing about this!"

He reached out his hand, and both Burt and I gave it a solid shake. "They're all yours, Mr. O'Keefe." My mom sighed with relief and said she'd be home later.

We passed Officer Farnsworth in the waiting area. I saw him quickly slip his cell phone into his shirt pocket. *Nice try*, I thought to myself. *Nice try indeed.*

CHAPTER FOUR

FrightMare

Without so much as a single word, Mr. O'Keefe led us from the headmaster's office, across campus, to the privacy of Mendel Greenhouse. Once inside, he erupted with the loudest belly laugh I'd ever heard! "Mr. O'Keefe," Burt said, "why did you do that? We weren't anywhere near you today. Why did you cover for us like that?"

He removed his scally cap and smoothed his wavy brown hair. "I know you boys no more made that girl disappear than Mr. Griffon himself!"

"You knew my father?"

"Aye," he nodded. "They're just trying to find a quick scapegoat!" He pulled an apple from his coat pocket and took a big bite. "Fact is, I knew that girl took a toss at ya."

I immediately turned to face him. "Wait a minute! You saw the whole thing? Where were you?"

"Aye," he said, adjusting his hat. "I am the eyes and ears of this school. I know who makes trouble fer whom… I know who the bad seeds are… I know who loses cell phones and who finds them…" His eyes pierced mine. "Fact is, I didn't really see it happen; I heard you lads talking 'bout it. Later, I found your necklace on the ground along with the murder weapon." He grinned and took another bite. "I knew it t'was yours because you're never without it!"

"Wait! You found it?" I shouted. "Where is it?"

"I was gonna give it to your mum when she arrived for festivity preparations, but I thought it best I give it to you. Didn't want to make trouble fer you," he whispered.

I gave a solemn nod. From the recesses of his pocket he produced my most sacred possession. "When I asked your whereabouts, she said something 'bout a skateboard accident and the business with your eye. Then the stir regarding Ms. Polanski gone missing and Stillwell's account….well, I knew they'd be gunnin fer you." He removed a piece of neatly folded cloth from his pocket and gently placed it in my hand. Burt hovered over me for a glimpse. We looked at him in amazement. So much had happened; I'd didn't even remember losing it!

"Oh, thank you, Mr. O'Keefe! Thank you!" For a minute there I'd completely forgotten myself and gave him a big hug! I could tell he wasn't used to affection. He stiffly patted me on the shoulder.

"I fixed the clasp fer ya." He cleared his throat. He looked a little embarrassed at my show of gratitude. I covered for him by switching the subject.

"Should I give the phone back to them?"

"No boy, you did well. If they knew you had it, they'd hang you both out to dry and not just for Isabelle's disappearance either! The fact is, they'd like to pin this entire thing on a couple of throwbacks like you, no offense, of course!" Mr. O'Keefe knew more than I gave him credit for. Part of me wondered if we hadn't kept quiet about the closet incident, would we still be in Packwood's office. He went on, "…that way, it focuses negative attention away from the school, the mystery is quickly solved, and things can go back to normal."

"What should I do with her phone?" I asked.

"Whatever you do, don't answer it. You haven't, have you, lad?"

"No sir," I said swiftly. "I think that cop tried to call it while I was in Mr. Packwood's office, but before then it never even so much as vibrated. Why do you suppose that is?" I asked. "Isabelle's parents' said they tried to call, but she didn't answer.

Mr. O'Keefe thought about it. "Maybe the storm interfered with the reception. Bad weather is always causing problems with the school's landline phones. I'm sure cell phones are no exception. Anyway, none of that matters," he said, shaking his head. "I heard the Polanski's talking with Farnsworth. It has some sort of satellite tracking on it! If you answer it, you'll lead them right back to you! Then, your gooses will be cooked all right! Just turn it off!! Hide it somewhere no one will find it!"

I nodded. Burt was looking through the greenhouse windows. "What should we do in the meantime?" he asked.

"Well, both of you need to carry on as normal. Go ride your skateboards, help me with the Masquerade Ball, but most importantly, stick to your story and stay out of trouble!"

"Mr. O'Keefe?" I could hear the fear in Burt's voice.

"Aye?"

"What do you think happened to her? What do you think happened to those other two kids?"

"I haven't figured that one out yet, laddie…not yet. Now, you boys better scat before they think we're getting our stories straight! If anyone asks ya, we were talking about job assignments for the ball. Here," he said, handing each of us a work schedule and a doily dotted with pink and white flowers. "Pick a job from the list. Take it with you. We can discuss it in more detail once you've decided which positions you want. Made the doilies me self." he said proudly. "They're fer your mums."

Before leaving we generously thanked him then made our way back to the cottages. I slipped the talisman around my neck. It felt like home. Every once in a while, Burt would look over his shoulder just to make sure no one was following us. "Will you relax, Burt! We're covered. He knows we didn't do anything."

"It's not him I'm worried about! Did you see Mrs. Polanski staring at us? I think she knows something…and that policeman… He gave me the willies."

I tried to ease the tension by doing my best cop impersonation. Pretending to have a notebook in hand, I began asking him all sorts of dumb questions. "How do you spell tic-uht? Wait a minute! How do you spell Farnsworth? Forget that! How do you spell Mississippi? I'll ask the questions around here, son!"

In the middle of a good laugh, he stopped cold. "What do you make of that notebook? Your name was splashed all over it."

"I don't know. That's been bothering me a little. Isabelle never showed that she could stand me, let alone 'like' me. I do know one thing. I think they'll be watching us closely."

Burton heartily agreed. "It's best we do as Mr. O'Keefe instructed then. We should just proceed as normal, maybe lay low for a while and make real sure we don't get into any trouble. What are you going to do with the phone?" he asked.

"Not sure. For now, I'll find a safe place to hide it."

"It's getting late, Creed. I'd better get home before my mom calls."

"Chances are my mom's already called yours. Just stick to what Mr. O'Keefe said. Okay?"

He nodded, then ran toward his front porch and waved before going inside. My house was quiet except for the television. We had forgotten to turn it off before we left. The news was still covering Isabelle's disappearance, except now they were reporting the possibility that she'd run away. I turned it off. My brain had enough stimulation for the afternoon. There was still the issue of the mysterious letter, but my mom would be home soon. Hopefully, she wouldn't notice the missing corner. Besides, now was not the time to get caught snooping. I needed time to sort out what happened. The words "lay low" played over and over in my mind.

I decided to wait and see if she would fill me in. She'd acted pretty strange this afternoon, and she was fairly quiet about the entire Isabelle ordeal. I could tell from the look on her face in the office that she knew we were innocent. But she also knew that we weren't with Mr. O'Keefe at the time he'd said. She just seemed preoccupied again.

I sat at the table reading over O'Keefe's job choices for the ball. What did I want to do this year? Last year, Burt and I had been welcoming attendants. Not my first choice, I know, but at eight dollars an hour, and all the food we could eat, it wasn't half bad. Masks and appropriate attire were always mandatory. At least no one would recognize me! Devonshire provided free costumes and masks to anyone working the event. Last year, I had gone as an Egyptian slave and Burt went as a scribe. My mother always disguised herself as some sort of royalty or goddess. It was her tradition. One of the few stories she did tell me about my father was when they first met. She only told me of it one time. I absorbed every detail as if it were as vital as air. She was dressed as Isis and he, Osiris. Her laughter would eventually turn into tears. I finally settled on welcoming attendant.

"Creed?" I came out of my chair like a rocket! "Creed honey, it's just me." She began descending the stairs. "I thought I heard you come in."

I managed to ask, "Where's your car? I didn't see it parked outside."

"Oh yeah," she said exasperated. "When Quinn, I mean Mr. Packwood, called me, I raced to get to his office. He just said that it pertained to you and was very important. I was in such a hurry that I left the lights on and drained the battery! I couldn't find anyone with jumper cables, so Mr. Packwood brought me home. I didn't mean to scare you. But never mind me, how are you doing?"

"I'm okay," I said, searching her eyes. "Today was a rough day. It was pretty creepy. They actually thought I was the reason why she's missing. They believed I might be the cause for those other kids' disappearances, too! Mom, I really want you to know…" There was a brief moment where I wanted to tell her the truth about what really happened. I wanted her to know I really hadn't done anything… I didn't start the fight… "That I didn't have anything to do with Isabelle's disappearance, or anyone else's," I blurted out!

"I know, son." The reassurance in her voice was calming. "I believe you, and so does Mr. Packwood. He was just following orders from the police department. It seems Ms. Stillwell told the authorities she'd heard you and Burton fighting with Isabelle just before she disappeared. She couldn't see the bullies; she could only hear voices in the hallway. Apparently, the voices sounded like yours and Burt's. She met Isabelle walking down the stairs just after it happened, but reported she was fine. Isabelle didn't even infer an argument had occurred. Ms. Stillwell's account states that she watched her head toward the parent pick-up station. Anyway, that's why the police wanted to speak with you. Stillwell said you were the last ones to see her before she disappeared.

"No, wouldn't that make Stillwell the last one to see her before she disappeared?'

"They've already questioned her Creed. She does have a solid alibi. It's seems Ms. Stillwell and a few Latin students were working on their entry for the ball. Emptying the garbage only took her a couple minutes before she was back in the classroom with the other kids. Witnesses corroborate her story. The police are satisfied with her account and wanted to focus in other areas. "You mean me."

"Yes, but none of that matters anymore. Everyone now knows you were with Mr. O'Keefe. Don't pay any more mind to it. The police were just doing their job. They have to follow up on every lead possible. You never know which one will help them solve these mysteries."

I took a deep breath. "Mom?"

"Yeah honey?"

"You know we came home after school..." Her eyes became glued to mine. "You were here. We weren't with Mr. O'Keefe at the time he said…and, and…you know it."

She gave me a sympathetic look and put her hand on my shoulder. Her voice was gentle, but firm. "I've known Mr. O'Keefe for more years than you've been alive. He isn't the type to stick his neck on the line for just anyone. He has his own reasons for what he did. And he knows as well as I that you had nothing to do with Isabelle's disappearance or anyone else's. I am honored that he would believe in you so strongly." I felt a little relief, but something else was bothering me. She sensed my concern. "Do you have anything else you want to tell me?"

My reply was awkward. I studied the carpet beneath the table. "I didn't think Isabelle liked me…let alone *'like'* me. She was always making fun of me, so I played pranks on her, but she played just as many on me. I feel bad…" I continued to flounder for words.

"It's okay, Creed. People have different ways of showing they care for someone or maybe different ways of trying to hide their feelings. Some people believe that loving someone makes them vulnerable. Therefore, they act the very opposite of how they feel.

For now, I just pray they find the poor girl." She began fixing dinner.

I nodded. "Me, too." And that was the last of our discussion.

Minus the ten dollars for my good report card, the rest of the evening was fairly quiet. We both picked at our meatloaf. Occasionally, one of us would turn the television on for updates, but there never was new information. As I got ready for bed, she sat at the table, as always, sorting out bills. I was too mentally tired to bring up the letter. "I almost forgot. Mr. O'Keefe made this for you." I removed the lavender doily from my backpack. "Well would you look at these pretty flowers! That man never ceases to amaze me!" she said with a smile. "I still wear the scarf he knitted for me last Christmas. "G'night Mom."

"Night honey; I love you." She gave me a peck on the cheek.

As I walked upstairs I could hear Burton's faint voice calling me on the walkie-talkies. I ran toward my room and shut the door. "Creed?" he said in whisper. "Creed?"

"I'm here," I said.

"Is it safe?"

"Yeah, it's clear."

"See you in a minute then!"

"Okay," I shot back. I cleaned the area in front of my window and brought out our homemade ladder. I saw Burt's figure outside.

"What's the password?" I whispered.

"Whydah."

Of course the Whydah was a pirate ship that sank off the coast of Cape Cod. It went down with a huge sum of booty. The wreckage had been discovered years ago. Burt hoped that one day we could go there and search for left over remnants of the treasure. I tossed the makeshift rope down to him. It disappeared somewhere within the ivy-covered exterior. He climbed up in record time.

"My mom's working late tonight."

"How'd it go?" I asked.

"You were right. Your mom called her and told her everything. She's just happy we're both okay." I nodded. "Did you hear about Stillwell?"

"No," I said, shaking my head.

"Well, my mom wanted to make sure everything was smoothed over from today. She called the headmaster. After talking for a while, he told her that Ms. Stillwell thinks the ball should be cancelled! That'd be a first in the history of Devonshire! She feels it's unsafe for students to attend because of all the disappearances. Packwood is going to call an emergency meeting in the morning. Just thought I'd warn you in case your mom comes home in a really bad mood. At least you'll know why. What about you?"

"I'm doing good, but my mom never even mentioned that letter."

"After a day like today and you're worried about some letter?! We need to stay focused. Maybe it doesn't even really concern you!"

"No. There's more to it. I know that much. Something's wrong..."

"Oh there's something wrong all right! Forget the stupid piece of paper! What about the phone? Did you hide it?"

"You mean this?" I said, pulling it out from the hollow space under my dresser. "I haven't had a lot of time to think about it. My mom was home when you dropped me off."

"Where's the car?"

"Battery issues." He gave an empathetic nod. We spent the rest of the night talking about the day's events until his mom's headlights crossed the driveway.

"I'd better get home before she finds out I'm not in bed!" He climbed down the ladder quickly. I watched him disappear into his bedroom window. I made sure Isabelle's cell phone was still off and put it back in its hiding place. I didn't even remember falling asleep, but I do remember the nightmare…

In the darkness their immense shadows spilled out from the woods behind my house. They began pacing beneath my window making strange clicking noises with every step. The first creatures I caught site of resembled hideous hounds with long necks and snouts. Their ghastly bodies could be likened to that of a well developed man, but covered in black shaggy fur. Instead of hands and feet they bore oversized paws which furiously slashed at the ground. Hair about the neck and back stood up like spikes on a razor's edge. The horrid creatures were salivating and frothing madly all the while exposing prominent, protruding, fangs. The remainder of the pack watched and waited with great expectancy. In a frenzy I tried to wake myself up, but nothing happened!

Their presence was suffocating. The stench radiating from them was entirely putrid! And as the beings drew nearer, I was overwhelmed by something quite extraordinary. It too was horrific, but in different sort of way. It was a menacing atmosphere…a presence…an unseen oppression that was impossible to escape. Such a suffocating ambiance was like none I'd ever known before. It was an understanding…an immediate awareness of what it felt like... It was as if they'd brought an aura of death with them… And in those terrible moments, I experienced emotions felt by their victims in the last few minutes of life, as though it were really happening to me…the last breath, the feeling of one's body shutting down, terror, hopelessness, shock…disbelief. Truly, I was experiencing what it was like to die!

Without warning came the resonating sound of people crying and pleading for freedom. I was mortally terrified! It was getting harder to breath. "Let us out…Please… let us out! Do something!" they shrieked. But let them out of where? Such a destructive force both repelled and immobilized me. I wanted to run! In panic, I froze and was forced to look on. My fears intensified as their numbers grew more plentiful. I witnessed yet another terrifying species seep up from the ground, seemingly out of nowhere! They were brought into existence in the shape of a small black funnel cloud not even disturbing the very soil they sprang from. It was like watching dark fog rising. After a short but graceful display of swirling and spinning something evil stepped forth from its core. The moonlight allowed me to capture my first true glimpse of the beasts. Their entire bodies were caped in a majestic cloak comprised of black smoke. As they moved, pieces of the shroud would pinch off forming vial, hideous, creatures.

I was a spectator to the hair-raising conception of a grotesque black bird. A segment of smoke bubbled away from the rest, producing the repulsive head of a crow atop the winged body of a scorpion! It was enormous with razor-sharp claws and serrated beak. The deformed creation revealed the strangest, most intense blue eyes I'd ever seen. Swiftly it scuttled across the ground before taking flight. After circling overhead, the loathsome fowl rejoined its master simply by touching the outside of the garment. Suddenly, it vanished!

Buried within the confines of the cape resided the framework of a human form consisting of a skeleton surrounded by a transparent, yellowish fluid. It was as if their bones had been dropped in a vat of cooking oil and it molded around them like skin! The liquid inside this external casing flowed and glided with movement. I could see no organs, just ghostly images bearing contorted faces.

They floated and swirled amongst the viscous matter using it as a medium to transport themselves around the creature's insides. In slow aqueous motion, I watched the devoured souls pull at their eyes and mouths. They moaned and wailed most grievously. Such torturous cries were something I wouldn't soon forget.

After a short while, I was able to determine what was making those strange clicking noises. The glittery shine gave the secret away. Every creature bore a hooked ivory-colored talon in place of where their big toes should've been. Some were blood stained due to excessive use. However, each one was exquisitely decorated with the gold and black tally marks! The imprinting created patterns and designs that glimmered and sparkled with movement. And in a peculiar sort of way, they were hauntingly beautiful. I could only assume such markings kept record of the number of kills each creature had acquired. With every stepping movement, the knife-like extension pierced the ground making contact with rocks in the soil. Click...Click...Click... I looked on as other creatures moved beyond a partial cloak shift. Some performed a complete transformation. The plasmatic form melted away into the darkness, producing the same hellish hound I'd seen earlier! They snarled and shrieked with demented excitement! They tore at the dirt for no reason!

Then, all of the commotion ceased. I began to hear a particular being speak in a language quite foreign to me. It didn't dawn on me till later that I had the ability to fully understand him. As it talked, captive souls continually tried to escape through its mouth. With each attempt, a huge, forked snake's tongue erupted from between its lips and swept them back inside. "He's here. I think... I think I might sense him," it hissed. "Yesssss....He is watching us right now." As the creature spoke, imprisoned souls floated behind the orbits of its eyes using them much like one would use a pair of binoculars. They were taking turns looking out into the realm of humans! One minute it appeared to have the likeness of one person's anguished facial features and the next change completely into someone else's. Somehow, this evil monstrosity was their window to the outside world. And there I was, left to stare at the mortifying kaleidoscope of countenances! "We must be very cautious until we know for sure. We will find it before he does! Then, he's ours for the taking!" I saw a brilliant flash followed by intense heat.

CHAPTER FIVE

Giests Don't Play Fair

J awoke to the sound of thunder and the smell of fresh waffles. The rain and the wind were hitting the window so hard I could barely make out the soft knock at my bedroom door. I felt a persistent burning in my throat as if I'd been screaming all night. "Creed honey… Time to get up. I've got a lot of things to do today. Creed?" She timidly entered the room. "Creed…what happened in here?"

I'd like to say I sat up in bed, but it looked like I'd never made it there. My room was in shambles, and I lay on the ground in the middle of it all. Dresser drawers had been thrown open and stacked on top of each other six high! The clothes from inside now lay in one big pile. My father's prized history book collection… ripped from the shelves. The contents of my closet were totally emptied and the telescope I'd received for my twelfth birthday had been knocked over. She conspicuously muttered, "If that's how you treat costly gifts, I might as well buy socks for your next birthday present."

Then she caught sight of my dad's books. She looked hurt but didn't say anything. Instead, her nose pinched the air. She smelled something odd. I could smell it, too. It was a light pungent stench of resembling a burnt sour odor. I couldn't quite place it. "Creed! Clean this room up immediately! Have you been eating in here? It smells as though something's spoiled. I don't have time for this! Mr. O'Keefe will be here any minute to help me get the car.

"You mean you get to ride on his motorcycle?"

"Creed, be serious! He's picking me up in his work truck. Now forget about that. I'm counting on you to be good and do the basics, like keeping your room clean and staying out of trouble! I've got a lot going on with the ball and everything…Please Creed…"

I didn't even have time to explain, not that I could have. "I'm sorry. I'll clean it up," I heard myself say. "I'll start with Dad's collection." She gave a sigh of relief.

"I'll be back late. Mr. Packwood has called an emergency meeting about the ball and with only less than a week left," she said in exasperation! In the distance I could hear Mr. O'Keefe's truck horn. "I've got to go."

"Tell him I've chosen welcoming attendant!"

She glanced back, "Okay. There's a plate of waffles down there with your name on it." She managed to muster up a weak smile as she surveyed the damage one last time. "Love you," she yelled.

I heard the front door close. Mr. O'Keefe's pickup accelerated and then was gone. I was home alone. I got up slowly. It felt like I'd been kicked in the head. The burning in my throat worsened. I tried to rub the outside of it, but flinched at the first touch. As I put the books back on the shelves, I noticed the strange fragrance still lingered. I opened the blinds to let light in… "Creed?" It was Burt on the walkie-talkies.

"Yeah, it's me."

"Is it clear?"

"Yeah buddy, come on up. My mom just left for the meeting."

Minutes later, he came in the front door. Chances are he smelled the fresh waffles.

"Help yourself," I yelled. My throat felt like it was on fire! I managed to find clean clothes and Isabelle's cell at the bottom of a pile. I put the phone back in its hiding place and got dressed. Burt was sitting at the table with a stack of waffles and syrup.

"Save any for me?"

He spoke as he ate. "What happened to you? It doesn't look like you slep..." He swallowed a mouthful of waffles. His eyes were fixated on me. "It's a little early for Halloween don't you think?" I touched the outside of my face and neck. It made me wince. "Did you get sunburned or something?"

"What do you mean?" I shot back. "It's pouring outside!"

"It's your face," he stammered. "Here, come and see." He was motioning me to the hallway mirror. It looked as though I had come in contact with some intense heat. My face and neck were sunburned and painful to the touch, sort of like when you get a sunglasses burn from snowboarding all day. But the oddest thing was that an exact copy of my talisman had been burned into my throat. It had been traced to a painful perfection. The lingering stench I'd been detecting came from being touched by one of those awful creatures. "Are you okay? Does it hurt?"

"I don't believe this," I whispered. I couldn't answer his questions fast enough. For the next half hour, I proceeded to tell Burton about my dream. I spoke with so much fervor and zeal that he became absolutely engrossed in my story. He even let his waffles get soggy in the syrup. I ended the entire drama with, "So what do you think?"

"I don't know," he said, shaking his head. "Did you put any acne medicine on yesterday? I know that stuff can make skin sensitive to the sun." I shook my head. "What about an allergic reaction to a new...laundry detergent or facial soap?" Each new suggestion was shot down. "Okay, let's just say something did visit you outside your window last night. It's possible, right? Maybe make its way into your room and trashes it. What was it looking for? Wouldn't they leave a trail?" We locked eyes. He beat me to the front door. I grabbed my shoes, a rain jacket, and followed him. "Show me where you thought you saw them."

"Over there," I pointed. We searched the woods in the pouring rain for about an hour. Burton poked at different mounds with a stick while I investigated the area underneath my window. We didn't find anything but a dead mouse!

"It's okay, Creed. I believe you. There's got to be a reasonable explanation for all of this! Maybe it's a genetic thing or something." I watched as he continually searched the ground for clues. I had been on many of his treasure expeditions, but none of his were as crazy as this.

"Come on," I offered, "let's go inside and finish our breakfast before we get struck by lightning."

"At least your eye isn't so puffy anymore," he added.

"Yeah, I guess so." After breakfast we went upstairs. We talked as I cleaned the catastrophe in my room.

"Do you remember Wendell Colby?"

"Yeah, I think so," I said curiously.

"Well, his mom worked with my mom in the dining facility."

"Yeah, and?" I added.

"Well, according to my mom, that got it directly from the dish washer who knew his mom, Wendell was a chronic sleepwalker." I took a minute to dissect what he was trying to tell me. "He would always do weird stuff in his sleep, like walk outside in his pajamas or fall asleep in his closet. Then, when asked, he would never remember anything about the incident. So, you think that maybe…"

"Maybe I made this mess in my sleep?"

With confidence, he proudly declared, "It is possible!"

"Okay Sherlock, then how do you explain my face?"

"I've been thinking about that one. I don't have any answers for you yet, but maybe we can use the school library or its computers for help. I'm sure there's a reasonable explanation for what happened."

I mulled over his suggestion. The storm picked up strength as I put the last of my clothes back in the drawer. "There. All done!"

"Not too many staffers at the library this time of year… if any. They've probably shut it down for summer maintenance. And, it is broad daylight!"

I knew what he was hinting at. A year before last, while trying to hide from Mr. O'Keefe, we found ourselves inside of a stairwell closet. We discovered that one of the floorboards was loose so we pried it up. The secret compartment housed a ring full of keys that looked to be as old as the school. At first we thought they were just useless until finding out that one of them actually opened the library doors. Being that the school was usually occupied, we hadn't had much time to discover what the others unlocked. But, we didn't really care. This particular key was a highly prized possession affording us entrance to our new secret getaway. During one of our escapades we discovered where Mrs. Murtaugh hid the teacher's computer pass codes. And last year, during Christmas break, Burt and I snuck inside and played races on the sliding book ladders! It was a feat punishable by expulsion!

But I guess you really have to consider the library to understand our excitement. It's no ordinary run of the mill book mobile. It's an enormous structure that has been classified in professional circles as a great work of art. Internally, it is circular in shape, similar to that of a lighthouse or the turrets atop the Great Hall of Devonshire. Mrs. Murtaugh likes to call it the sea of knowledge. At the time of its christening, builders from all over the world hailed it as an innovative, architectural masterpiece. It was constructed to encompass multi levels, stained glass windows, marble flooring, pillars, and of course, books from floor to ceiling. The building's trademark is the humongous rounded archways which climb to the peak of the stained glass dome overhead. Together, they form a continual letter "m" that stretches around the entire building. They help give the library its rounded appearance and also double as inset bookcases. Most archways are occupied by volumes upon volumes of literature. Various sections contain openings leading to computers or private reading areas. Spiral staircases give access to such levels above. Ornate wrought-iron railings protect those of us who wish to venture higher. It's a facility that rivals many of the finest in the world.

Occasionally, Devonshire would allow tours. Visitors traveled from all over the globe just to revel in its magnificence. According to the tour guides, the grandeur of the library was due to the finances of one passionate academy donor. His quest was to make sure that Devonshire students would not want for literature on any subject. He achieved his goal. His name? Anvil Hollingsworth, and the library, accompanying wing, and museum were rightfully named in his honor. Various portraits of Anvil hung among such places. Without fail, each depiction showed him holding a rather strange looking tobacco pipe. The stem of the pipe was mahogany red. The tobacco bowl was black and held in place by a black dragon's claw. Resting its chin on the bowl was the dragon's head, mouth open, facing inward, so that the each time he took a puff, he was looking straight in to the beast's vicious expression. It too was black, and its eyes, the color of fire. Several guides declared it was the only one of its kind ever made. Others went as far as to claim that when passing certain portraits of him, one could smell a robust woody-sweet tobacco aroma! I don't know about any of that.

We grabbed my backpack, some snacks, the keys, and took off. The walk was a wet and rainy one, but it assured us that not too many people would be out on such a day. The cool rain felt good on my face. "What if we get caught?" Burt said cautiously.

"We can just say that the door was already open and we walked in." He seemed to find my answer satisfactory.

As we approached Hollingsworth Library, the storm grew more persistent. Drawing closer, we witnessed the lights in the building pulse on and off. "Did you happen to pack a flashlight?" He sounded nervous and curious at the same time. I assured him, I had. I'd survived many a storm here and learned to be somewhat resourceful.

It was quiet upon entering the Anvil wing. There was plenty of evidence that preparations had already begun for the ball. We approached the library, but ducked inside our familiar closet. Voices could be heard. It sounded like the decoration committee was hard at work. I chuckled. "Well, it looks as though Ms. Still-well didn't get her way after all!" I could tell Burton was having second thoughts.

"Maybe we should come back another time," he whispered.

"No, we'll be just fine. We aren't doing anything wrong. If they want to kick us out, we can tell them that we are doing library cleanup for Mr. O'Keefe." He forced a smile. Just then we caught a glimpse of Professor Howelgood. He was walking briskly while shoving a large quantity of papers and clothing into a big duffle bag. "What's he doing here?" whispered Burt. "You don't think he's up to what I think he's up to do you?"

"Of course he is! By now, he's discovered that Loremont took his demonstration materials…but he can't prove it." I turned toward Burt. "What's a little more trouble, heh? I could use a good laugh...You want to have some fun?" He grinned from ear to ear.

"I'm in."

"Then follow my lead." Casually we exited the closet. We stepped out just before Howelgood passed by. The look of utter shock on his face was priceless!

"GGGood evening, boys!" he stammered.

"Going for a late night workout?" I offered.

"Oh, you know, just clearing out old papers this and that...end of the year stuff."

"Got a body in that bag?" I asked jokingly.

"Maybe he's stealing priceless antiques?"

"No, no" heckled Burt. "The coffee in the teacher's café is irreplaceable, so he drove all the back here for an iced chocachino."

"You wouldn't be '*borrowing*' English supplies would you?" I added chidingly.

Howelgood bowed his head and sighed. "Alright boys, you caught me. Someone took some very important materials needed for our science exhibit. I have a pretty good idea who that *someone* is, but of course *he'd* never admit to it!"

"Save it," I said laughing. "We have something to confess. We saw Loremont running across campus with your stuff the other day."

"Are you sure?!" he exclaimed. We nodded. "Well did you tell anyone?"

"No," I said remorsefully. The next thing I knew, he'd grabbed both my shoulders and shook me!

"Good man, Griffon!" he yelled happily.

"One of the beakers had blue fluid in it," said Burt cautiously. "I think the other contained some sort of yellow liquid in it. He had a mess of wires and other things, too."

"I KNEW IT!! That no good dirty low down literary lunatic!!!!!!!! Thank you men! Thank you! Can I count on you to keep this hush hush?" We both nodded.

"THIS MEANS WAR!" he shouted.

"But don't '*you*' want to tell someone?" inquired Burt.

"And ruin a time honored faculty tradition? No way! Besides, this is the perfect opportunity to get even with that preppy young punk once and for all! I'll be seeing you men!" he yelled stomping adamantly toward the door. "I'll use science to get my revenge! He'll rue the day he ever entered my lab! By the way Creed, put some sunscreen on next time you go outside!" And he slammed the door behind him. Burt looked at me, mouth open, and in total amazement.

"Whew! That was a close one," I muttered. "I have a feeling Professor Loremont's Bunsen burners are set to be torched!"

We silenced our laughter as we neared the entrance to the library. Extraneous voices grew louder. We overheard a lady say, "The ball is only four days away and we still don't have all of the decorations up! We don't even know where the Science or English entries will be exhibited!"

"I think they'll be strangling each other, that's where they'll be," murmured Burt.

We entered the room with great caution. No one acknowledged our presence. However, I did see Mr. O'Keefe in the midst of the gathering. It sounded as though they were arguing over the placement of the big dipper constellation. Mr. O'Keefe looked up at me, rolled his eyes, and put his head back down. "Okay," I said, "we're in! Where should we start?"

"I can go up on the second floor where they keep the medical books," he offered. His voice still held a tinge of nervousness.

"Yeah, good idea. I think I'll use the school's computers to see if I can find out some information. I'll meet you back here in about 30 minutes," I whispered!

He grabbed a flashlight from my bag and scrambled up the spiraled stairs. The committee was heavily embroiled in their debate. The lights dimmed a few times as I made my way to the third floor. I could hear the rain hitting the stained-glass windows.

The computer floor was barely lit. The faint flickering glow of the computer screens gave light to the room. I saw a figure seated at the last row of terminals, probably one of the neglected left here over vacation. Thinking it would be too obvious if I used Ms. Stillwell's account number, I logged in with my student identification code. The World Wide Web popped up. Immediately, I began my search query. I didn't know just what to call my problem. I looked up red face, sunburn, genetic sunburn, but I didn't get many results I could easily understand.

Suddenly, from the rear of the room, came the resonating sound of growling... The hair on the back of my neck stood straight up. Slowly I looked behind me and saw three figures sitting at individual terminals! That's funny... When did they get here? An intense flash of heat caused me to face forward again. I turned just as the left half of the forked tongue wisped a desperate soul back into its mouth! The right side stayed behind to guard against further escape attempts. As before, its head and body were cloaked in a flowing garment of black smoke. Up close the voluminous covering appeared plush and soft. However, I knew what lurked beneath those luxurious folds. The high temperatures it radiated was almost unbearable. It was the equivalent to standing directly in front of an open kiln or fireplace. I used the computer's keyboard to shield my face until realizing the pulsing heat had stopped. But it was the creature's stench that was absolutely unforgettable. Up close and personal, the smell was nauseating and best described as the essence of intense rotting flesh. Obviously, it was the beast from my nightmare! Only this time I wasn't asleep!

Click…Click…Click. Those bloody talons were as comforting and unforgiving as nails on a chalkboard. As the demon was within arms' reach, imprisoned spirits took turns intermittently floating behind its eyes…nose…mouth. They hungrily observed me within its face bearing demented smiles and malicious expectations. They were undeniably chilling to look at, but I dare not take my eyes off of it or them! Effortlessly, the demon dramatically fanned its cloak, in then out, arrogantly displaying what lie beneath the smoky gatherings. Amidst the dim light, the same distorted spirits writhed inside its body. They were screaming in a void of silence agonizing over their plight. Until without warning it addressed me! The tormented souls spoke in unison to form one collective voice. Painfully, they growled and hissed out each word!

"I see you're still wearing my calling card," it said. I looked around the room speechless. The sound of disturbed laughter echoed behind me! I stood paralyzed with disbelief! Was this really happening? *Snap out of it Creed*, I told myself. "You won't find any information about a Giest's sear on that machine. Most don't survive it! Especially not twice. However, it did help to i-dent-i-fy you quite easily." More unnerving chuckles came from the henchmen in the back of the room! I could hear them scurry closer. My brain was warning me to escape, but it was too late. I'd been surrounded! "If it weren't for your father's Quetral stone around your pretty little neck, our task would be complete!"

I looked down at my talisman. "So, since I can't necessarily claim you for the time being, why don't you tell me where it is? I promise when the time comes, I will take your soul quickly! You won't suffer…much"

"What are you talking about?" I managed to choke out.

"Come now, did you really think you could hide forever? After a few centuries, one would think you'd catch on!" Its vacant black eyes narrowed all the while flashing a demented grin. Shortly thereafter, a new set of despairing eyes filled in the dark openings. I watched as the huge, reptilian tongue swept back and forth across its hungry lips.

"What are you talking about? Who are you? I, I don't understand! How do you know my father?"

For a moment it stared at me as if trying to read my thoughts. Coming to my senses, I clutched my flashlight like a weapon. "You truly don't know?" it said tauntingly. "Aaah, I see," it mused. I could hear the voices mumble and pause, trying to solve this riddle "…less knowledge, less power, less attraction….nice…yes, very nice! I shall remember that," it hissed! I gripped my necklace. It froze in fear. The creature's eyes, now abandoned, watched nervously, waiting for me to do something. It nodded to the demons behind me. "And yet it is possible you are lying to me," it snarled!

I felt for my backpack, ready to run, when out of my peripheral view I saw movement. I looked in the doorway and there stood Burt with a stack of books in his arms. Not wanting to be distracted too long, I turned my eyes back to creature, but it was gone! I looked behind me. They were gone, too! The room was silent. The only sound that followed was Burton hitting the floor.

CRAPCER SIX

Who's Afraid of the Dark?

he school doctor informed Ms. Woods that Burt's fall had caused a minor concussion. It's something that happens when your head gets struck hard…or you faint and blindly hit your skull on the ground. In other words, his brain sloshed to the other side and back, causing swelling in certain areas. After staying for a short observation, he was released and told to lie in bed for a couple more days. I was just thankful he was okay. But in a way, I couldn't wait to find out what he had seen. I didn't want to push it though; he was pretty groggy. Mr. O'Keefe was the first to answer my cry for help. "What in the name of amber ale happened, lad?" he shouted!

I heard myself come up with a quick cover. "I think he tripped with a stack of books in his hands, sir."

He eyed me for a moment, waiting for more of an explanation. I watched him check the ABC's: airway, breathing and circulation. "Grab his legs," he ordered! "Thank God I brought me truck tonight!" A few of the ladies from the decoration committee screamed when they saw us carrying Burt down the stairs. They frantically crowded around us. "Make way!" screamed Mr. O'Keefe. "Were takin him to see Doc!" When we finally reached the parking lot, we found his truck. Carefully we laid Burt down in the bed of it. I sat with him while Mr. O'Keefe drove like heck to the emergency clinic on campus. Burt did not stir. He did not wake up.

What's happening? I thought to myself. *What did they do to him? Please be okay!*

The emergency staff took Burt right in while we anticipated his mother's arrival. After a long wait involving absolute panic, tension, and confusion, Burt was deemed stable enough to go home. I felt so guilty. He'd only been hurt because of me. But how could I tell everyone that a bunch of soul thieving snake men were responsible? I wasn't even sure if Burt had seen any of them…And if he had, would he remember? He was woozy from the pain medication by the time the nurse wheeled him out. Mr. O'Keefe sat patiently waiting to drive us home. Of course, Ms. Woods protested, saying that he had already done too much. But Mr. O'Keefe was determined. He stayed through the entire ordeal. He did nothing but show genuine concern for Burton's welfare, and I was thankful for the extra support.

No one had really asked what we were doing in the library. I don't think anyone suspected that it would be the optimum location to stir up trouble. Burt's accident did have a bright spot for me. It caused so much drama that my burn almost went undetected. My mother did notice it, but was easily convinced I'd spent a little too much time in the sun. What was she thinking? It had only been raining for the last few days! "Creed, lad, grab your pal's belongings and help me wheel him to the truck!" Ms. Woods was busy discussing last-minute details with Doctor Whitmore. I saw her sign some sort of release papers. In turn, the doctor gave her a prescription to fill.

"We'll take him right home, Ms. Woods." Mr. O'Keefe sounded tired.

"Thank you, Clancey. You have been such a big help."

Clancey? Mr. O'Keefe's first name was Clancey? I started to laugh out loud! I did everything but point! "You can still call me Mr. O'Keefe," he said, addressing me with a stern smile. He wheeled Burton out the door and motioned for me to follow.

"We'll see you in a little bit, honey." My mom reached toward me for a hug. "I'm going to talk to the doctor a bit longer and then we'll need to stop at the pharmacy."

"Don't worry; he's in good hands," I assured.

I caught up with Mr. O'Keefe just in time to help put Burt in the front seat. The drive home was awkwardly quiet. Burton was starting to come to his senses. "Hey buddy," I said nervously, "how are you feeling?"

He shakily answered, "I feel like I've been run over."

Mr. O'Keefe produced a nervous laugh. "You'll be in your own bed in no time, lad. Fer now, you need to rest. We'll stay with you until your mum gets home." We pulled into Burt's driveway. Mr. O'Keefe helped him get out of the vehicle and in the house. We carefully corralled him over to the sofa.

"Creed," Burt said in a weak voice, "what was that thing? I don't remember falling…it was like a great explosion forced me to the ground."

Mr. O'Keefe's eyes held mine in silence. "Hey buddy, I think you hit your head too hard. I don't know what you're talking about. Just get some rest," I added calmly. I propped his head up with a pillow and covered him with a blanket from the back of the couch. It didn't take too long before he passed out from all the excitement. I only prayed he wouldn't talk in his sleep. O'Keefe sat at the table uncomfortably quiet.

"Can I get you something to drink?" I offered.

"Creed?"

"Yes sir?"

"I, I need to know if…well what happened in library?" He shocked me with his direct approach. "T'was there someone up there with you? Did someone scare you lads?"

I couldn't answer. I tried not to let the silence be my answer. He would think I was crazy! I thought I was crazy. I could just see it now, crazy boy kidnaps girl and tries to kill best friend… I spent the entire time at the hospital trying to make up logical explanations for the bizarre things that had transpired. "Or," he said, "did some '*thing*' scare you, lad?" He looked at me with such a knowing. I was ready to spill it all. Ms. Woods broke the tension. In they walked with armfuls of groceries and the prescription.

"Clancey? Still you act as an angel of mercy! Thank you so much for watching over these two! I don't know how to repay you!"

Mr. O'Keefe just smiled and waved his hand through the air. "I don't need anything, ma'am. I'm just glad the lad is okay." His eyes locked with mine once more. "I best be going fer the night." He stood up and adjusted is suspenders. "We've got a lot to do for the ball this week. Can I be counting on you, Mr. Griffon, fer some assistance?"

"Yes, sir," I said confidently.

On his way out, he whispered something to me. His voice was riddled with a chilling sense of caution. "Do not take off your Quetral stone, lad…your dad's talisman… They're out there ... If you want to see tomorrow, don't take it off fer nothing!" I don't even remember shutting the door behind him. I heard the roar of his engine as he drove away. What was happening to me? The sting from my burn brought me back to the present.

"Come on, honey, we need to leave these two to rest." My mom's voice was urging me toward the door. I heard her tell Ms. Woods that she could call us for anything, day or night. "I'll send Creed by in the morning to look after him, okay?" His mom smiled thankfully at me. I felt for my necklace. It was the only thing that made me feel safe as we stepped outside. It was pitch dark. The walk home was the longest one of my life. I heard every wind surge and rain drop for 20 miles around.

"Creed, why are you so jumpy?" She was obviously aggravated. I fumbled for our front door key and escorted her inside. An eerie absence of sound filled my ears. But nothing felt out of place. I did a quick check around the house for signs of any disturbance. I was sure about a few things: I wasn't tired and I didn't want to fall asleep! I was afraid to close my eyes…and Mr. O'Keefe… He knew! He knew something! I had to talk to him!

That night, I lay wide-awake in bed. Everything I'd spent the day denying was turning into my reality. That thing knew my father! Why did it call my Talisman a Quetral stone? And why did Clancey use the same term? And most of all, what was it looking for? My mind spun endlessly. I watched every hour go by until around dawn. Then I slipped into a deep slumber from exhaustion.

CHAPTER SEVEN

Steak Knife or 911

"Time to get up. He's been asking for you! C'mon! Amanda and Burton need our help." My mother's voice was pressing. "It's getting late." I looked around the room half dazed. Everything was in order. It felt like I'd only fallen asleep minutes ago, but I was glad for the daylight.

I dressed quickly and left for Burt's house. Ms. Woods greeted me on her way out. "I've got to go to work, Creed. Thank you for looking after him!"

Burt's gruff voice retorted: "Would you like to chew my food for me, too?!"

She halfway leaned back inside the door. "Don't forget to take your medicine." He grumbled something at her. She smiled. "He's all yours. After work I'm going to stop by the school and help your mom. I'll call and check up on you to see how things are going." She grabbed her raincoat and left in a hurry.

I walked on in. I tried to hide my shock. I'd never seen him in such bad shape! He looked far worse than the time he'd gotten the flu! He appeared very pale and run down. His brown hair was matted to the sides of his face like he had been sweating all night and his bright green eyes were dull. "So, what do you want to do today?" He supplied a sarcastic look.

"Well, I guess hang gliding is out." He cracked a smile. I suggested watching a few movies and flipped on the television. The news was still covering Isabelle's disappearance. So much had happened, I'd completely forgotten she was missing! Burt didn't take notice.

"Looks like you'll be working at the ball without me," he said.

"I didn't think you wanted to go."

"It's a different thing all together when you can't go."

"I'll split my tips with you," I offered.

"Thanks Creed, but that's okay. Have you gotten your costume yet?"

"No, I think Isabelle's disappearance threw a wrench into everything. I heard my mom tell her assistant, Mrs. Knorr, to phone the entire planning committee. They'll be working round the clock to complete the final details."

"Creed?" He said my name in such a way that it made me lock eyes with him. "What happened to me?"

"What do you mean, Burt?" I tried to sound convincing. "You hit your head, buddy."

"No, I mean what really happened up there? I'm not sure if I dreamt it or what I saw happened before I hit my head, or because I hit my head I saw them... I can't seem to get them out of my mind! They looked so real! I don't remember fainting. I've never fainted in my life! You know that...I do remember a great force knocking me over..." I was at a loss for words. He knew me too well. There was no denying it. I couldn't hide the expression of fear on my face. "They were real, weren't they? Just like in your dream!!" I silently nodded. He closed his eyes and took a deep breath. "What did they want?"

"I don't know, Burt. The one in the front said a lot of things that didn't make sense. They want to hurt me. I know that much!"

"So, is that what happened to your face?"

I nodded again. "It called it a Giest's sear." His jaw hung open as I told him what I'd experienced in the computer room. I went on to tell him about what Mr. O'Keefe said. He sat quietly for a long time.

"So your dream..."

"It wasn't a dream," I added.

"And Mr. O'Keefe?" he said questioningly.

"I haven't figured that out yet. I think we can trust him. I don't know how he knows…but he does."

"Are you afraid?" he asked.

"That would be an understatement. I don't know what's happening, Burt. This summer started out so strange. I get hit with an apple, she winds up missing, the police suspect us, you fall, and my nightmares are real! I want to talk to O'Keefe, but I don't want to do it alone." He wholeheartedly understood.

"I'm feeling better. Maybe we can find him today," he said hesitantly.

"No, you need to heal. Besides, your mom would freak out if she thought you were out running around so soon after your accident."

"Creed?"

"Yeah."

"I didn't faint!"

"I don't think you did, Burt. I think one of those things pushed you down!"

"I think they did more than that," he said. "Let me show you what I found this morning." He leaned his head forward. His chin touched his chest. "Come here and take a look at this." I drew near with caution. In doing so, I caught a glimpse of something about the size of a nickel on the nape of his neck. He moved his hair out of the way. It was clearly an image of a snake, and it had been embossed into his flesh!

"Does it hurt?"

"Not really. It feels sort of like a bee sting. It kept bothering me, so I used my mom's makeup mirror in bathroom for a closer look." He straightened up and faced me. "So, what now? I think we shouldn't be alone without some type of protection...witness... My mom won't mind it if you keep me company while I get better," he added. "You can stay here tonight!"

"I'm worried about my mom," I said.

"You don't think those things will hurt her, do you, Creed?"

"I'm not sure. I know she'll probably be staying late at the school this evening. I don't believe she'll mind if I stay here." He gave a faint smile. "It asked me for something. It said it knew my father and something about me being in hiding for centuries. I don't know... I think we should try and get a hold of O'Keefe. Does your mom have the staff phone book anywhere?"

"Yeah, over there," he pointed. I rummaged through an end table and found it.

"I think I'll give him a quick call. Maybe he can meet us?" I found his number under custodial services. Burt looked on intently. "It's ringing." A minute later, it was still ringing. "He's not home," I said.

"Maybe he's helping your mom. The ball is in two days. From the sound of it, the committee is behind. I'm sure he's helping out somewhere." I listened to his voice of reason and hoped he was right. "So what now?"

"Well, the most important thing is for you to feel better! Let's wait for Mr. O'Keefe and ask him what to do." We found ourselves waiting and waiting, and waiting... Our day was spent playing board games, chess, and watching lightening streak across the sky. I made lunch: bologna sandwiches and chips. Ms. Woods called a few times to check up on us. I assured her everything was fine. My mom called late in the afternoon, too. She was destined to work into the wee hours of the morning. Apparently, there was a misunderstanding with the caterers. Then there was a problem with the decorations. I listened to her endless list. She was tired and frustrated.

"I asked Burt's mom if it was okay for you to spend the night there, honey." I sighed with relief. "The storms have caused problems with these old phone lines. I've had one heck of a time getting through! I tried calling you with Mrs. Knorr's cell phone but that didn't work at all! I'm just glad I finally got a hold of you."

"Don't worry Mom. Things will work out."

"Oh Creed, it just keeps getting worse! Mr. O'Keefe left on some sort of emergency! He was my go-to guy! Now, I'm afraid I have to find someone else to help me."

"Did he say when he'd be back?!" My question sounded a little too urgent.

"No. Creed, are you okay?"

"Uh, yeah Mom, I just didn't get my costume from him."

"Oh, in that case, I can bring you one."

I made an effort to sound light-hearted. "Make it a good one!"

"You bet, sweetie. Give Burt my love." I could hear voices in the background. "I have to go now, dear." The ongoing dial tone snapped me back into reality. I hung up in defeat. Burt lay back down on the couch.

"Mr. O'Keefe's gone, isn't he?" I couldn't even look at him. "Now what?"

My response was slow and unsure. "What time does your mom get home?"

"I think she closes tonight, which means she won't be home till around eight o'clock, but I overheard her talking to your mom about the ball. When she gets off work, she's going over to the school to help out."

"How are you feeling?"

"Okay, I guess." His answer was somewhat uncertain.

"Maybe we can do what they do in the military. We can sleep in shifts. You take the first watch, then it's my turn."

He began rubbing the back of his neck as he spoke. "What happens if they come back?"

"I haven't figured that out yet, but we have a few hours before it gets dark."

"I don't think darkness matters," he mumbled.

"What do you mean?"

"Because it wasn't completely night time when they found you in the library!"

"I wish you hadn't said that."

"Maybe we should try O'Keefe again?"

"Good suggestion." I ran to the phone and dialed his number. It rang and rang. Burt looked on with great expectancy. I shrugged my shoulders. "No one's home."

He kept rubbing the back of his neck. "Are you okay?" I asked.

"Yeah, this thing stings quite a bit."

I had become very familiar with that feeling. My face still bore the signs of the sear. I went over to the sink and wet a dishtowel for him. "Here," I said wrapping it around his neck. He thankfully accepted. I caught a quick glimpse of the snake. I could've sworn it had gotten bigger, but I was tired and evening was approaching. Occasionally, I got up to check outside for signs of something, anything, but before too long the darkness overtook the light. We were left with dim shadows cast by the street lamp. Ms. Woods called a few more times. She would in fact, be joining my mother at the school. They wouldn't be home until early morning. I made sure all of the doors and windows were locked. We kept the phone nearby in case we needed to dial 911. Although I wasn't too sure how they would help us against soul-nabbing creatures.

Burt and I armed ourselves with steak knives from his mom's cutlery drawer. I made my bed on the floor while Burt stretched out on the couch. "Why don't you catch some z's for a while? I'll wake you up when it's your turn."

I was already a little groggy, so I didn't protest. I clutched my talisman in one hand, steak knife in the other. In record time I drifted off to sleep remembering Mr. O'Keefe's instructions: "Do not take off your Quetral stone. Do not take it off for anything!"

CHAPTER EIGHT

Borraye Constriction
by Death Bite

J sat straight up in the darkness… panic-stricken, still gripping my stone and knife. The sound of Burt's snoring was loud and deep. The clock on the microwave read 1:00 a.m. Poor guy must've passed out and forgotten to wake me. I grabbed his flashlight and shined the beam of light around. Carefully, I peaked outside, but didn't see either of our cars. I guessed they were still planning for the ball. Burt's breathing grew heavier. *He needs all of the rest he can get*, I thought. I tip-toed around the room checking each window. I froze for a moment only to disregard a strange sound…a whisper… "No," I said out loud. My stomach began to growl. I was starving! Trying to be quiet, I made my way to the refrigerator for a late snack.

My efforts were interrupted by another strange sound. I stood motionless and listened. I couldn't deny it! I was hearing something. I was hearing some type of voice! It did cross my mind to wake Burt up, but it was obvious he needed sleep. I headed in the direction of the stairs. I could hear the sound of someone calling my name. "Creed…. Creed Griffon… Are you in there?" The voice was coming from Burton's room. My feet slowly made their way up the steps as if anchored in cement. "Creed?" I walked down the hallway toward Burt's door. I was shaking so badly I found it hard to grip the knife. I closed my eyes and gingerly pressed my ear against the door. "Creed, lad, it's Mr. O'Keefe." The familiar static from Burt's walkie-talkie accompanied his urgent tone. I quickly pushed the door open and flooded the room with light. It was creature free. The sound of radio garble helped me easily locate the device.

"Mr. O'Keefe?"

"Yes, lad. It's me. We've got to move quickly! I need you to listen carefully. Have they come back yet?"

"No sir. We've been waiting all night."

"Aye. That can only mean they're planning something." He sounded quite confident. "They will bring more." I felt my stomach churn.

"Mr. O'Keefe, what's happening?"

"All in due time, lad. Right now, we need to keep you safe. Has she told you about the chronicle yet?"

"What's a chronicle?" I asked in exasperation.

"Your mum… Has she given it to you?"

"Mr. O'Keefe, she's not even here. What are you talking about?"

"Let me in, lad!"

My response was tentative. "What? Where are you?"

"At the front door, lad. Now let me in before I become folly fer Thoth!"

"How do I know it's you?"

"Because I fixed your necklace with a clasp in the shape of an infinity knot; it matches the one on the pendant."

Immediately, I spun the necklace around. I saw the new clasp in the shape a figure eight. Now why hadn't I noticed that before? I ran for the front door. Burt was snoring loudly on the couch. Knife in hand, I turned the knob. Finally, some help! I took a deep breath, preparing for a hearty greeting, but choked as he entered the doorway. It turned and spoke into the darkness."

Mallanot, Vesh, guard the house!" I heard footsteps running away in opposite directions. It turned back toward me and closed the door! Shrouded in darkness, I saw the shape of a man, but he was camouflaged in the shade of night. His movements were fluid; his form like a liquid black shadow. I could see a mirror image of Burton's front door, rain and all, still reflected in his outline. As he strode forward, he shifted back into human likeness. It was as if someone had showered him in water and washed the darkness away! I stood in front of Burton, who was still sleeping, preparing to defend us both!

"Down lad," it said. "It's me, Clancey." It in fact it looked like Mr. O'Keefe, but I was still in shock and great doubt.

"How do I know for sure?" I stammered.

"Because if I were Thoth, I would've tried to kill you by now!"

I let down my guard a bit. "Who is Thoth?"

"Aye, he is Lord Denegaul's servant and grand leader of the Giests."

"Huh?"

"He is the one who left his sear on your face!"

"Oh, the face changing snake guy," I muttered. My description made him chuckle. "What are you?"

"Years ago, you taught me how to shift the night into submission. Do you remember?" I stared blankly at him. "It was in the temple of Dendura," he said impatiently. "I can see you have much to remember, but luckily that is *not* my area of expertise. Right now, we'll need to take care of your friend before he is constricted to death by the Borraye snake!"

"Burton? What do you mean, death?" He slowly raised his hand in the air as if he were asking a question. "Vecht Lore Aviatan!!" I turned just in time to see Burt's body gently roll over onto his stomach. "Come here and see," he urged! Burt's breathing had turned into wheezing. "Look here, lad!" He pointed toward the snake. It had grown large enough to cover the back of his entire neck. I could see reptilian skin emerging from its outline. "Borraye snake," he pointed. The small tip of the Borraye's tail was wiggling from within Burt's flesh. "It is from the death bite of a Giest. They strangle slowly. When the victim dies, the reptile completely disintegrates. The soul is then taken by the Giest who left its mark. It will choke him by dawn if I don't get him to the Ivy cottage for help."

"What can I do?"

"You will stay here and act like nothing has happened. We need to contact your mum, but not raise any suspicions. They have not yet detected my presence, but any sudden moves and we will be swarmed by some of the nastiest creatures this side of Polaris! You can count on one thing. They are out there watching and waiting…waiting fer us to find it!"

"You mean the Giests?"

He put his head down. "Aye, the Giests, and the Fallon, even the Gheddons. There are many more that no longer follow our ways." He stood up and said something strange. "Amanat duat!" Immediately, I heard a soft tap at the door. In walked two silhouettes encompassed in the same color of night O'Keefe had camouflaged himself in. "Mallanot, Vesh, meet Creed." They turned to me and bowed. "You will take Burton to the Ivy cottage! He needs assistance from the Dorn. He has been bitten by a Giest." Burton effortlessly glided through the air toward them. As he floated past, I could clearly hear his labored breathing. When his body came in contact with the guards, it vanished!

Clancey shut the door behind them. "He is in good hands, Creed. The Dorn have fought the Giests for many years. They know how to heal his wound." I sat down on the couch. It was still warm from heat of Burt's body.

"What have I done? I've sent my best friend off with some sort of invisible night beasts!"

Mr. O'Keefe touched my shoulder. "He'll be okay. I promise." The voice I had just heard sounded like Burt's! I looked up. It was Burt, in the flesh, with a big smile on his face! I reached out to give him a bear hug.

"You idiot," I yelled! "You're back! It worked! You're okay! I can't believe…"

"No, no, no, lad, wait! Wait! It's me, Clancey!" I blinked a few times. This was all happening way too fast. I was seeing Burt, but hearing Mr. O'Keefe!

"Burt?"

"No, Creed. It's me, lad. I've shifted. Someone has to take his place while his wounds are being treated. We'll raise fewer suspicions this way." His voice immediately transitioned into sounding like Burt's with an occasional O'Keefe adage.

"Oh," I said sounding disappointed. "It's just…well, he's my best friend. I'm responsible for whatever's happening to him. This isn't the first time I've gotten him into trouble, but it does qualify as the worst."

"I was your best friend long before Burt. Can't you remember?"

"I'm sorry; I don't even believe this is happening. I'm just waiting to wake up."

"Aye, lad, it is real." His statements were sure and cold. "Soon you will see and know things that you could never imagine. Some you'll wish would go away by blinking your eyes…but they won't. Don't let doubt and unbelief be your excuse for failure."

"Can't you fill me in? What's going on? What are you?" I knew I sounded pathetic, but I hoped he'd provide a logical explanation for everything.

"Did your mum ever tell you about your dad?"

I stared at him. "She told me he died when I was very little. I've only seen a few pictures of him. She doesn't leave them out for display." I adjusted my stance. I wasn't sure what he wanted to hear. "I actually stole one of his pictures from her special scrapbook. I returned it the same day, but not before scanning it in the library. I kept a copy for myself. I was just tired of trying to remember what he looked like!" Clancey continued to listen intently. "Do you want to see it?"

He threw his hands in the air like I'd been reciting an afterschool special. "I should've known she wouldn't tell you anything!"

"Tell me what?" I said harshly.

"Why your dad of course! He isn't dead!!!" He took a deep breath and began to spew information faster than I could absorb it.

CRAPTER NINE
One Big Freaky Field Trip

"*Y*ou are the Son of He!" His expression was wide-eyed and expectant! It was as if he wanted me to stand up and cheer. I desperately tried to piece together what he was saying, but the disbelieving stare gave me away. He instantly became frustrated. "We don't have time for all this, Creed! Your life is in danger! We need to plan for what's coming!" He scratched his head and started to pace. I was still trying to get used to the shift of O'Keefe masquerading around as a Burton's look alike! Not to mention the fact that every once in a while he would startle me by using both hands for dramatic effect.

"Your father...his name is Holgraham." He said this with such absolute certainty that it angered me. "Now wait a minute! You've gone too far! You don't think I know my own father's name?! His name was Augustus Griffon!" He dismissed my comments and repeated himself rather forcefully.

"Your father's name is Holgraham, I tell you! He paused to regain his composure. We made direct eye contact. "He is, in fact, The Genocent of Dendura, Gate Keeper to the Realm of Magic, Grantor of Immortality, Author of the Great Work, and Propagator of Honorable Craft! Dendura is the sacred place...and you; you are the Son of He." Still nothing... With each statement he became more agitated. I didn't know how I was supposed to react. According to him, I'd won the lottery or something.

"Why, everyone knows who you are, Creed! Our only problem is that *you* don't know who you are! Your craft is legendary! Your powers are rivaled only by the Genocent himself!" He was painfully aware I'd still made no connection.

"Look, what do you know about Egyptian history?" he asked impatiently. He searched my face deeply, looked over his shoulder and continued. "Egypt was a grand civilization, a mighty dynasty that flourished in the sands of the desert for thousands of years! Their empire influenced the development of many ancient cultures in the Mediterranean world and beyond. They held a vast knowledge of medicine, astronomy, science, agriculture, mathematics, arts, architecture…anything you could think of!" He startled me by thrusting his index finger in the air. "But they were not limited to just worldly understanding!" This was said with such passion and fanaticism, I was afraid to breathe.

"Egyptians were also a very spiritual people. They worshipped multitudes of assorted of deities. So the eventual clash of scholarly knowledge with spiritual knowledge was inevitable. Arising from this conflict came a question that even they could not answer." His words became slow and halting. *"How –is –immortality- achieved?* Tis a quandary no one could solve…or could they? Over time, Egyptians grew absolutely obsessed with the afterlife." I couldn't hide my growing indignation.

"This is insane! I'm sorry, but what does *any* of this have to do with me? Where did you take Burt?"

"He is in good hands! Do you want to learn or not?!"

"Of course I want to learn, but I don't see what Egypt's past has to do with me!"

"Then I'll help you to see," he said. "Come closer."

From his head he plucked a single hair. He held it taunt then blew through one of the ends as if it were a straw. It emitted a stream of white mist. The vapor produced a good sized rectangular cloud confined to the area in front of him. The fog billowed and rolled forming illusive shapes within an unseen canvas. Certain outlines primitively resembled human shadows. There were at least three from what I could tell. The portrait consisted of swirling misty silhouettes with vapor for color and images that seemed to need facial features.

"We could do with a bit of pizzazz don't you think?" He pulled another hair, only this time; it was from his eyebrow and repeated the same process. A rainbow of colors erupted from the strand's tip. The liquid bounced about the picture similar to that of miniature pinballs, washing everything in its path with various shades. An image of a young boy came into focus first. He looked a little older than me and had shoulder length hair the color of hay. One lone braid rested near his face. Two smaller boys were hiding from him in a tall grassy field. Everything appeared life like... So you can imagine my surprise when they actually starting running and laughing. I watched just as if I were staring at them through the front window!

"Whoops! Wrong memory! Hold on a minute." He furiously waved his hand through the images scattering them until they were gone. The smallest boy escaped dissolution and Clancey had to chase him around the room. When he was finally captured Clancey tickled him! The boy giggled as he faded into thin air.

"Sorry 'bout that. I'm a little bit out of practice." He let out a sheepish laugh. "I'll get on board in a second." From scratch he ritualistically repeated the hair pulling process and before long I was staring at a very different recollection. "I'm no scholar but is that..."

"Egypt," he said finishing my sentence. "Yes. This is where it all started. It was a much simpler time," he whispered. I couldn't believe my eyes! I was gazing upon the inside of some sort of Egyptian Temple. Natural sunlight illuminated the magnificent room. Hundreds of colossal pillars held up a vast stone roof. Dazzling hieroglyphs ornamented every column, ceiling and open space. The attention to detail coupled with the endless palette of bright colors was astounding.

"I recognize this!" I exclaimed. Clancey got excited! "You're serious?! Do you really, lad?!"

"Whoa! Wait a minute! I mean I recognize this from my father's books. Only those pictures don't have all of the vibrant colors! This is amazing! Is this how it really looked? Everything seems so alive!"

"Come," he said. "We must move quickly." In unison he placed the back of his hand on my forehead and the other on his. Then he brought the palm side down over our mouths. He performed the last step by placing a hand over his heart and mine. "Rembrenerick!" I felt a strong pulling sensation as if someone were yanking me forward by my shirt.

The next thing I knew we were standing inside the temple! I was no longer an observer! I was a participant! Real live Egyptian men and women were scurrying past us although they took no notice of our presence! "They don't know we're here," he whispered. "We need to hurry." I understood that to mean no more questions, but I was so excited… He began narrating the scene of events.

"Now, there were many dynasties in Egyptian history. Various pharaohs ruled each one. The pharaoh was king, supreme ruler, but revered as so much more! The position of pharaoh in the ancient world was essential! The belief was held that he alone could commune with the gods and intervene with the supernatural beings that controlled the destructive forces of nature.

"In walked a reverent procession consisting of one man followed by a company of servants. He wore a sacred head dress made of blue and yellow striped cloth. It covered his head and shoulders. Perched on his brow were two golden images, one of a vulture, the other a cobra. Blanketing his chest was an elaborate breast plate decorated with hundreds of exquisite jewels. His lower half was wrapped in a white linen cloth and held up by a golden belt. Even his sandals were embellished with precious stones and embroidery of the most lavish sort. I knew better than to ask. But if I had to guess, this was pharaoh!

"The pharaoh was regarded as more than just a king; he was seen as the actual living incarnation of a god!" I observed a few of the servants as they walked up a set of stone steps. The stairway led to an immense throne atop a grand platform. They placed incense around his chair just as he was preparing to seat himself.

"Without him, it was believed that society and the world would collapse into chaos! Common people gave him immense authority, respect and tribute. He was exalted by priests and scribes. No one was more obsessed with the afterlife than pharaoh! He so desperately wanted to maintain his powerful status in the present as well as eternity. In his position, who wouldn't?" He began speaking in a low whisper. I leaned in closer.

"Thousands upon thousands of years ago, the great pharaohs of Egypt formed a secret society, The *Ankha'ni'sis*. It means giver of life." Pharaoh waved his hands and the entire entourage left, all except for two helpers who stood on either side of the throne. Shortly thereafter, in walked who I assumed to be the Ankha'ni'sis. They moved in unison and in block formation, three across and four deep. Out of reverence they kept their heads bowed and proceeded toward the great king. Each priest wore a white hooded ceremonial cloak that covered him from head to toe.

"Only select priests were chosen to oversee this clandestine project. Their main goal? To ensure the pharaoh's position in the world of immortals. You see he wanted extra insurance that he would live forever as he'd been promised. Many, many failed. But it was the mighty Genocent... Yes, your father! He was the only one to succeed in this quest!!" I listened as his voice began to crescendo. He was so caught up in the moment that he didn't notice one of the priest's heads was raised. It was cocked sideways as if he was straining to hear something. Not wanting to break ranks he began discretely peering around like he'd lost something. And although I could not see his face, I got the distinct impression we were being watched.

"It was he who wrote the great magic thereby introducing humans into the world of Dendura! The chronicle documents his craft, incantations, and spells. All the knowledge we so desperately need! Sadly, its interpretation is limited to the chosen few...Exodus!" he commanded. I felt a backward pulling sensation. Before I could breathe we were standing in Burt's living room again!

"Let me guess," I said breaking the ambiance, "I'm one of the chosen." I just couldn't take it anymore. A combination of fear, exhaustion, and overload befell me. I realized the sarcastic laughing I'd been hearing was coming from me! "I'm sorry, Mr. O'Keefe, Burt, whoever you are…This is really neat and all, but you've got the wrong guy! Did you see that pharaoh?! I'm no god! I'm Creed Griffon. You know, mediocre student, plain, simple, throwback... Everyone knows this! This is just a dream…Yes, I'm sure this is just another wicked dream! Burt and I will have a good laugh in the morning and all this will be over!"

"Oh, you think this is a wicked dream, do ya, lad? Heh, Heh, Heh," came his mocking laugh. He pretended to wipe a tear from his eye. His voice was sure and unwavering. "You can do better than that. Pah-lease! You're just as stubborn as you ever were. You can deny all you want, but it won't change what's coming..." I tried to protest but he loudly spoke over me.

"And if your regard for yourself is based solely on what others believe, then mediocre is all you'll ever be...

By the way, I never said you were a god. Your father was a member of the Ankha'ni'sis. He is the man that bridged the world of humans to the world of magic. It was he who learned the secrets to immortality and the hidden portal which led to the Infinity. Of course it is the Infinity that houses the realms of magic... At first the Semigents and Intelligents residing there questioned whether pure blooded humans should be allowed further access to their mystical world. But over time Holgraham gained their trust. And in return, they showed him favor by revealing their coveted secrets. The Genocent was taught how to bring genuine humans into the world of magic by writing the city of Dendura into existence. The chronicle was penned out of necessity! It is the sacred writings that reserve a place for Genocists; you know humans of magic and sustain their prolonged existence within magical realms. You, Creed, are his Apprentice."

Silently, I mulled over the inexplicable experiences I'd had the last few days. As angry and confused as I'd become, there was no denying the extraordinary happenings. My extra insurance? Burt had seen them, too! "What does my mother have to do with all of this?" His impatience grew.

"We have no more time for pleasantries, lad! They'll be coming! And we must be ready!"

I adamantly repeated myself. "What does my mom have to do with all of this?"

"Fer the chronicle, of course! Use your head!"

"How do you even know she's got it?"

He glared at me as though I'd punched him in the gut. "We don't!" he said sharply. "She's always kept her distance from me unless it was work related. We had an understanding. She didn't offer and it was not my position to ask. She relied on me to do my jobs and my performance was never questioned! Implicit trust!" he said bowing his head. "However, if she does have the sacred writings, it was never mentioned to me…maybe out of concern for everyone's safety? I don't know," he whispered. "We need that chronicle to keep our people alive… And your mum is our last hope."

CHAPTER TEN

Impossibly Possible

My persistence earned me more than I'd bargained for. "Now, that's out of the way, you hungry?" he asked. "How about some eggs and toast?"

"You're kidding right?"

"No, I'm quite serious. I don't like to plan on an empty stomach."

"How can you think of food at a time like this? According to you we're preparing for the apocalypse!" He cast a jolly smile and shrugged.

"We should eat while we can. In our line of work that's an important rule! I don't expect we'll be seeing much human food after this. Besides, a few near death experiences is good for a body. It'll be like old times!"

"Are you serious?" He happily breathed in a deep invigorating breath. He looked as though a heavy load had been lifted off of him. "There's more to life than just book learnin', Creed."

"Aren't you scared?"

"Awe!" he said with a devious smile. "But that's what makes it all worthwhile, don't you think? You can't say you've really lived until you've been scared out of your skivvies once or twice! Now how about those eggs?"

"None for me…thanks."

"Then don't mind if I help me self." And he did just that, rummaging in Burt's kitchen and through his refrigerator like he lived there!

I sat at the table and listened to his account of my mysterious past to the tune of banging pots, pans, and slamming cupboards.

"When Holgraham disappeared, we found that the chronicle had gone missing, too. At first we thought that perhaps he'd taken it with him on another one of his long journeys, but it's different this time... Dendura is beginning to show signs of decay. I never thought I'd see the day," he whispered softly.

"You see, something must've happened. He's not continuing the great work. Surely if it was in his possession he'd do so! Around the same time our enemies were enlightened as to our unfortunate situation."

"How do you know he hasn't been captured or something?"

He just shook his head and stirred the eggs. "The indications would be quite evident. Horrific destruction, chaos, the unimaginable would rule in this world, as well as our own. Trust me, he's no one's prisoner."

"And his great work?"

"Where's the hot sauce?"

"The what?"

"Hot sauce...You know, red spicy liquid...You can't have food without hot sauce!"

"Over there," I said pointing.

"The great work is the continuance of the chronicle. Only the Genocent or his offspring can write in its holy pages and by doing so, Dendura and its inhabitants continue to exist while the wicked ones are kept at bay. But it's not just the Genocists' existence that is at stake. Because they've become a major force within our worlds, all realms are threatened. Even this one..."

"Holgraham knows better than to let Denegaul find both of them together. This means we still have a chance!" It sounded as though he was trying to convince himself that there was still hope.

"Whatever reason for his disappearance, we believe he entrusted your mother with the book, instructing her on what to do when the time was right. It's a risky move, I know, but he must've felt your memory alteration was foolproof." He seated himself at the table and began shaking hot sauce over his plate.

"That's it! Excuse me? What did you say? Was it memory alteration? You did say mem-or-y alt-er-a-tion, didn't you?!"

"And a right powerful one at that!" he added with a mouth full of eggs. "Your mum kept the past from you to protect you. We all did. We had to prevent you from remembering at all costs. Just about anything can elicit a memory from your subconscious mind.

"You sound like my mother," I added.

"Why thank you! She's the one that taught me that."

"I don't believe any of this! You speak about it so casually… as if we're talking about the weather!"

"It's best if you don't fight it, Creed. As I was saying, most anything can cause a memory to surface. It could be a smell, a picture or even a word… We were very, very careful. You see, if your subconscious memories were somehow triggered, the knowledge and craft would be irrepressible. For your safety we couldn't allow for that. No sir! The wicked Lord would be swift to zero in on you! Even now, the seeds of magic are being nourished inside you. It's growing because of what's going on around you. We must be very careful from here on out."

"Wait a minute. This is all happening too fast. I don't even feel any different."

"You don't have to. It's the slower way to get you back to normal, but it's all we have right now. More importantly, because your craft has been reawakened it will continue to grow stronger and stronger. Eventually it will vehemently attract the wicked lord and the legions that wish to kill you for it!" He took a deep breath and proceeded to drink the hot sauce straight from the bottle.

"It's really very simple. They can sense the use of magic no matter how minute. All magic folk have this ability, but we're taught early on how to conceal such things if need be. You're too new at all of this to know how to mask it just yet. There are three elements to keep in mind: size, location, and awareness!" He licked his thumb and then held it up. "One, you have to be looking for the source of unmasked magic. You have to tune in to it much like a frequency on the radio." He spoke out of the side of his mouth, "And trust me, they are. Two, Three!" He abruptly thrust his first and second finger in the air. "The greater the size of blatant magic conjured the stronger the beacon especially in Rogue territories not known for using plentiful amounts of craft on a regular basis. This signal will serve as a locator of sorts.

"And if you're near someone that's summoned a great deal of magic that's not disguised or hidden in any way, it's like a forceful pull on your personage. You can actually feel it tugging at you. Not in a violent sort of way, but in the sense that something's been stirred within you. We don't want to stir the wrong side. No sireee," he added with a chuckle. "I'd liken it all to thunder. You can be going about your daily business when you hear it roll in the far off distance…no big deal. You don't pay it much mind. But if you hear an ear shattering crack right up close and personal, it gets your attention! There's no guessing as to where it's at!."

"But how can they sense magic I don't even know how to use?"

"On the contrary, you will…It'll just start happening. Can't stop it now, even if we wanted. You've seen too much….heard too much. This is why we need to be very careful."

"So the more powerful the disclosed magic, the harder the pull can be, especially if you're close to it? And if you're looking for it, you'll find it."

"That's it!" he said proudly. "Maybe I'm not such a bad teacher after all! When someone throws a large ruckus of magic like that, it's hard to miss, particularly if you're nearby. The threat is after you're restored to your old self, or should you accidentally dispense any serious amount of noticeable craft before then, it will be like wearing a huge signal that screams, HERE I AM! Most likely your lineage isn't helping us either. I wouldn't be surprised if you're naturally emitting a slight magical ambiance already. Why I've heard that some of those beasts can pick up on the slightest quiver…"

"Do you think that's how they found me to begin with?"

"Hard to say, but not to worry," he added. "I'm workin on that one."

I didn't want to hurt his feelings, but I had to ask. "Have you considered the fact that they already know what I look like? They know where I live."

"Yeah, they may know all of those things, but whose house are we in right now?"

"We're in Burt's," I replied.

"At the moment you're not anywhere you shouldn't be. We're safe for the time being. We also have a little added insurance because we have a few friends watching the perimeter. It's when they find out that you are not where you're supposed to be… that's when trouble starts. But no fears, Holgraham taught you the mysteries of the ages. And in time, you will remember them all to include continuing the great work." He lightheartedly buttered and jellied a piece of bread. "I was hoping when you saw me shift the darkness, it might bring back that night in the temple. But so far, you seem pretty lost." He momentarily studied me, and then haphazardly slapped me on the shoulder. "Nothing has worked so far!"

"But I don't get it! If all you need is someone to write in a book, why can't you do it?" He gave a modest laugh.

"Because, I've already told you, I'm not his progeny, Creed. That's your department. Besides, Holgraham put a Clysmic spell on it. If anyone other than 'the chosen' so much as scribbles in it, they'll be instantly banished to the shadow worlds. Nasty business! Trust me, not a good place," he said peering at his 'new' likeness in his knife.

Then he did something peculiar. He leaned in to me and began whispering even though we were the only ones present. "But, there's another way, a faster way… If we can find the chronicle before them, you need only lay hands on it and your memory, knowledge, and power will swiftly be restored! Of course, we'll take all precautions necessary to do that properly… But at least this way, we get the book and you can better defend yourself should the stone begin to fail you. I admit it's a little dangerous but it's better this way, then the way they have chosen for you. After we gain possession of the writings, and you've been restored, you will finish your training. Then you shall be a mighty force, ready to take your place among your people."

"But you're the custodian!" He laughed.

"Yes, for years now. My true commission was to watch over you, make sure nothing bad happened to ya! And might I say, you've been quite the handful, sliding book ladders and all…"

"But who…how?"

"Your mum asked me to be your guardian long ago."

"Then you must know why they want to kill me! I've done nothing to anyone! And who exactly is this Denegaul you spoke of?" His countenance unexpectedly changed. He put his fork down and pushed the plate away even though it was still heaped with food. His fists clenched and his jaw tightened. He stared off into nowhere for a very long time. I got the feeling that I'd said something very wrong. He forcefully shoved his hand into his pocket. I could hear his fingers fiddling with something that made crinkling sounds. His words came out rather abruptly.

"Aye Denegaul is a friend to no one," he spat. His eyes briefly flashed a red glow. "He answers to many names, but he is in effect, the dark lord, ruler of MalDracaena, the shadow worlds, and the wicked realms. A whole list of other titles follows his name…none of 'em good, I can tell you that." He ran his tongue over his teeth and began rocking the chair. "You have the right to know of his atrocities although I have no right to be schoolin ya in such things." Then he pounded the table so hard that his fork somersaulted backwards! Immediately his hand shot up with all five fingers spread wide, signaling for it to stop. The fork came to a screeching halt just before impaling itself into the wall. Gently it came to rest on the counter.

"If you remember nothing else, remember Denegaul is the pinnacle of dark magic, propagator of evil and hatred, a most clever and ruthless opponent. He's the reasons we're in this mess. And all that is vile bows its knee to him. At one time the evil lord and his followers were immortal like Holgraham. But after the Genocent uncovered their plot of overthrow, he cursed them with the Demigent spell.

Before I could ask, he answered, "Regardless of our bloodlines, most of us *are* Demigent which means we're semi-mortal. We are capable of living much longer than the average Rogue…You know non-magic humans… The drawback is that we are just as susceptible to their everyday ills and weaknesses. We simply have a longer life span to try and dodge the inevitable." "*The inevitable?*" He rolled his eyes. "Why death of course..." "Oh, I see..." He shook his head. "Anyway, few have been granted the rank of immortal. However, it's a different ordeal entirely when an immortal falls to the levels of a mere commoner like the rest of us. To be purposefully cursed...ripped from such an exalted status simply to face one's eventual demise??? Now that's a horrific and humiliating tragedy! Only those who have tasted of eternal life can understand this affliction. That's why they desperately seek the chronicle!! Their life supply *is* dwindling. If they've managed to evade death this far, *and in their line of work it ain't easy*, the curse will ultimately kill them... sooner than they'd like... "

"So they need one of us to interpret the book in order to regain immortality?"

He gave a solemn, "Yes. Make no mistake; Denegaul is the poisonous root behind every cunning attempt on your life thus far, and many more to come. One thing you can be sure of, he'll stop at nothing to learn the secrets in that book!"

I found myself trying to rationalize the totally irrational. Reality was ever so slowly sinking into my thick head. There was no getting past certain events. I was talking to Burt...But it really wasn't' him! My real best friend had been taken away by some liquid camouflaged men. And those Giests...I couldn't come up with reason enough to discount them as being imaginary. In all sincerity, I asked, "But what does Denegaul have against me? Did I do something to him personally?"

"It's not what you did, it's who you are. With your father's whereabouts unknown, you are the evil lord's last chance to regain eternal life. As long as it was just your father, obtaining an interpretation of the sacred book was a remote possibility. But then they would've had to capture the Genocent, which is next to impossible. Oh, they've tried countless times to kill him for it, but his powers are too great!"

"So my father is immortal?"

"Yep."

"Are there a lot of immortals in your world?"

"Nope. You can thank Denegaul for that, too. Originally, the Genocent made all humans who entered the great city immortal. But because of the overthrow, he quickly realized what a drastic mistake that was."

"Well if he's immortal, then why does he run? Why does he hide?"

"I don't know the reason for his absence. I suppose repeatedly fending off malicious legions can be quite tiring powerful or not… The constant attacks and betrayals must've been not only demanding, but disheartening as well," he mused. "Maybe he just got tired of it all and needed a rest. Who can be sure?

"I do know there are three conditions in which immortals can succumb to death, but I've only learned about one of them. In a nutshell, immortals are said to be subject to death if they renounce the magic that originally brought their immortality into existence. This doesn't imply they die right away either. It basically means they've been turned Demigent by one of two ways, willingly or unwillingly. I can't think of too many that possess the ability to cast such a potent spell. Even so, the Genocent is more than capable of deflecting such a hostile bewitching. That leaves us with willful denouncement which is unconscionable for such a man as He. No, it's something else. I can feel it.

"Despite that fact, neither Denegaul nor his minion's have been discouraged from further attempts. It's possible they know something we don't."

"Like numbers two and three?" He gave me a snide grin.

"I'll have you know those particulars ain't common knowledge or even uttered in everyday chatter," he scolded.

"Regardless, in order to receive the translation, one of you must be sacrificed. It's the only way the book will give up its secrets to anyone *other* than the appointed. So it's nothing personal."

"This just keeps getting better and better," I said cynically.

"At first it was only the Genocent that was pursed… During the dark times, servants of the wicked one secretly infiltrated Dendura. Evil demons they were just waiting to betray him! And because of this, he was not hard to find. Thankfully, he's too powerful to catch. Although, that didn't stop the attacks! Those fiends clawed and grasped at every chance they could to bring your father down." He bowed his head and spoke in such a low voice that it was hard for me to understand what he was saying. "One fateful day, it was revealed that Holgraham had a child…a son he'd been training up while in hiding…That son was you. When news of your existence leaked, our enemies went ballistic. They believed chances for survival to have increased in their favor. I'd liken it to a pack of wolves chasing their prey. If there's a weak or injured one among the group, they will attack it first."

"So I was weak?!!"

"No, quite the opposite, but you were just learning… You were his Apprentice." He licked a spot of jelly off of his mouth with his tongue. "Denegaul figured you'd not be as strong as your father. Of course you were just a young boy, right? But that's where he was wrong. Under your father's teachings your powers quickly superseded your age! They were beyond what anyone ever expected! We were all so proud yet amazed at your extraordinary skills. On the other hand, Denegaul was consumed with efforts to capture you believing that he and his armies could undeniably overpower one boy. We would conceal you; they would find you; we would barely escape! At the same time, additional legions of the dark lord were methodically searching for the chronicle. This scene played itself out over and over again…It was a deadly game of cat and mouse.

Meanwhile your craft was becoming more powerful by the day making you harder to hide because you didn't possess the full ability to mask the potent magic you discharged. Inevitably, your power drew the enemy like bees to honey. We didn't know who we could trust. Your safety was constantly in jeopardy," he said shaking his head.

"After the discovery of your existence, Holgraham tried to keep you close by to protect you, but together you made more of a target. In the end he simply yearned for you to have a normal life free from fear and impending harm."

"What makes you think anything is different this time? I'm still just a boy. Apparently one who can't remember…"

"Oh yeah, about that…I recognize that things aren't necessarily in our favor right now." He put his plate on the counter and started filling the sink with hot soapy water. "Honestly Creed, your memory alteration was done out of desperation…It really was a dire situation… What you don't understand is that you had to use your powers to practice your skills. Unfortunately, you also had to use them to defend yourself. Point blank, you had to use them one way or another. But it was the exertion of your craft that created the very problem we were trying to avoid. Eventually it was found by withholding your memory; your knowledge and power would cease, making it more difficult for our adversaries to detect you. In order to save you, the great magic was used to put you into a deep slumber. All remembrances of your past life were completely wiped away!

"It's a simple equation. No memories = no remembrance of craft = no powers = no attraction. We returned you to a somewhat younger state in order that you should create a new past, and new recollections of your own. You were finally safe. And when it seemed as though the terrible season had passed, we awoke you, free to start again!"

"So how many childhoods am I supposed to have had?" He wiped his mouth with his sleeve.

"Two, this one and your first one." Hearing him actually say it so bluntly left me speechless. My mind couldn't even begin to find the words...

"And our plan seemed to have worked, at least for a while that is. Then the rumors started. Subtle whispers that were followed by questionable signs. Shortly thereafter, it was confirmed that Holgraham had truly disappeared and the chronicle was nowhere to be found!

"He's been gone far too long. Dendura is crumbling and our people will die... all because there is no one to write in the sacred pages! That's where you will come into play. Except now, our adversaries know your true identity! The evil lord cannot afford to let you slip away this time. And because of your encounter with Thoth, he suspects your memory to be impaired." There was a hint of nervousness in his voice.

"This weakness can be used in their favor. You can bet they will increase efforts to find the book. Once the chronicle is in their possession, they seek to capture you and force the knowledge to come forth. Make no mistakes about it, after you've served your purpose, he will take your life without a second thought! Obviously, he doesn't want you hanging around challenging his new-found authority. And if they succeed, no more Dendura; Denegaul and his legions live forever. Every realm, every world will be ruled by his cruel hand! It will be a dark eternity."

CHAPTER ELEVEN

The Collected

She awoke to find herself on the floor of a small damp cell. There were no windows, neither were there any doors. She was cold, wet, and dirty. A single candle dimly lit the room. The dying flame was surrounded by splashes of dirty wax. She gasped for air quickly remembering what she'd thought was a bad dream. Sitting up, she realized it was no dream at all. "Please!!! Can someone tell me where I am? My name is Isabelle Polanski!!! Please!!!! Someone?" Immediately, she felt for her cell phone. No luck. Using the wall as a brace she stood up slowly and in doing so, hit her head on the dirt packed ceiling. The sound of water dripping was the only reply. As her eyes adjusted to the poor lighting, she began to feel her way around. The enclosure was no bigger than an average sized walk-in closet. In her short travels she stumbled upon a cot. Next to the makeshift bed was a huge pile of jackets, purses, and extraneous outerwear. She promptly sat herself down. "Where am I?" she whispered.

Out of the darkness came a calm response. "We're in some sort of underground holding cell..."

"Who said that?!" Isabelle screamed.

The unfamiliar voice emanated from a dark silhouette in the opposite corner of the room. "My name is Walter Winchell...Please don't be frightened...According to my guessti-mate you've been here for about three days. I've been waiting for you to wake up. See, look here." A faceless shadow grabbed the solitary candle and held it up to the earthen wall. He was pointing to the tally marks he'd made. "It's hard to tell the time of day in this place. But I've done what I could…"

Then he held the candle near to himself so Isabelle could see what he looked like. He appeared fairly tall; because he couldn't stand upright so much, he leaned sideways to avoid hitting his head. He had short blond hair, glasses, and when he smiled he brandished a set of perfect white teeth. He offered his hand up for a shake. Tentatively Isabelle reached for it. "Nice to meet you," she said. "I guess you've already heard who I am?" Walter laughed softly.

"Where am I?"

"The best I can tell we're in some sort of underground prison. From what I've gathered, they collect children here, but for what I'm unsure… Most of them seem to be about our age. Up until approximately three days ago, I shared this cell with a girl named Fiona Talbert. Do you know her?"

"Yes! Yes! I mean no…well sort of… She's the girl who went missing from Pemberton Academy!"

"That's her! I'm really worried," he said shaking his head. "I woke up the other day and she was gone! I didn't even get a chance to say goodbye. The next thing I know, I wake up, you're here. I've had so many roommates, Isabelle… each time it ends the same way. I won't allow it to happen again. I can't take it anymore." The grief in his voice was quite evident.

"How long have you been here?"

"It's hard to say," he said despairingly. "I've lost track. I can't tell you much except for the fact that they feed us twice a day." From his pocket he removed two golf ball size pieces of something that resembled bread dough. "Here, are you hungry?" Isabelle shook her head no. "Then save this for later," he added handing her a piece. "You may need it. But more importantly, are you okay? They didn't bruise you up too bad or anything?"

"No, I'm pretty good other than being dirty, tired, and frightened out of my mind!"

"How did you get in here?"

"I'm from Devonshire," Isabelle replied somewhat dazed. "The last thing I remember is walking to meet my chauffer...and...and..."

"And what?" he added impatiently.

"I don't want you to think I'm nuts or something, but I stopped to talk to one of our teachers along the way and the next thing I know the teacher turned into a.....It all happened so fast," she said quietly.

"Into a student?" he added inquisitively.

"Yes, right before my eyes! How did you know that?"

"Because that's the same thing Fiona said. The others were too frightened to talk about it, but she told me everything."

"Did she happen to say what the student looked like or maybe give a name?"

"Yes, in fact she did say a name. It's was sort of an unusual name." Walter adjusted his glasses and thought for a moment. "His name was Creed, Creed Griffon. Yes, that's it."

Isabelle fell back on the cot completely flabbergasted! "It can't be," she said in awe. "I just can't believe it! I mean I thought it was him, but my mind didn't want to process the idea! Of course we've had our differences, but mostly I just thought it was all in good fun! I don't get it. Why would Creed be collecting kids?"

She continued to argue with herself until Walter interrupted. "So now we're getting somewhere! I only know what Fiona told me about him. Said she knew him because of a school function? Anyway, he's the one who lured her off campus…She didn't want to go with him because he was always getting into trouble… And now look what he's done to you! If I ever get my hands on that guy, I'll kill him!"

"It's okay, Walter. I'm okay. I'm not disagreeing with you about the trouble part, but the fact of the matter is, he gets into *trouble* because he's usually defending himself…And to be completely honest, some of the teachers are more partial to the wealthier kids and so they side with them right or wrong."

"What do you mean and why would you make excuses for a loser like that?" he spat.

"He just sort of doesn't *like* to fit in with the rest of us. It's not that he can't. I was once made to go to a dance with him as a punishment. Do you know that he stayed clear on the other side of the room rather than be sociable and hang out with my friends? Either that or he just really didn't want to be around me."

"I've heard his name enough to know that where he goes trouble follows. First Fiona, and now you! I bet he was the one responsible for Timothy, Sandy, and Kim Lee, too! Tell me, did he ever give you the slightest inkling that he might be different?"

Isabelle adamantly shook her head no. "There never were any indicators that he was 'different' so to speak. Actually, he's very smart. I think his problem is that he's not really into the school's atmosphere. I don't know. Lots of kids at our school drive fancy cars, wear expensive clothes…that sort of thing. I suppose looking at it from his perspective; Devonshire can be a stuffy place… He seemed turned off by the whole scene. In retrospect, I can't say I blame him," she admitted. "But frankly, he never gave the slightest hint that he had magical powers…or was a shape shifter of some sort! It's amazing!"

"You believe in such things?" Walter scoffed. "I meant 'different' pertaining to raving lunatic...How do you know we weren't drugged or something?"

"Of course I believe in magic! Don't you? You're here and all...How did you get in here anyway???"

"Wait a minute. Forgive me," he impatiently added. "This is the first solid connection I've been able to find!" Isabelle watched him pace with staunch determination. "Maybe if we can find a few more similarities between your stories, it may lead to us getting out of here! Fiona said there were others. Did you see anything else?"

"Yes." Isabelle's voice quivered. "While he was talking two black funnel clouds came creeping up from the ground on either side of me. And out of their centers stepped something revolting." Walter could see that she had started to tremble. "They couldn't have been human. I, I tried to run..." Isabelle cried softly. He sat down next to her. "My parents must be so worried...Well, at least I think they are. They're having *'problems.'* I was sent away to Devonshire as always. I don't even know if they've worked things out. I don't know if I'll ever see them again. " Her restrained tears soon turned into sobbing.

Gently, Walter removed a dirty tissue from his pocked and dabbed her cheek. "Don't cry. Please don't cry." Carefully, he tucked her brown hair behind her ear. "We'll get out of this place somehow. I promise.

"I, I want to show you something. Fiona and I believe it might be a way out of here," he said almost inaudibly. "Come see." He picked up the candle once more and walked over to the other side of the cell. "See here." Isabelle got up from the cot and followed after him. He was bending over a small section of freshly dug earth. "If they knew I had this they'd kill me for sure. It was left behind in one of my prior roommate's jackets. He never knew what he had poor chap. I recognized it immediately. I was hoping Fiona and I would get a chance to figure out how to use it, but well…like the others she's not here anymore." He bowed his head. "I don't know how much more of this I can take, Isabelle. His fingers quickly excavated the soft dirt until he came up with a small object.

"It's called a Fenestra. It's how I landed here and I'm pretty sure it's how some of the others ended up in here, too." Amidst the meager luminescence Isabelle could see a silvery, shiny coin. "Most simply put, it's a window maker," he said. "I was walking home from school and found one similar to this one on the ground. Like anyone else, I picked it up."

"Why it's a quarter," mused Isabelle.

"No, that's what they want you to think. I mean who would pass up money lying on the ground? Certainly not me! When I first saw it, I already had plans on how I would spend it. I could easily buy a new slate and some chalk for school. Of course my mom was always complaining that we never had enough sugar in the house. I was going to buy her the biggest bag that the mercantile carried!"

"Aren't you afraid someone will find out?"

"They haven't so far."

"So how did you end up in here?" she asked curiously.

Walter shrugged. "It seems so long ago…It doesn't matter anymore." He took a deep breath, closed his eyes and began to recall a story he seemed to want to forget. "I didn't go to a fancy school like you. I went to Brixford."

"I'm sorry, I don't know too many schools that aren't…Well you know, like Devonshire" Isabelle said somewhat embarrassed.

"Don't worry," added Walter. "You're not missing much!" Their laughter soon turned serious again. "To answer your question it all started when I was walking home, from school. I remember my dad wanted me home right away to help with the farm work. As always, I passed by the mercantile. They had a water spigot. It was a long walk home so I decided to get a drink. I put my books and slate down. When I was finished I gathered up my things. I happened to notice a coin on the ground near where I'd set my stuff. I thought to myself, *It's my lucky day!* But as soon as I picked it up, it was as if time had unzipped itself right in front of me and there it was…a window to an entirely different place. I know it sounds crazy, but…" He abruptly stopped mid-sentence. He peered around frightened.

"Shhh!" hissed Walter. "They're coming!"

"Who's coming?" Isabelle asked shrilly.

"Our captors," insisted Walter. "You'll be okay! Just do as I say!" Isabelle strained to hear something…anything…dripping water was the only audible noise. Just as she was prepared to say he'd made a mistake, Walter walked over to the wall and began conversing with it! "Yes, she sees…and believes. She says he does not conjure his magic. It is as we thought. If I could have more time…Yes, my lord."

Isabelle began wondering just how long Walter had been cooped up in the dungeon. But it didn't last long. Unexpectedly a portion of the wall twisted and opened up! With unshakeable confidence, in strode the most hellish creature Isabelle had ever laid eyes on! It was Thoth himself dressed in his most decadent ceremonial garb! You'd think something that smelled so awful wouldn't be that confident. The black garment swaddled around him precluding Isabelle from seeing his face in its entirety. But that didn't matter. A pink fleshy snake's tongue erupted from his mouth. One half of the forked appendage preened his robes emphatically while the other half stayed behind to guard against escapees. Isabelle screamed bloody murder! "THAT'S THE THING!!! THAT'S IT!! THE FUNNEL CLOUD!" Blindly, she grasped on to Walter's arm!

Strangely enough, Walter's arm didn't feel like a normal arm should. It felt unusual and somewhat fluid filled. A chorus of demented laughter filled the chamber. Immediately, her eyes swept to his face. The blond hair and glasses were nowhere to been seen. Staring back at her was the hideous face of a Giest.

CHAPTER TWELVE
Sugar Fix

"Look, I know this is all one big blur. But you've got to trust me."

"So, if what you say is true…" Clancey rolled his eyes. "Where could he have gone? Where is my father?"

He bowed his head. "We don't know. We have endlessly searched him out. It seems as though he's vanished! Genocists' say he has gone off to create a new chronicle. Others say that Denegaul has him on the run. We tried to keep his disappearance a secret so as not to cause alarm. But like our adversaries, we, too, are running out of time. They know as well as we what is coming. We need your craft, Creed…please. We need you to continue your father's great work. If Dendura's present situation does not stabilize, its inhabitants will be forced to live in this world, or within the realm of spectrals; some may choose to dematerialize all together. Trust me; none of them are good options."

"Okay, so tell me, what are Genocists again?"

"This isn't Latin class master. You've got to pay attention. There are two types of humans. The ones that know magic are referred to as Genocists. Ones that don't are referred to as Rogues; *R*ude, *O*verbearing, *G*reedy, *U*nbelieving, *E*gotistical *S*pines!!"

"Whoa! Wait! That's where I draw the line! Don't EVER call me that again!"

"You misunderstood me! I'd never call *you* a Rogue!"

"No, No! I don't care about that! *But,* I am NOT your master. I'm just a kid…like you, I think?"

"Oh. Then what should I call you?"

I thought about it for a second. "Friend."

He grinned. "Then it is, like it was!"

"You know what I think my problem is? I'm trying to make sense of it all when you can't make sense out of any of this. Maybe we can make some sort of deal and just give the book to them?" I'd realized as soon as I'd blurted it out, that it probably wasn't the smartest thing to say. But my mind was swirling with heaps of information and I was too tired to make excuses for it. Little did I know what happens to him when he gets really, really, angry…

He slammed the silverware down in the sink and stopped washing dishes all together. The room grew sharply silent. There was rage in his face. I heard a crackling noise. It sounded as though I was stepping on the potato chip bag Burt and I'd ransacked for lunch. *'No, no crinkly bag down there…'* Looking up, I couldn't help but notice his skin had changed color. At first I tried to convince myself it was the lighting, but then the left side of his head began to twist and bubble! Slowly, the right side followed suit while his body grew to enormous proportions! It all happened so quickly…I stood in awe wondering if it was safer inside or outside! Razor sharp spikes emerged from the tip of his hairline, and back behind his skull. Those that erupted from his spine tore through his clothing leaving nothing but shreds to cover his massive body! The sides of his muscular arms burst into thousands of thick dagger like projectiles! Burt's phasaud had completely disappeared! As crazy as it sounds, the creature started to look alarmingly familiar. But where had I seen a man with an animal's head before? Suddenly, I recognized its likeness from one of my father's books. I was in the presence of a Minotaur, but none like the pictures I'd come to know. This was the mutant version including bonus features.

The metamorphosis continued with the manifestation of two huge ram horns. They spiraled and wound in a circular pattern behind his head, eventually ending in razor sharp points that faced forward. Each antler grew almost instantaneously, encompassing his brow with their immense form! His ears became nonexistent and were immediately replaced with a set of small spiky ones. His nose flattened producing a bull like muzzle. Rows of razor-sharp teeth erupted from inside his mouth! I was on my way to being completely mortified when I spotted the little, spunky, white lamb's tail he dawned on his backside! Such an innocent feature stood out like a kazoo at a violin concerto. I started laughing out loud! I couldn't help myself. That particular warm and cuddly attribute didn't belong on such a monstrosity, and it didn't make sense…but then again a Minotaur in Burt's living room didn't belong or make sense either! I was so floored by everything else that it took me a moment to realize the iris in his right eye had completely disappeared! I came to my senses and darted over to the other side of the room finding my knife on the way! Lamb's tail or no lamb's tail, this thing was far from friendly! I was half way up the steps when it addressed me. He wiped the froth bubbling from his lips and spoke in a low growl.

"Khemphre Fortall!!!" He took a piece of foil wrapped candy from what was left of his pocket, tore it open, and popped it in his mouth. His face calmed instantly, similar to boiling waters suddenly without heat! The transformation ceased! "Never say ANYTHING to me again about giving those plunderers the book! They've destroyed EVERYTHING that was important to me…everything I cared about!" he screamed. "We will not *GIVE* it to them," he hissed. Next, and with great restrained passion, he told me what they would do to me. "As a rule they will kill you only after you've laid hands on the sacred writings, then and only then will the translation be released and they in a secure position to take it from you! Unlimited waves of fury will follow suit! Evil from the likes you have never seen will devour anything in its path! Oh there will be GREAT suffering," he growled.

"The wicked one must NEVER learn the secrets in that book! Don't you get it? Denegaul will become the most powerful force known to spirit, man, or beast! He will enslave all living things! We will NEVER give those traitors the advantage unless today is the day YOU wish to DIE by their hand!" His breathing was erratic. He'd used every last ounce of his breath to convince me. He reached into his pocket for another piece of candy. About that time, I recognized he was shifting back into Burt's likeness.

Mental Note: Never mention anything ever again about giving the chronicle away. It was obvious I'd pressed him to his limit. I ached with so many unanswered questions. Confusion did not begin to describe how I felt. "Then why didn't they capture me in the library?"

"Because," he said hastily grabbing a clean shirt and pants from the laundry room, "you're wearing the Quetral stone, of course! Its origins are as old as Dendura itself! It is said to be formed from the primordial mound that gave birth to Dendura! You have one half and your mother is wearing the other. It's protecting the both of you! I'm sure it hasn't slipped your notice that it doesn't stop their continual attempts to detain or locate you. It simply means, for the time being, that their magic won't entirely work on you."

"Then why should I be afraid of what's out there?"

He threw his hands in the air and in doing so finalized his shift back into Burt's resemblance. "The Quetral stone is a direct reflection of Dendura's wellbeing. Slowly, it will erode, much like our home is starting to do. Its strength will weaken, thereby leaving you defenseless! That's what they're waiting for! You will need to generate your own craft to protect yourself." Before I was able to ask any more questions, we heard the sound of keys turning the lock. Our attention focused on the front door. In walked Ms. Woods.

"Burt? Creed? What are you boys still doing up? Burt what are you doing standing up?"

"I just came back from the bathroom. Besides, it was getting late and we got worried about you. We decided to wait for you to come home."

I stared at Burt's new twin. He looked, acted, and sounded like Burt, but it was Clancey…Mr. O'Keefe in there. "That was so sweet of you guys. Look! You even tried to clean up!" She gave Burt a kiss on the forehead. "How are you feeling, honey?"

"I'm doing better, Mom. Creed took care of me all day. He even made me lunch and dinner."

She spent the next five minutes telling me what a "great kid" I was. During which "Burt" made mocking faces at me behind her back. "Creed, your mom probably won't even make it home tonight. When I left, she was trying to solve a costume fiasco. By the way, she sent this one home for you." She held up a costume neatly folded inside a storage bag. "You can try it on tomorrow. It's very late. Why don't you stay with us tonight."

Yeah, I thought to myself, *like I want to be alone right now*! "Sure, Ms. Woods. Thank you." She saw to it that we made our way upstairs. Strict instructions were given to "get some rest!"

"In a few more hours your mom will need help finalizing last-minute details for the masquerade ball. She's counting on you, Creed. We don't have too much longer till show time and no one knows where Mr. O'Keefe is. I hope he's okay," she muttered. "Now, get some sleep you two! Burt needs all the rest he can get right now." She turned to me. "I'm trusting that you'll take that into consideration." I got one of those "motherly" looks before she closed the door.

"I think she means business, lad. I'll take watch the rest of the night."

"But what about my questions? I have so many. I am so confused!"

"You can't quit now!"

"You heard his mum. Anyway, you need rest, Creed. Many a poor decision has been made due to lack of sleep. I have some planning to do. I'll take advantage of the peace and quiet." I'd taken only a minute to turn down the bed, but when I was finished he'd seated himself at Burt's study desk. A set of knitting needles and a ball of yarn were rhythmically being maneuvered through his hands. "I know of worse habits!" he said defensively. "Besides it helps me think." I lay there for quite some time trying to piece everything together while he knitted and slowly rocked himself back and forth.

Then a horrible thought occurred to me: "How will I know my mom will be safe? We've got to hide her or something! Don't we?"

He let out a sigh. "She's got the other half of the Quetral stone...and she is well versed in taking care of herself.

"I don't understand any of this? Why did he leave us?"

"That'd be a question best left to your mum's explanation. But if I had to guess, I think he did it fer your guy's safety."

"Well if he's so powerful, you'd think he could sneak a visit! My mom really loves him! She cries and I feel so helpless!"

All he could say was, "In time you will understand."

I didn't feel like talking too much after that. As I lay there, I tried to stop my mind from coming up with more questions. It's not every day you find out your dead father is alive…or he's some sort of a god…or that your entire life is a lie! I managed to fall asleep only because I wanted to forget everything…the monsters…Isabelle…a past I could not remember… There was still a slight chance I'd awaken from this strange and horrible dream.

CHAPTER THIRTEEN
No Time to Doubt

The morning of the ball came quickly. Ms. Woods left a note saying she'd already gone to the school to begin preparations. My costume lay neatly folded on the kitchen counter. According to her, Burt was to stay home and I was to meet them at Devonshire to begin final set up. The house was abnormally still. After a short investigation, I realized I was alone! I clutched my Quetral stone for reassurance. I wondered where Burt…Clancey had gone. I still wasn't sure what to call him. All I could remember was that someone was impersonating my best friend.

I grabbed some cereal and sat at the table. I had so many questions to ask my mother, but knew better than to run out the door on my own. What did he mean by craft? And what mysteries had my father taught me? I strained to remember something, anything, from this distant past, but nothing surfaced. I closed my eyes and tried to imagine my father by my side. It just wasn't happening. I became frustrated. It left me to wonder what I actually could remember about my 'first childhood.' My earliest memories were of Burt and how we'd met in kindergarten. As I recall, we almost collided on the playground. We were trying to catch a baseball hurtling in our direction. Neither one of us managed to do so and fell flat on our backsides laughing! The smile disappeared from my face. Now I was supposed to be an Apprentice? An Apprentice of what? What in the heck is craft? I shook my head and laughed.

Jokingly, I raised my hand as I had seen Mr. O'Keefe do. Three words came to mind. Without much forethought, I sarcastically voiced them: "Vecht Lore Aviatan!" At least I think that's what he'd said… After that I don't remember much.

When I came to, Burt was standing over me. He sounded concerned. "You okay?"

"Yeah," I said, rubbing my head. "I think so. Is it really you, Burt"?

"Sorry to disappoint you lad, but it's still me. How's your head?

"I'm not sure what happened."

"It looks like you were assaulted by the remote. I think the remote got the worst of it though." He expelled a nervous laugh. "Try not to do that again, okay? Remember the beacon and all." Pieces of black plastic and electrical components began coming into focus. I rubbed my forehead.

"Where were you?" I asked, rubbing the tender spot.

"You were still sleeping, so I decided to check the perimeter. I wasn't gone long, but when I came back, you were on the floor out cold! The television still works." He cleared his throat. "Tried the retrieval spell, did ya?" He gave me an annoying grin.

Disregarding his comment, I asked, "What time is it?"

"We have a couple of hours before we leave for the ball."

"Did you see the note?" I asked. "You're supposed to stay in bed today."

"Yeah, but I've got that one taken care of. It's a masquerade ball, isn't it?" He flashed a devious smile. I stood up slowly and rubbed my forehead. Maybe there really was something to this craft I'd been told about. "Next time, I think I'll turn the television on the old-fashioned way. So, what's your plan?"

He pushed the cereal box aside, then took a map from his pocket. In the background I heard something about a breaking news report. "Have you already been to the school?"

He looked up from the map. "Aye, tis a sight to behold! I snuck a peek I did... Your mum has really outdone herself this year!"

"Yeah," I kidded, "I don't believe we'll be staying for dessert though." He didn't answer. Instead, he walked over to the TV and stood in front of it. "What are you...?"

"SSHH!" His hand swatted the air. I realized what had caught his attention. The news reporter was interviewing our school doctor.

"Hey! That's Burton's doctor!" The camera panned to Officer Farnsworth. He was holding my school backpack like he'd caught a ten-pound trout. According to Doctor Whitmore, I'd left the pack in his office.

"You must've left it there the night we brought Burt in!" My mind went racing back to the events of that horrible night.

"I remember helping you get him inside your truck. I'm not sure if I had it with me or not."

"Wait a minute," he said fearfully. "Look!" From inside the canvas sac, they pulled out something small and black. I recognized it immediately. It was Isabelle Polanski's cell phone! "I thought you told me that phone was hidden?!"

"It was!" I snapped back. "I turned it off and stashed it underneath my dresser! How did they get it?"

In his interview the doctor stated he was, "...alerted to the backpack when the cell phone began ringing. When he answered it, someone hung up. The next thing he knew police cars surrounded his office!"

"The satellite tracking must've located it," I said in disbelief!

"Incredible! Shush! Hold on," he said.

"Police are also on the lookout for these individuals." When they were done parading my mug shot, one of Burt's replaced it! Next was a picture of Clancey! An image of the make, model, and license plates of his truck and motorcycle flashed across the screen also. "He is the custodian for the illustrious academy. He has disappeared mysteriously. Mr. O'Keefe is wanted by the local authorities for questioning."

"Well, I'll be," he muttered. "Thorough little varmints, ain't they?" He started pacing. "This is a set-up!"

"What do you mean?"

"Don't you see? They're going to keep you from running! Because of the stone, their magic is limited where you're concerned. And without your craft it's hard for them to keep track of you. But with a little conventional help... The cops will be here and not just for you, I might add. They're getting the cops to do the dirty work for them! Once they have us in some detention facility, our enemies will know just where to find us...any time of day or night. It will make finding the book so much easier when they don't have to worry about you slipping away! When they get it, no prison wall will keep out a Giest, or a Gheddon, for that matter. We'll be like sitting ducks!"

"Now what?"

"We've got to run!" For the first time I heard panic in his voice.

"I thought you said, a few near death experiences does a body good!"

"I'm always in for a good fight...not a slaughter!" His statement was no confidence builder!

"Where can we run to? Can't you just change into something and 'poof' us out of here?"

"Poof? Don't I wish." I didn't try to hide my bewilderment.

"Things don't work like that. It is a lot more complicated than what you might expect. For starters we aren't leaving without the chronicle. Secondly, I can't just go summoning craft in front of unbelievers. Not that it would really matter anyway. Most Rogues can't see us or the magic we evoke unless of course we want them to. But such risks aren't worth taking," he added vehemently. "This entire ordeal is becoming far more unpredictable by the minute...Oh well; I guess that means more fun for us, huh?" And he rubbed his hands together with much excitement.

"Can I ask you something else?"

"Sure," he said curiously.

"What day was it when you lost your mind?" He raised one eyebrow and laughed cynically.

"You see, we were confident you'd never be located. I would've hoped by now you'd be in possession of some of your magical gifts. I could really use the help."

"But what do you mean when you say you can't do any magic, craft, whatever you call it, in front of unbelievers?!"

"I'll give it to you in cliff note version. In the first place, I'm what you might call a little rusty," he said nonchalantly. "Most of us are taught progressively and according to the manifestation of our giftings. If we're lucky, we receive additional training. I never got a chance to finish mine. I guess you could say I'm a dropout of sorts. It's not something I'm proud of but I've made my way."

"Well what about your shape shifting back there? That was pretty impressive!"

"Thanks. That's a compliment coming from you. But transformation is one of my gifts. I'm what you might call naturally talented as far as altering my appearance goes. In other words, I don't have to try too hard or use much craft to make it happen...It's the outcome that can get a little bit out of control." He tried to hide his embarrassment. Clearing his throat loudly he continued. "The problem is when things get a lil'…I mean if I get really, really, angry I can shift, into creatures beyond the rudimentary levels of practical magic. I haven't learned how to fully manage it yet… so sometimes my transformations are somewhat off from standard text book. Maybe if I'd have finished school things would've turned out differently. I don't know."

"Well don't beat yourself up over it," I said jokingly. "I thought you were incredible with those spikes and horns and teeth and everything! You scared the bejeeberz out of me! I knew you were a Minotaur, but you added your own wicked twist to it! I'd have to say your version of that beast was a lot scarier, unique even!" Of course, I'd meant every word I'd said to him. His creation was brutally chilling and one I'd soon not meet again. I knew better than to mention the lamb's tail. I didn't want to embarrass him.

He shrugged and gave a perplexed smile. "I've never thought of it that way… Still, it was cleared up right quick don't you think?" I nodded. "Honestly when it comes down to it, I'm more reliable at beckoning the basic magic I know," he whispered. He could tell from my expression that I was waiting for more of an answer.

He scratched his head then exhaled with plenty of gusto. "Enough about my qualifications! To answer your question bluntly, we'd be crazy to throw magic around in an unsecured environment with Denegaul's henchmen hidden who knows where! I've already told you. Not only can they sense the most infinitesimal use of overt magic but they wouldn't have to search very far for it if it was right in front of their faces! Frankly, we need to be very careful how and when we use our Craft or it will bring them right to us." He turned and abruptly began muttering to himself while keeping count on his fingers as to the reasons why we weren't supposed to. "Not to mention the fact that we'd probably be outnumbered. And then of course we are forbidden to do such things in front of the Rogues, especially the children! There are those whose faith we'd soon not rekindle…."

"No offense but why didn't they send someone more…you know…equipped to handle the situation?"

"You won't like the answer," he said swiftly. "They're preparing for war. I was the most obvious choice anyway. Besides, my teacher always said…"

"Your teacher isn't here right now. I guess we need a plan."

He shook his head. "With all due respect lad, you are my pedagogue, my teacher…at least you were…and will be again." He smiled radiantly.

"What does that mean? And what exactly is this craft you keep talking about? Is it like witchcraft? Are you a wizard or something?

He kept shaking his head. "You have much to remember. Sorcery, Witchcraft, Gheddoncraft, Giestcraft…. Our ability came long before any of that. In the beginning it was simply referred to as craft. And that is the name we've claimed for centuries. Craft is magic in its purest state. Many followed after its inception and tried slapping their own label on it. The label you'd best understand, yes, is 'magic'. Although when some people think of magic they associate it with a magician. His folly consists of optical illusions, well practiced tricks, or sleight of hand type of stuff. No, no," he whispered ominously. "Our magic is very real. There is no pretending here.

"Regardless of its name, since the beginning of time good and evil have always existed, Creed. If you possess magical capabilities and use them for good it creates a positive synergistic energy. In turn, if you have powers and use them for evil, it creates a negative synergistic energy. These are fundamental principles on which all magic is based. You don't have to know magic to be evil. You don't have to know magic to be good. Everybody has the capacity to be one or the other. Inevitably however, one force will always outweigh the other. It is our overall choices that determine which way those scales tip." He began putting things in to his back-pack including a bottle of hot sauce.

"Of course it's hard to remain honorable in a world so full of opportunities to go astray. In fact, every society not only makes it easy to do what's wrong, they condone it. They make excuses for it. However, it takes tremendous strength do what is right… to remain committed to that innate sense of truth in each of us… not just once, but until it becomes imbedded in every fiber of your charac-ter to where you do what's right when no one is looking, without recognition or reward…because your reward *is* the privilege of knowing you're a person of integrity. That is so very precious and rare, and so very powerful! Tis a much sought after commodity. Goodness at its purest and most selfless state formulates cata-clysmic energy ready to be harvested by those who know how!

"To put it simply our form of magic, which can also be referred to as craft, is generated from the collective souls of the good. It forms the portals from which we link. It is the well we con-tribute to. It is the well we draw our mighty craft from. He paused. And yet there are those who know such secrets but prefer to con-jure their magic from a very different source and for a very differ-ent purpose… That is but another story." Without warning, the casements began to rattle. The noise was a foreboding one. We looked out the window. It was peaceful. No wind or rain in sight! "Whoa! Would you look at the time! It's getting late. Get your stuff," he commanded!

"What stuff? Everything I own is next door. This is Burt's house, remember?"

"Well then, I guess you're ready to go."

"Go where? I can't show up at the Andromeda Ball without a disguise! The cops are looking for us, and so are the snake men! They'll nab us for sure!"

He stopped and faced me. "Do you trust me?"

I didn't hesitate in giving my answer. "Yes, I do!"

"We need to get to your mom without raising suspicions. Cops are easy to spot. Fallons and Gheddons are another subject entirely! I'm sure by now that one, if not both, will be waiting for you at Devonshire." Things just got a whole lot more complicated.

"I guess we'll have to change to plan b...stupid Farnsworth!"

He raised his arm and made a motion with his hand, as if turning an imaginary doorknob above his head. A small, red, glowing globe materialized in the air above. He didn't give me time to ask. "It is called a Xenolin sphere. No wand needed," he said arrogantly. His magic, basic or not, was amazing. Of course I was an utter rookie, but I'd hate to see what his definition of 'powerful' meant.

"I didn't think you were supposed to use your craft in front of unbelievers," I said curiously.

He looked around. "Do you see any here?"

I was beginning to really like this guy. "So what does it do?"

"It summons for backup." Effortlessly, he hurled the orb at the floor. There was no sound of breaking glass! There was no sound at all, just the sight of the sphere exploding into a million tiny fragments. We were showered in strange, red, leaf-like particles, which dissolved when I tried to touch them. He started rummaging through his knapsack. "You'll need to change into your costume." I paused momentarily, waiting for something extraordinary to rise from the broken pieces. His impatience grew. "What are you waiting for, lad? Get a move on! We've got to go!"

I ran toward the kitchen. My costume still lay neatly folded on the countertop. I removed it from the storage bag and held it to my shoulders. The material unfurled itself and fell to my feet. I rummaged through the layers of plush velvet folds. What kind of costume did she bring me? Clancey broke out in uncontrollable laughter. I was confused…until I took a good look at the costume, of course. I read the label. It was a replica of Queen Elizabeth's coronation dress! "Just so there's no misunderstanding, I – am – NOT – wearing – this…this thing!"

"Actually lad, it's the perfect disguise for you. It really is!"

I gave him a look of disgust. "No, you don't get it! I'm not masquerading as Queen Elizabeth! In case you haven't noticed, this is a dress; she was a woman! I am not a woman! If I'm going to fight, I'm not doing it in a dress!" He kept pursing his lips, trying not to laugh.

"Okay! Okay your highness! I don't blame you! We'll go as is. There's no time to fuss over disguises! I've got a friend or two in these here woods; they'll help us out. Quickly now! Our backup should be close."

"I just thought of something," I said. "This has got to be my mom's costume. It's tradition for her to go as something like this. She must've had a completely different costume picked out for me. I don't even know who or what I was supposed to be! That means I don't know who she will be at the party! Hundreds of people will be there! How will we find her?"

"Have faith, Creed. We will find her." He grabbed his knapsack and opened the front door.

CHAPTER FOURTEEN
The Realm of the Willow

J stepped into the night ready for anything. I had to voice my thoughts. "I can't believe I'm really doing this! It's crazy!" The air was cold and crisp. "Can't we run back to my house? Maybe I should call my mom? It will only take a minute."

"The longer we stay here, the more dangerous it becomes. I sense it. We need to move fast. Now keep quiet!"

From where we stood, I could see the school's festive lights shining brightly. He motioned for me to go in the opposite direction of Devonshire. "Where are we going?" He held his first finger to his lips.

We walked without event past the other cottages. How I wished I could be safe inside any one of them. Porch lights lit the way until we came to the end of the sidewalk. Beyond it was nothing but a wall of forest. I looked back at the houses fearing I would never see my home again. I could hear faint police sirens in the distance. I knew they'd be here any minute. "Are you ready?" I nodded. "Do as I do," he ordered! I fell in behind him. We began trudging through the most rough, uncut, terrain. Burt and I knew the trails around our houses very well. I dare not say it, but wondered why we couldn't just use one of them. We came upon a thicket of trees so dense I had to move branches out of the way just to go forward. The limbs were gnarled and kept snagging pieces of my clothes. At one point, I lost total sight of him.

I continued to clear a path, but soon noticed something strange… I wasn't brushing against branches, I was pushing something away…it was…it was arms! Within seconds, I found myself walking in step with an army of warriors. Their movements were fluid and inaudible. I was afraid to breathe for fear of being the only one to make noise. At first I wasn't sure if they were on our side. I heard Clancey's reassuring voice whisper, "It's okay, lad."

A minute ago I had been fighting my way past nature, and now I was surrounded by some sort of mystical escort. I gave up trying to make reason out of it.

"Hextal, Shorgwin, katana sticks!" commanded Clancey.

Immediately, two of the cloaked beings took off ahead of us running at top speeds! During mid sprint both sentinels brandished a large samurai sword which instantaneously materialized into a small, thick, piece of wood. They held these objects out in front of them while maintaining their foot race. The baton was roughly the size and shape of a rolling pin. Before I could think to ask what it was for, the guards gripped both sides of the wooden object like the handles of a motorcycle, made a small leap, and flung a leg over an invisible saddle. After straddling the mount, they positioned their bodies in a forward lean and silently rocketed to the air overhead. Besides the riders, the only things visible were the katana batons used for steering. The transports themselves were completely invisible. I remained quiet but that wasn't too hard. I was awe struck.

I snuck a quick sideways glance at my new companions. There were at least 20 of them. They wore full-length ceremonial-looking robes. Each garment was forest brown and trimmed in shimmering gold. Their faces were discretely hidden within the folds of material that formed the hoods. I looked for any sign of human characteristics. I found that to be an odd thought, but after remembering the beast Clancey had become, it wasn't a bad idea.

Their hands were masked by black gloves. Even their feet were shod in dark-laced boots. One could've easily mistaken them for a procession of monks, but the double-edged swords sheathed across their backs told me otherwise. The moonlight gently exposed the sickle-shaped ends of each weapon…definitely not monks.

I was carefully guided toward the center of the formation. But instead of going around each soldier, I was passed right through them as if they'd never existed! Upon contact, they would simply disintegrate and reform once I'd made my way! Our movements were uniform and swift. We walked deeper into the woods. I was trying to get my bearings, but didn't recognize anything. I got up the nerve to cast a glance back. I saw nothing but forest and swirls of fog where we'd been. I was sure the police were at my house by now. "Enjoying the parade?" I spun my head back around. It was Burt, obviously still being impersonated by Clancey.

"What are we doing?" I whispered.

"We're taking a different route to Devonshire," he said.

I insisted, "The school is the other way! You know that!"

He became agitated. Stretching out his arm, he whispered, "After you." I looked in the direction of his invitation. There was nothing but a grove of massive willow trees. "CEPHEUS INCAR-NATO!" As he spoke, the soldiers fearlessly presented their doubled-edged swords. Then one by one they hurled them in the air like a boomerang! Miraculously, every weapon returned to its owner but remained spinning similar to helicopter blades, just above the guards' heads. Without delay, the veracious instruments shot electric flames from their jagged tips! The sickles continued to turn as each warrior reached up, grabbed the spiraling weapon, and brought it back down through his own body! Upon an explosive contact, the guardsman's form was erased, one rotation at a time! Eventually no trace was left except for a few shimmering particles.

The last of the cloaked soldiers were the two aerial riders. They turned to us, bowed, presented their katana sticks, and tossed them into the air. The wooden batons transformed into spinning swords amidst the dimly lit sky! Both claimed the appropriate blade, then disappeared as their predecessors had done. I realized my mouth was still hanging open.

Clancey leaned in and spoke out of the side of his mouth. "Not bad for someone who doesn't pull a rabbit out of a hat. Quick!" he urged.

I was motioned toward the largest willow tree I'd ever seen. *I don't remember that being here. How could I have missed this?* I thought to myself. Its long green branches effortlessly cascaded from unknown heights above. In a way, they reminded me of jellyfish tendrils I'd seen at an aquarium once. I was captivated by the tree's colossal size. Carefully, I parted its enormous limbs and journeyed forward. The realm of the willow engulfed me. I was cut off from the outside forest. It was absolutely peaceful. Looking overhead, I caught sight of the moonlight creeping past its emerald lochs. A subtle wind stirred them softly. Gracefully, they brushed the ground. Fireflies whimsically danced and bobbled in the tranquility.

As I drew near to the gigantic trunk, I could see a small archaic door carved into its bark. A single black rung served as a handle. My hand was quickly shooed away when I reached for it. "No, No, No, Creed! Where are your manners? We must first be invited in! By the way, Druix don't like it when you look 'em in the eye, so whatever you do...don't do that!" He slapped me on the shoulder. "It's a long story, but the truth of the matter is, if you pin 'em down long enough, their eyes will foretell your future, past....sometimes even death! And since we're on the subject you might also want to know that there's a slight possibility of going mad with any of those scenarios… Not to mention the fact that'd you be nuts to try it in the first place. But we've got nothing to worry about." He chuckled nervously. I managed to cast a glance behind me. I could see the woods beyond the willow's surroundings. In that split second it crossed my mind to run. Those thoughts must've shown on my face, because he tried to reassure me…If that's what you could call it. "Not a comforting thought, I know, but many a man has wished to see his own end in order to know how to avoid it. Unfortunately, many have died tryin! But never you mind that…feisty little buggers…they love a challenge!" He spread his arms wide. "Why, I got a scar the size of a…." The door opened slowly. I was hit with a gust of fresh air and the sound of roaring water. I listened as it strained to be heard above the noise.

"Bless my! Tis Hem!" I looked over at Clancey who was still impersonating my best friend. His eyes did not rise from the floor.

"Aye, tis He, old friend. We ran into a bit of trouble with the humans."

"Why, off courst, ye dit! Umans ard nutin bit tribble! Present companist excludes."

"Thank you fer your gracious hospitality, Grapple."

"Twas nuthinga. We ard on nert tu half ye, Apprentisk. Pardons my no speck umans goot!" He opened the door all the way. "Calm end! Calm end!" His welcoming was enthusiastic. I found myself crossing the threshold.

"If it's not too much trouble, my friend, we'll be needing disguises to avoid capture."

"We kin tic cared off dhat!" He sounded like a nice enough guy. "How wasa dhe escurt, grit wund?" His voice was aimed in my direction. I assumed he was addressing me.

I replied rather cautiously, "Fine, thank you." With my peripheral vision, I caught rough sight of the layout.

"Oakley! Pliss tu bringa ourd gists saulm refresh und changed off closed!" I heard distant shuffling and clanging in the background. The smell of something sweet slowly drifted our way. Grapple and Clancey were busy discussing an entrance of some sort. Since I wasn't supposed to look at our host, I continued to survey my new surroundings.

We were inside the hollow of the massive willow tree. It was entirely warm and friendly. Varying shades of luscious green ivy intertwined with the mighty roots anchored in the earthen ceilings and walls. This combination seemed to fortify every room. The main entrance consisted of a y shaped corridor. The left branch was comprised of doors going down either side. The right fork gave off to a small sunken living area which in turn, led to more rooms. An enormous wooden tool rack filled with individual cubby holes arched over the door and outlined this entrance. Each slot was filled with some type of farming tool, such as sickles, shovels, or rakes. They were worn with use. Several instruments were completely unfamiliar to me. Regardless of the curiosities, it was very cozy for being in the center of a tree… Not that I had any other such house to compare it to.

I turned just in time to see Grapple walk down the torch-lit tunnel. He was wiping his dirty hands on a piece of cloth. The light cast funny shadows as he passed by. His stride was one of confidence. His appearance was truly dwarf like. He wore an oak colored tunic and pants. A large leather apron dotted with mud covered his work clothes. Its strings encircled his waist and were neatly secured by a knot tied around his chubby belly. His work boots were well worn and also covered with earth. I couldn't help but notice his arms were muscular for his size, and laden with strange scars. And it wasn't hard to miss the noticeable pair of pointed ears peeking out from beneath his brimless hat.

Momentarily he disappeared out of sight. This was followed by the sound of one of the back doors shutting. The noise of roaring water lessened. His footsteps were approaching. I was quick to lower my gaze, but not before taking into account one last detail. On his chin was an intricately woven long white beard. Its crisscross design was similar to that of a basket or placemat with each layer collectively forming a checkerboard pattern. But that was all I got a chance to see. They continued to hurriedly mull over their plan.

I was drawn into the sunken room by the warmth of a hearty fireplace. It was constructed of long malleable tree trunks no thicker than a soda can. Their smooth cylindrical shapes intertwined and twisted around each other to form the sides and hearth. I warmed my hands while observing an oil portrait hanging over the log mantle. Innocently, I grabbed a piece of kindling to feed the flames. Without hesitation there came a loud snapping and popping. Incredibly, the hearth and mantle crackled, twisted, and glided forming an enormous fiery mouth! Its hungry lips opened wide as the grate assumed the role of gnashing teeth! "Feed her!" hollered Clancey running toward me. "Feed her!!!" I stood entranced! It was so unbelievable! Before he reached me a molten tongue shot forth snatching the piece of wood from my hands! It rolled the timber up in a fiery ball and chomped it with its iron teeth! Instantaneously, everything calmed and returned to normal. The fireplace happily sparked and dusted the ground with embers. Clancey arrived out of breath and shaken.

"Are you all right, Creed? Did Sedona burn you?"

"No, surprisingly I'm good... What the heck was that thing?!"

"Why she's a fireplace of course! If you're gonna feed her, next time don't stand so close!"

From a sideways glance, I caught a glimpse of an unfamiliar profile bearing a snide smile. It was peering out from around the doorway. Due to embarrassment, I didn't bother to pursue the subject further so shortly thereafter, they went back to planning.

"Is it safe?" Clancey asked.

"No wund hast used id end quite saulm time. Tis shurt noticed. We'ef dunned what we kin. Hast hem calmed tu histself yed?"

"Saun off Hem...?" it growled.

In shock, I managed not jump. Remembering the warnings, I didn't look up or make eye contact either. There was a menacing taunt in his tone. His breathing was slow, gruff, and deliberate. I think it pained him to perform such a menial task. I was served a hot drink. It smelled sweet and tasted like thick, black, licorice. I couldn't help but stare at the infinite scars that saturated his arms. They looked like the ones I'd seen on Grapple. Several of his wounds resembled bite marks. Others appeared to have been made by some sort of blade. None looked recent, but each had been strangely outlined, possibly by a tattoo gun to highlight them. "Beautifulg ain't dhey?" He modeled both limbs for me, flexing his forearms and biceps like a bodybuilder. "Tist me badges off on nert! Druix ard warriorst," he exclaimed, pounding his chest! "Fearlest! Sooned we willled seed what ye ard mate off Apprentisk..." His words were carefully spoken in such a way as to try and frighten me.

I intentionally dismissed him as if he were menial servant. "Thank you, Oakley, you may go now."

It was quite evident what he was implying. I must've looked like an incompetent fool with the entire fireplace ordeal. Still I gave the impression that his statement had not moved me. I'd survived countless verbal attacks from the kids at school. His didn't make me flinch, either. Still he stood, waiting for some sort of retaliatory response. His presence created an awkward social pressure. I ignored him and decided to focus my attention to my unique surroundings. Hopefully he'd get the hint.

Opposite the fireplace was a small recessed, dining area. Its sphere shape had been dug into the clay walls. The eatery resembled an old-fashioned restaurant booth. U-shaped bench style seating was molded from the soil and outlined the wooden table held at its center. I intentionally scooched my way around the seat to the middle. Thankfully, it was just out of Oakley's view. I set the cup on the table behaving as if I were a regular. Eventually, he left defeated, surrendering two changes of clothes. I sipped my drink and unfolded one set of black garments. A pair of black boots fell out of the center. The clothing appeared baroque but meant for a boy. I didn't care. It was a better disguise than the get-up I'd left behind! They looked warm and good enough to wear to the Andromeda Ball.

"Saun off hem?" I recognized Grapple's friendly voice.

"I'm over here." His footsteps drew near. "Tis goot tu seed your'd made self ad home. Yezdt?"

Not forgetting my manners, I kept my eyes focused on the table and replied, "I am very thankful for all that you are doing for us."

"Much bliged," he said softly. "Ye ned changed ocake? Pliss tu used bist rums. Watched your'd furdst stepped."

It was at that instant I felt the bench seat pull away from the wall, slowly twist, and lower me down into the earth below.

"Went your'd dunned jist calm beck upped dhe stairst," his voice echoed.

He stood waving at the top of a staircase that had just been my seat… then walked away. In the distance came the sound of Grapple and Clancey planning again. It was somewhat comforting. I had been lowered into what I assumed to be Grapple's personal living quarters. It was absolutely breathtaking! The area was circular in shape and the size of a small bedroom. Several torches in iron floor stands gave the room soft light. Carefully placed vines embellished with tangerine colored flowers hung down to the floor. The foliage added a sweet honeysuckle scent to the air. And as I brushed by them, their petals fell. Just before they hit the ground they burst into an array of vibrant sparks! I watched the mini fireworks display in amazement. Each flaming ember bounced about the room and eventually found itself within one of the hanging vines again. Wherever the sparks settled, new white flowers bloomed. Despite my shock, it was pretty cool. From somewhere up top came a warning from Grapple.

"Dun't titch dhe flowerds ocake? Dhey cand made ye sleeps ford dayst." My mouth hung open. I didn't even blink. Carefully, I withdrew my hand from the petal I was about to pluck.

"Right. Got it!" I yelled back. *"I've got to be out of my mind"* I muttered. As I stepped deeper into the room the subtle light revealed something most extraordinary. It was the walls. They were moving! Drawing closer, I realized they were entirely comprised of glass from top to bottom. Behind this transparent barrier lay an infinite underwater microcosm! The breath taking scenery momentarily quelled my fear of water. "So this is what it looks like under here," I said to myself. Brilliantly colored fish chased each other about the room and over head. The water bubbled and bounced in a soothing motion while filtered rays of light penetrated the waters from somewhere above. Everything was peaceful until a foreboding thought occurred to me…I couldn't help but picture the catastrophe …It was just that barrels of surf kept rolling and surging against those glass barriers... *And I wondered if in fact the glass was strong enough to hold it all back...* I wasn't about to tell them I couldn't swim. I tried to reassure myself while taking a few deep breaths. *I'm sure Grapple wouldn't leave me in a death trap...* But then I reflected back to the flowers...

Hurriedly, I began to undress. Next to his nest-like wicker bed was a small night stand which featured a miniature version of the same picture I'd seen hanging over the fireplace. I heard laughing. No one had entered the room as far as I knew. The sound had probably come from upstairs…I continued to take off my shoes. There it is again! Something moved in my periphery…No, it can't be, but it was! A school of full-fledged mer-people had taken up residence behind the glass. At first they didn't really faze me. I mean why would they? Of course I'd run into worse creatures. From waist up they exhibited human features draped in vibrant shells and seaweed. And from the waist down they donned what looked like dolphin's tails! They seemed friendly enough but continued to point and giggle. "I'm a monkey in a zoo," I said in disbelief. "If you only knew how strange and out of place you are in my world!"

But then the craziest thing happened! The gathering parted and a mysterious mer-girl made her way through the center. She was dressed in rippling seaweed dotted with pink and white flowers. Strands of seashells decorated her long brown hair. She didn't appear any older than me. Curiously, I approached the window. When I was within a foot of her, she gingerly slipped her hand right through the glass as if it didn't even exist! The barrier did not crack or break and not one drop of water so much as seeped through! The arm that had penetrated into my world was completely dry. Just on the other side she floated calmly. Her hand innocently beckoned me closer. "You want me to go with you?" She nodded. "Can you speak?" She did not reply. Her mannerisms, facial expressions...her very presence offered intense tranquility. She was mesmerizing...so difficult to describe... I knew I couldn't swim...I was petrified of the water...But I didn't feel any of that now. I only craved the peace she so desperately was trying to give me. Slowly I reached out to her.

"Apprentisk!!! Dun't titch dhe mar gurld sheed willed drowned ye!" ordered Grapple. My hand snapped back! My eyes popped wide open! She did nothing but smile sheepishly behind a set of wicked yellow triangular teeth. She withdrew her offer as if nothing happened. I watched as she swam back to her people. They encircled her, and then she was gone!

"Keep your head about you, Creed!" I said to myself. "Don't touch anything!

I used one of Grapple's homemade quilts to change beneath but not before testing the bed. I poked at it with my new shoe first to make sure it wouldn't eat me if I sat down on it. Thankfully, it didn't try to harm me in any way. It simply was a bed. *I wonder what other surprises he has down here?*

By the time I'd emerged from the blanket, the mer-people were nowhere to be had. Not forgetting about the bursting wall scenario, I promptly tidied up the area and compiled my clothes. I finished buckling my shoe half way up the stairs. In doing so, I saw a peculiar shadow dart through the water. But as I turned to focus on it, there was nothing but swirling sand and swaying kelp. Curiously, not one sea creature was present, not even a fish! "I guess they thought the show was over." One last glance around the room and I thankfully ascended the steps.

Clancey was waiting for me. He took my clothing and shoved it inside his satchel.

"Were almost ready. I'm going to change and then we can be off." He grabbed the other set of clothes and disappeared down the hallway.

Once again I found myself observing the painting over the fireplace but in more detail. This time I knew to stand a bit at bay and not to feed it. The portrait was of some sort of dwarf with a very long, razor-sharp nose. He had the largest green eyes and stark white pupils I'd ever seen. *Come to think of it, I'd never seen white pupils before*...I observed more unusual characteristics such as his ears. They were rather pointed. I only took notice because he had no hair on his head to cover them! His salt and pepper mustache was crimped at each end with a small golden hoop. He donned a long white beard that had been braided down the center. And on its tip he wore a charm with tiny leaves on it. In one hand he held a brimless hat; much like the one I'd seen Grapple wearing. In the other, he proudly displayed a double-edged sickle. I felt a hand slap me on the shoulder. It was Grapple.

"Twas me brudder tilld dhe Fallern gotter old off hem." I heard him pause. I caught the glint of a handkerchief wiping his nose. "I know'd ye willed fight ford us, Saun off Hem. Ye willed shields us frum dhe adbersariest' slingas und arrows...und we willed dood our'd part...yezdt, we willed dood our'd part," he declared. "Calm, we musta moofed swiftlies."

CHAPTER FIFTEEN
Bowling with Bridge Trolls

Clancey soon joined us and together we followed the Druix down the narrow corridor. I realized that Grapple had changed clothes too. He now wore a plush green emerald cape. It flowed as he walked while draping his shoulders and back. Instead of brown, his brimless hat matched the color of his mantle. Around its center was a decorative strip of tiny precious stones and beads. He'd even changed his shoes! I got the feeling he was wearing his finest traveling attire.

Periodic torches hanging from the walls lit the way. He stopped at a rounded doorway. I could hear the voluminous sound of rushing water behind it. "My willed guide ye ast fard ast dhe waterfauld. Frum dhere ye ard on ye owned." Not an uplifting statement I had to admit. "Beed caredfuld off dhe root serpends. Dhey no likes strang gers downed dhere." And with that, he opened the door. We descended dirt-packed steps that led deep into the earth. It grew very cold. The sound of fast moving water filled my ears. As we neared the choppy river, the ceiling became lower and the walls squeezed in closer. At one point, we had to walk single file down the passageway.

The area opened up considerably as we approached the bottom. We'd entered some sort of underground sanctuary. Without really understanding how we'd gotten there, I found myself standing on an incredibly high plateau. This raised terrain connected to the border of an extremely, lofty wooden pier. It spanned approximately 500 feet across the roof of the cavern but did not stretch all the way to the other side. It promptly stopped at a nowhere point a quarter of the way across the cave. Overall, the wharf's massive height could be likened to that of a sky scraper. "It's as if they didn't finish..." I whispered. I stood gazing upon my impending fate.

The contraption was held in position by a myriad of thin wooden stilts angled this way and that. Worse yet, the walkway itself sagged at certain points and had no side railings! Curiously, it was littered with piles of assorted debris. I was able to determine some of the fragments were feathers and cloth. They had been intermittently strewn along the platform. Adding insult to injury, and dangling off its most distal point was a rope ladder which led to a...

"Grapple, what is that down there? Why, it looks like a...a...car!"

"Off courst id's a card! Id's a tunas bot! Dhey nod mate likes dhat anymored!" he said proudly.

"Clancey... Uhh, that's a car! And it's floating in the water! What's it doing down there?"

"Relax Creed! It's a 1968 cherry red Chevrolet Camaro! It's our ride! Grapple's seen to it that we have only the best!" He slapped me on the back and pulled me in closer. "That *car* is his baby," he whispered. "See to it you don't insult him!"

In disbelief, I watched the active current toss the Chevy back and forth. Its tires bobbed in and out of the water. *This is crazy*, I silently mouthed. One slip anywhere on the pathway was the equivalent of a two to three hundred foot drop into rushing waters! My reward? A ride in a tuna boat.

A feeling of uneasiness overtook me. I didn't voice it, but thought we'd have a better chance with an empty milk jug tied to each arm. Now was not a good time to let everyone know I'd never been on a boat slash floating car before…or that I had a paralyzing fear of falling into that water!

"Ye furdst," said Grapple and he pushed me forward. "Tu dhe bot!" Of course, let the hydrophobic new guy try it out. It's funny the tricks your mind can play when terror stricken. I thought I'd taken a few footsteps in the forward direction. I could even see and hear the rushing water between the creaky wooden planks. However, in reality I stood frozen at the start of the pier. My foot had not budged one inch! "What's taking you so long, Creed? We've got to move!"

I became fluent in excuses. "I'm sorry guys. I'm just a bit hungry…I haven't eaten in a while and I'm sort of out there…you know?"

"Oh well nice! What did I tell you about the food rule?" chastised Clancey. "You should've eaten the eggs while you had a chance. I may have some candy in my pocket. Hold on, let me take a look…let's see here…"

Of course being hungry wasn't entirely true. In reality, everything in me wanted to get down on all fours and just crawl my way across the mess. I could never let them know how petrified I was. After all, I was supposed to be their rescuer…Wouldn't Oakley love to see me now?

I took a deep breath and repeated the acronym: F.E.A.R. stands for false evidence appearing real. But I couldn't help but think to myself, *This is really real!* Unexpectedly, I remembered something else my mom had shared with me. And because of it, I was able to take a step forward. Although, it felt as though I was wearing lead shoes. "Fears are okay, as long as they don't rule you, Creed." Well my fear was very real… and it wasn't going to go away anytime soon, so I was left with nothing *but to do it afraid.* ..Sometimes you've just got to do it afraid! Either that or I'd go down in history as *the* spineless legend.

Clancey's frantic footsteps interrupted my breakdown! He blew past me and on to the bridge causing it to violently sway and shake! I could've sworn I heard him laughing as he sprinted by! Pieces of feathers and trash blew off in his wake. I fell to my knees! Thankfully, that was excuse enough. I grasped at the swinging walkway and held on for dear life! "Ouch!" Something sharp cut my hand! It was a small chard of bone! Fortunately it wasn't mine. I promptly plucked it from my palm.

"Bridge Trolls!!!!!!!!!!"

"What?"

"Bridge Trolls!!!" he screamed. "MOooove!!!"

Whatever they were, it didn't sound good. I started out in a frenzied low crawl. The timber boards shuddered, swayed, and creaked beneath my weight! Pieces of garbage stuck to me like glue. There was no going back. Behind me, Grapple was yelling in a fit of rage! Bright flashes of light exploded within the sound of his voice! Out of nowhere, I was pummeled by a slimy, greenish, black weighty ball. It rolled up my back, hitting me in the head and knocking me flat on my stomach! I clung to the swerving steps! The sphere was slightly bigger than a basketball and covered in a gooey gelatinous coating. Instead of just rolling off of the side, its outer layer allowed it adhere to the pier. Clancey was screaming, "Get up! Run Creed!!!" Somewhat dazed, I watched the sticky orb unfurl and in doing so, expose a pair of spiky, webbed hands and feet. Its nails looked painfully sharp and were dripping with viscous goop. At the same time, something was unsuctioning itself from the underside of the boards I'd been resting on. I looked down. A pair of pinpoint eyes glared back at me through the fissures in the wood. They didn't look happy.

Without warning a couple of sharp claws busted through the plank next to me! On impulse, I rose to my feet and broke into an all out sprint. I was being chased! Water or no water, I sprinted down the bridge hurdling the remains of dead victims as I went. I didn't know how many trolls had joined the hunt. I wasn't about to look backwards. There was no need to. An entire horde of them were running with me but they were running on the underside of the platform! A few spun out ahead anticipating my passing. The walkway swung erratically! I tried to maintain my footing while heading for the car. It was an awkward display of clumsy acrobatics. Meanwhile, the creatures in back of me kept rolling into the bottoms of my feet attempting to knock me off balance. I was involved in a lethal game of bowling!

Clancey stood motioning wildly at the end of the wharf. Making it to him would not be an easy task. Both of his hands were outstretched and waving in my direction. I couldn't understand what he was screaming. I had been forced to stop. A number of trolls had accumulated on the path in front of me producing a formidable barricade. They maintained their circular form but pulsed as I drew near. The sphere closest to me wasted no time and began shifting from green to neon red. As before, a pair of webbed hands and feet sprouted from its center. The rest of the ball flattened, forming a thick stocky body. The transformation produced a short, anatomically human little guy wrapped in primitive garb!

Two thin colorful membranes unfurled exposing his face. The coverings were the shape of old-fashioned pleated fans, just like the ones that Chinese women used to carry. Except his had frilly edges with extraneous bits of foreign material hanging off of them and were not pleasing to look at. I couldn't tell if they were actually ears or wings…Each appendage scintillated and fluttered forming a circular outline around the periphery of his face. After their dramatic presentation they folded accordion style and came to rest at the back of his head. His skin was reptilian brown splotched with patches of neon green. He had wide set bulging eyes and what appeared to be slightly pointed ears that were recessed into the sides of his broad head. Maybe those fluttery things were wings after all? I could see nothing that resembled a normal nose but in its place were two slits where one should've been. A series of tiny jagged teeth filled his mouth and caused it to hang open ever so slightly. Interestingly enough, one lonely tuft of blond hair rested on top of his head. And every time he moved or spoke with the tiniest bit of aggression, it fell in front of his left eye.

"The Apprentice is not to pass. No he is not to pass! Evil! Wicked beast!" he screamed in a shrill voice.

"Excuse me, but who are you and how do you know who I am?"

His plump lips pursed sideways as he blew the hair away from his face. "Who am I? Who am I? Why I am Trumpkin! And you will not pass Son of He because you did not ask permission, that is why!" Again he repeated the same blowing motion.

"Permission for what?"

"Why permission to access our bridge of course!" It was hard to perceive him as any sort of threat. I mean I really wanted to get off the bridge, and the only thing stopping me was a midget having a temper tantrum. He looked so silly angrily blowing those unruly wisps of hair. It was hard to keep a straight face which was a benefit, because it made me forget where I was! "Oh, so this is your bridge?" I said sarcastically.

"Yes, and it has been in my family for generations!"

"And what a fine bridge it is. But what's the harm in my friends and me just passing on through?" More trolls began hatching from their pods. My question infuriated him.

"You do not have permission!" he shrieked. Suddenly the creature's wings violently snapped open! They fanned and quivered threateningly against the sides of his head! ...*Not a good sign...* Both appendages flashed alternating colors of red and orange underneath the translucent skin. In the process of creating such a colorful distraction, he vomited a stream of milk-colored slime! It came spewing out of his mouth in my direction! Fortunately, he missed.

"Gross!" I yelled. "Hey, say it don't spray it!!! I thought all trolls were big and stupid! At least you've got the stupid part down! Maybe you'd actually hit your target once in a while if you cut your unmanageable lochs princess!" Sorry to say, he didn't find my comments amusing. He fiercely spat again, and this time, he didn't miss! The mucus struck my shoe.

I tried moving but realized he'd cemented my boot to the pier. I yanked as hard as I could! I wasn't going anywhere. I was surrounded in every direction and virtually incapable of moving! The look of panic on my face further roused them. I dodged another shot of goo followed by yet another and another, until both soles were firmly glued to the planks! I was completely immobile just like they'd planned. When it seemed that taunting me provided no more amusement, the entire mob started approaching, wings flailing, teeth gnashing, and claws tearing at what would soon be my flesh. What happened next occurred within the blink of an eye.

Without any warning, I was spectator to the barrage of approaching trolls simultaneously being plucked from the pier! "Did I do that?" One second they were ready to rip me apart, and the next fiercely being catapulted from the platform! I maintained my footing while the bridge convulsed in all directions! Everywhere I looked it was raining trolls! They screamed like angry pigs all way the down to the water! WHEET WHEET WHEET!!! Bang! Splash! Plop! But what was even more shocking was the fact that not one of them flew, glided, or defied gravity in any way shape or form! They fell to the earth like a safe to the ground! It was over! We'd won!! Or so I thought.

It didn't take long to register the endless pairs of livid eyes staring through the spaces and cracks beneath me. Throngs of trolls had effortlessly suctioned themselves to the underside of the pier. They remained thoroughly unharmed! More importantly, the little beasts far outnumbered those who had been ejected from the topside. And yet as soon as I acknowledged their presence, they too were torn from the pier's underbelly! Gut instinct told me what was about to occur. The aggressive release of such weight started a tremendous whiplash effect like none before! The platform viciously jolted, then rippled upward with tsunami force! There was nothing to hold on to. I was thrown into the air prepared to meet my doom… Except when I opened my eyes, I realized I was still glued to the planks! Wave after wave, followed, but I rode out the swells and upsurges arms outstretched and postured like a professional surfer! Trolls and fragments of debris whirled around me! The angry squeals ceased to make themselves known. I'd like to think I was good enough to maneuver such a feat unscathed, but if I hadn't been stuck to the boards I would've fallen off for sure. In trying to kill me, they'd actually saved my life! Somehow the pier and I were still standing!

Clancey was pointing. I took a quick glance behind. I wasn't alone; more reinforcements were on their way. I tried going forward, but neither foot would budge! I was still stuck! As I struggled to break free I could feel my feet moving inside of the shoes. Hurriedly, I did the only thing I could think of. I removed both feet from their sticky shackles and ran barefoot through the chaos.

I approached Clancey at full speed! He was jumping crazily as if I were making the winning touchdown! The rope ladder was unfurled and was resting inside the car via the sunroof. The churning water bounced the vehicle up and down. I wasted no time. White knuckled, I threw a leg over the side and found myself descending the ropes one horrifying step at a time. I was comforted by an odd thought. The ladder reminded me of home. Burt and I made use of something similar for getting in and out of each other's windows. Those memories seemed so distant now. *Burt,* I thought as I lowered myself through the sunroof. I prayed that wherever he was, they were taking care of that Borraye bite! We'd been through so much together. It felt strange without him. I even remembered Isabelle and secretly prayed she would be found alive and well. But I knew better than to let my mind continue wandering. I needed to stay in survival mode. I needed to focus. Eventually, I found myself sitting in the passenger side of the 1968 vibrant red muscle car… telling myself to breath. I buckled the seatbelt while water foamed and lapped at the windows. I remained seated, out of breath, and completely amazed.

"Wow! I did it! I actually did it!"

My elated disbelief was momentarily disrupted. The current caught O'Keefe's footing just as he stepped on board. He fell straight into me. I lurched forward and grabbed the door in a state of alarm! Until then I'd completely forgotten about being in the water. "Sorry 'bout that, Creed. Why of course you did it! It's just like ole times!"

The choppy waves sobered my excitement. "I mean I really did it. Did you see me?" He just smiled from ear to ear while situating himself in the backseat.

"What do you think of our transportation?"

"It's pretty cool."

"You bet your bottom Drexel it is! Grapple takes good care of his collection! But whatever you do," he said looking over his shoulder, "don't let him turn on the radio!"

"What?"

"You heard me. He…"

Our conversation was cut short. The Druix descended the ladder legs straight out and stiff as a board. He slid from on high, down through the sunroof, and landed smack dab in the driver's seat. He didn't even use the rungs! "Done that once or twice have ya?" said Clancey from the back seat. I think the dwarf smiled. He started the engine. It powerfully rumbled and roared. Then we drove away from the dock as if it were a completely normal event. Subconsciously, I kept telling myself, *It's okay, Creed. You've made it this far! Relax! You've just survived a bunch of crazy bridge trolls. You'll be just fine. Try and act normal. Breathe. Just breathe!* Water passed over the hood and bubbled off the sides creating a good-sized wake. Grapple and Clancey were busy discussing the attack.

"Did you see my take? I got at least a hundred and fifty of the bothersome little stress balls!"

"I dested mored dhan ye!" He let out a raucous laugh. "Dhat Trumpkink tink hem owns alls! Tupid laddle candidbulls!"

"Did I get any?" I asked excitedly. "Did I make them fly off the bridge?" The laughing stopped.

Clancey's answer was tentative. "Well we did wait for you to generate something…anything… But I think you were just a bit overwhelmed … Don't you worry none. It will come in time."

I struggled for something to say in the uncomfortable silence. I didn't know whether to say thank you or apologize. I'd never needed 'help' defending myself in my life verbally or physically! But lately I was up against situations that even Einstein wouldn't know how to handle.

"Thanks guys, really."

Clancey slapped me on the shoulder. "It twas nothing. We didn't actually kill any mind you... Bridge trolls detest getting wet! Bunch of hydrophobic pansies if you ask me! Afraid of a little water!" They both erupted in loud snorts and chorkles.

I would've been completely humiliated if it weren't for the fact that I'd spotted a deep gash on Grapple's forearm. Bright red blood was trickling steadily from the cut. The vital fluid saturated a portion of his shirt. Clancey must've noticed it too, because he handed him a clean piece of cloth. "Camuro Steadies!" uttered Grapple. The car came to a complete stop in the middle of the unpredictable current. She held steady while the Druix began to dress his own wound. He flinched and at times held his breath while wrapping the bandage gingerly around his forearm. It was obvious he was in a good deal of pain but he was trying not to show it. He didn't look over at me, however when he was finished he punched me in the arm! "Wund tu adt tu dhe utters... Yezdt?" And he laughed.

I felt absolutely horrible. I couldn't help but wonder if I could've prevented him from getting injured had I initially run across the bridge like they wanted me to do in the first place. I sat silently embarrassed, completely humbled and thankful that neither one of them knew my dark secret. I continued to listen to the extraneous gloating clenching the dashboard less and less. We were tossed steadily through the water. Grapple steered the car as smoothly as though we were on pavement! For a change, fear of water wasn't my first priority, although it didn't mean I was cured. But it was fear of letting my friends down which now took an overall precedence.

"Turned dhe radyo ond." It immediately got quiet again. I looked back at Clancey. Wide eyed, he discreetly shook his head from side to side. The Druix repeated himself.

"Turned dhe radyo ond plead."

I searched Burt's face. What did he expect me to do? I shrugged my shoulders and obediently reached from the big black knob. Instantly my seat vibrated and shook to the sounds of music. Even the windows quivered! Who would believe me? We were cruising to the rhythms of winding guitars backed by infinite drums and base!

Fingers drumming and happily whistling, he maneuvered the Camaro through the voluminous waters. I was compelled to comment. "Grapple, I had no idea you liked rock music!" Clancey rolled his eyes.

"Addies mooziks id me faborite, bit my likes ald sords off mooziks."…And he wasn't kidding!

Without notice he removed his hands entirely from the steering wheel pointing and screaming, "Daultfinst off de startboard site!" The car shifted and drifted with the current. I was enjoying racing the dolphins until realizing we were heading toward the rocky shore! I kept waiting for the Druix to change course but he was thoroughly distracted by the song and the challenge of competition. Clancey's voice escalated.

"Grapple! Grapple! Pay attention! For goodness sake man! Can't you do two things at once? Look out for those rocks! No wonder you don't have a driver's license!"

*Well that's reassuring news…*Without a moment to spare; he gunned the engine and piloted us clear of the embankment.

"I'm thankful you haven't managed to add a cell phone to your collection, too!" heckled Clancey.

"Beck sit babby!" he grumbled.

"Where are we?" I asked.

"We ard end dhe fathoms," said the Druix. He gave the windshield wipers a pass or two and turned on the headlights. I began seeing small patches of lighted chambers along the shoreline. Each opening had a ceiling comprised of enormous gnarled roots. Inside every cave Druix men and women busily went about their work. They stopped to bow as we passed by. I was careful not to make eye contact, but in the dim light it was hard to determine where I was looking. As far as I could tell they were attending to the roots. Some were grinding things with mortars and pestles. They took the substance from the mortar and gently dabbed it on the roots.

"What are they doing?" He turned the music down.

"Dhey ard healding dhe treest," said Grapple. "Utters mate ingredients ford pochants. We tic, bit ard carefuld tu restored what we half ticken. Druix cared ford dhe eart und sheed give dust herd midsturis." We sailed past the assemblies of dwarves, each group diligently going about their business. Some were restoring trees; others were putting potions into tiny leather pouches. There were a few scuffles going on, but they immediately ceased upon our passing. The sanctuary was becoming noticeably narrower and pointed. The sound of rushing water continued to crescendo.

We made our way through the tapered passage. Grapple turned on the high beams. Within a few minutes the channel widened exposing a spectacular underground waterfall! I'd never seen one before, at least not in person. I looked on in amazement. It was easily a few hundred feet tall. Water crested then fell from its peak, cascading down toward the luminous pool beneath. The sound it created was thunderous. I strained to hear what Grapple was saying. "Ye kin rist heared tild yourd redies." He moored the car to a clump of roots and we stepped ashore. I was never so thankful to be on land in all my life! I tried to hide my euphoria.

I'd done it! I'd actually walked across the most unstable, towering pier, scaled the longest makeshift ladder, eluded bridge trolls, and taken a ride in a car boat all of which involved treacherous waters!! Grapple removed a torch from the wall and led us down the corridor. "I'fe seen tu id dhat ye half surplice." He opened a door to a small den. It was much like the one we'd come from, only its earthen ceiling and walls were plain. Instead of the usual table and chairs a small circular seating area had been dug into the ground as a replacement. Running along the border of the room was a little stream with fish in it. A small hallway led to another set of rooms in the back. Against the wall was an old, pot belly stove. I could feel the warmth it radiated. Something smelled good. Nestled in the corner were two small beds complete with pillows, all of which had been elaborately formed from the clay soil. They served only to remind me just how tired I was. "We dhaught yer mite beed needin dhese." He handed me my skateboard! It was inside a new backpack with a change of clothes and some personal items. He gave another satchel to Clancey.

I was flabbergasted! "How did you get my things?" I was so grateful; I made the very mistake I had been warned to avoid! In the process of thanking him I made direct eye contact! I scrambled to change focus! It did not go unnoticed.

Without hesitation, he grabbed my shoulder and pulled me toward him. I braced myself, preparing for vicious blunt trauma, but instead…he hugged me! I saw the shock in Burt's face. He pulled back, but didn't let go of my forearm. His voice was distant and trance like. I felt his grip tighten. His eyes were a mesmerizing, cat-eye green with those bizarre white pupils. It was as if I'd entered the most privileged of holies. Slowly, his pupils begin to transform and take the shape of dancing figures. I stared closer, unable to remove my gaze from his. And then…I saw him.

"Father?" He was just like my picture, except… No, something was very different. He was lavished in royal attire. His robes were heavily adorned with intricate embroidered patterns. His posture…his mannerisms…held a strong air of self-assurance. It was obvious he commanded immense respect. I watched him ceremoniously cross his chest with an Egyptian crook and flail. I recognized such instruments from pictures in his book collection. They were symbols used by the ancient pharaohs of Egypt. He stood fixed in the middle of a magnificent cathedral and in the background I could hear… uncontrollable sobbing? I didn't understand what was happening. The crying seemed so out of place in such a majestic setting.

I began to sense my father's overwhelming fear and confusion. And then the strangest thing happened. He turned and looked directly at me, as if he knew I was watching! Immediately, the vision disintegrated only to be replaced by Grapple's reverent soliloquy. Eerily enough the voice that came out of him was not his own. It was mine! My voice was coming out of Grapple! It was more voluminous and deep, but it was certainly my voice!

"What is the difference between wrong and right…good and evil?" He paused momentarily. "Head versus heart… Sinner versus saint… Mercy versus retribution, love and hate…Greatness versus mediocrity…?" A look of relief came across his face as he articulated his answer slow and deliberately: "A…split…second… decision." He released his hold on me as if the entire situation never transpired. "Surff us welled, Saun off He." The Druix reverently bowed, and then did the strangest thing. He vanished!

"In all my born days, I, I never…" Clancey was visibly shaken. "You looked him in the eye…you hugged him…and you have no scars. Do you have your senses about you, lad?" His voice rose higher the longer I waited to respond. "Are you okay, lad? Creed?"

I snapped out of it. "Yeah, yeah…I'm good… Just a little dazed really. I thought I saw something, but it was just my imagination. This is all so new to me…" I watched his expression relax. My excuse seemed to suffice. I wasn't sure what had just transpired, but I did know one thing. I'd looked a Druix in the eyes and lived!

CHAPTER SIXTEEN

Confronting a Bandolix

We gathered up our supplies. O'Keefe began to lay out his plan. "The school is right up there." He pointed in the direction of the waterfall.

"You mean it is right above us?"

"That's the general concept," he said.

"How do we get there?"

"Well, that's what's been worrying me a little. Plan A should've had us at the school by now, but with that cell phone mess and the police…Well, it threw a little bit of a wrench into things. The Druix have been cooperative enough to let us use the fathoms, but the rest will be up to us. Are you a good swimmer?" Obviously, that was the worst question he could've possibly asked.

"Why would I have to swim?"

"Well, because the way to Devonshire is through there." He walked over to the door, swung it open and pointed to the area beneath the waterfall.

"You're kidding, right? Are you crazy?" I yelled. "What do you mean, down there?" Fear was beginning to swell within me again.

He gave me a quizzical look and answered hesitantly. "About 125 feet below the falls is a house that sits on a flat ridge…it holds a hidden passageway that will bring us right up underneath the school. It's the safest way. No question about it," he said closing the door.

"So now it's an underwater house, huh? Have you ever taken this route before? I mean look what happened when we walked across a pier!" He breathed out, and then shook his head. "I can't believe you want me to do this! I've had enough!" I paused then took a deep breath. "I can't swim, all right!!!" In shame, I didn't bother to look at him. He did not respond. "Did you hear me; I don't know how to swim! I'm....I'm afraid of the water, okay! I'm as bad as those frilly bridge trolls! It took everything in me to cross that pier, and it didn't stop there! I even had a hard time riding in Grapple's car! I'd rather face a thousand Giests than do those things again! It's not too late for me to turn back! I can hide from these guys. I'll...I'll run away! You said they have a hard time tracking me..." Clancey's reply was straightforward.

"So you're afraid of the water?" He didn't give me time to answer. "Who crossed that bridge? Well, who was it? Say it!"

"Me."

"And who was it that crossed that mile high bridge over water with a horde of pesky trolls chasing after him?"

"Me."

"Then who crossed the water in Grapple's car, bad driving and all?"

"It was me..."

"Did you do them afraid?"

"Yes."

"But you did do them, each and every one, and that's what counts."

"What about Thoth? You didn't lose your cool. I know it didn't involve water but he's nothing pretty to look at! You did what you had to do scared or not and we got Burt out of there! *Sometimes it's better to look at what you've done before considering what you can't.*"

Grapple's strange rant lingered in the back of my mind. *A split second decision.* It was then I understood. Man is completely capable of altering his destiny in one moment of time… via one decision. The trouble was I didn't want to make the wrong one. Going forward wasn't the greatest idea, but it was painfully obvious that I couldn't go back. Direction-wise that left me staying right where I was at, and that wasn't a pleasant thought either. Burt's imposter searched my face as if trying to read my mind. Painfully, I realized that not all decisions afford us the time to be comfortable with the choice we've made.

But no matter what way my brain revolved around it, my heart already knew the answer. I needed to go forward. I'd come too far… done too many things afraid or not…But the fact was, I'd still done them. Burt was gone; I was fighting legions of nightmarish creatures. I had nothing to go back to but jail. I feared water would be one of my more milder enemies.

I studied Grapple's blood stain. He'd accidentally smeared it across my shirt when giving me a hug. I reflected upon it with the utmost accountability. Above of all, I didn't want anyone else getting hurt because of my disbelief, fear, or stupid mistakes…not Burton, Clancey, Grapple, anyone! People were really depending on me. Was I the Apprentice? I didn't know any of that. Until now, I'd just been blindly trying to stay alive! Everything occurred so spontaneously that I was never afforded the time to absorb the fact *that this was all real*! These creatures, this world of magic, I seen them first hand! I wasn't imagining and I wasn't dreaming! They needed me somehow. That much I knew. Who I was didn't matter. Such things could be sorted out later. What did matter was the fact that I wasn't going to be the one responsible for letting them down.

Reluctantly, I grabbed my pack. I heard myself say, "I'll go…I'll go. What do I have to do?"

"That's me boy! I'll be with you every step of the way. You won't even have to swim! I'll show you what I mean. This will be easier than you think. But before that, I need to school you in a few things. Sorry, it has to be the condensed version. But that's all we have time for." He took a deep breath.

"You're already familiar with what police look like along with their weaponry. You've encountered a few Giests. Their grand leader is Thoth. He is one of Lord Denegaul's right-hand agents. As you've seen they are shape shifters, usually a hound for a full shift or crow for a partial. But don't count on either of those. I've seen many a hideous creature form from within the confines of their manteaus. Make no mistake about it; no matter what form, they're a powerful force to be reckoned with. Mind you, if they are feeling particularly froggy, they'll opt for a slow death such as the one inflicted upon Burton. I was surprised to see he lasted as long as he did. He's one lucky lad. By all rights he should've been dead within the first hour!

"But that's the least of our worries right now. He's being taken care of. Anyway, as you've experienced, a Giest can sear their victim. It's another favorite of theirs. Your stone protected you, but others…let's just say it's a rather messy demise. They're considered most powerful when they transform their entire body into a singular identity or remain in their natural state, such as what you've witnessed. They will attack only the living and thrive on taking innocent souls…usually through the triad attack. It is their trademark. Two henchman followed by a Giest will harvest a fresh soul. It's not something I'd wish for you to see…It ain't pretty. The more souls a Giest reaps, the higher status they obtain, hence the tally marks on those deadly talons. Once inside a Giest, the forsaken spirit is eternally tormented. They're akin to walking sacks of suffering. When you hear that hooked claw, smell dead flesh, or sense death you know they're near. Mind you, only people of magic can smell them…lucky us!"

"Wait a minute! Wait a minute! Why are you telling me all of this? You said that we are forbidden to perform spells in front of Rogues. What about the people at the party? Won't they be aware of supernatural events? Giests flying through the air and so on?"

"I'm just trying to prepare you for the 'just in case scenario' because there's a good possibility it might happen. There are ways to handle such instances, but those should be avoided. They can be rather costly. It's most likely the guests won't see any of the unusual goings on if any... But should our enemies need to pull cheap shots or create a distraction, they may choose to purposefully make themselves visible to the Rogues…Then we'll have big problems…Aaah! Would you look at this!" he said pointing to his chest. "I got hot sauce on me shirt! See?! This spot is darker than the rest! Why didn't you tell me? Don't I look like the pig?" He removed a clean cloth from one of the cupboards and dipped it into a fresh basin filled with water.

"Believe it or not, their main concern is that you don't get hurt in the middle of all this, at least not immediately." He began rubbing the clean cloth over the stain. "Making themselves known would only incite mass chaos, and leave the possibility of putting you in harm's way. They need you alive and well to receive the translation. It's afterwards that you have to worry about."

I didn't need any more food for thought. I was preoccupied with having to face my worst fear. "So, what the heck does that mean?"

My frustration was obvious. "Look Creed, you'll find not everyone obeys the rules in our world, or in any world for that matter. Our adversaries, much like ourselves, don't want to be discovered. I'm sure you can imagine the pandemonium if the Rogues knew we existed! But more importantly the hearts of some humans are easily corrupted… One can never tell…We can't afford to underestimate them again," he declared. "Not to mention the fact that our foes have total disregard for mortal welfare. We don't want anyone getting hurt or killed! I'll level with you. We can count on them taking whatever measures necessary to capture you should the need arise. If they can get away with breaking the rules, they'll try. But that will be a task for the Time Benders. They're the 'professionals.'" He let out a warm laugh. "Bunch a bloody pirate if you ask me! To some not an amicable lot, but very efficient at what they do!" He rinsed out the small towel and laid it over the lip of the wash basin.

"Now, the Fallon are a different story. They're the bloodsuckers. The problem is, they look completely normal. It's like finding a needle in a haystack. They could be anywhere! So, we will have to be on the lookout! The tip-off is when you start to go numb."

"Numb? What do you mean numb?" My brain was still trying to compute 'hurt or killed.'

"You know, like when your leg has been in one position for too long…numbness and tingling in your limbs. It's a sign they're near. It makes it harder for the prey to avoid capture. A Fallon's presence alters circulation. They have an affinity for blood, but in turn the blood has an attraction to them also. They are not as picky as the Giests. They will feed off anything dead or alive. It doesn't matter."

"Like vampires?"

"Who? What? No, they don't use that method. They do take blood to survive though. They also can't resist the smell of fear. It entices them. If they smell any sort of anxiety, they'll chase! Fallons seize through long, spiked, pitch-forked fingernails!" He made an exaggerated upward thrust with his hand. "Their eyes roll back in their head when they transfuse. It's a nasty site to behold, but to them it's like spiritual communion. Their commander's name is Cultric."

"I heard you say another name…Gheddons?"

"We'll worry about those ones later. There's' something else I need to explain first: root serpents." I'd remembered Grapple murmuring something about that. "Root serpents live in the fathoms. They do not like strangers in their territory!! Pesky creatures they are. A tree may die, but the roots will live on. Some lower themselves deep into the soil never to see the sun again. We won't have to worry about them as long as we stay on the path. Stray from the path and they will pull you down into the depths."

"I can't believe I'm going through with this." I voiced.

He slapped me on the back. "The only way to escape them is this." He removed one of the tiny brown pouches from the table.

"What's in there?"

"Sinzibuckwud cubes."

"Excuse me….What kind of a cube is it?" He handed me the small leather bag. "It smells like maple syrup," I said.

"It is, only in cube form. It seems root serpents have a sweet tooth much like me! If one manages to get a hold of you, feed them this." He held up a small piece of brown dough, then popped it in his mouth.

"How do I fend off the Giest's and Fallon?"

"The best way to fend them off is not to get caught!"

"So basically, I'm diving into rushing waters filled with sugar-crazed serpents. If I survive that, then I get to avoid police and a legion of shape shifting, blood-sucking beasts."

"Well put, Creed! Well put! Don't worry, your Quetral stone should fend off the lot of them." The word "should" painfully stood out.

"How about my mom? How will I find her?"

"You've been to these masquerade balls before, haven't you?" I nodded. "Well then, ask yourself what she would be doing about now. How would she be acting?"

He was right. Every year my mother would spend the first hour or so behind the scenes making sure things were running smoothly. Then, like clockwork, she'd mingle, always with the current staff and students. Later on in the evening she would make her way down to the prospective enrollees. Once dinner was over, dancing would commence. She could always be found near the orchestra ensuring that the music and dancing went according to schedule. Sometimes guests were a little shy so her and the headmaster would start things off with a slow waltz.

"Here ya go, lad." He handed me a belt filled with stones. "Put this on. It will keep you weighted down in the water. Don't forget this." He handed me a small root bulb.

"What's this?"

"It's culpie root. It will allow you to breathe under water for about ten minutes. They're harvested down here."

"Impossible!" I gasped! "Of course I'll have to hold my breath or I'll drown!"

"Creed, you've witnessed so much of the impossible already and still you doubt?" He sounded disappointed. "Many Rogues' minds dwell in their own hopeless world...filled with impossibilities. They do not go forward, they do not go back. They stay right where they are because...they, too, do not dare to believe. They are limited simply by their own thoughts. And that is why most don't see us or the magic we summon." His head bent forward and he muttered almost inaudibly. *"Sounds like you've mistaken the unlikely for the impossible."*

He threw the pack on his back. "Time to go." Those words struck sheer terror in me! I felt as if I were in a trance as he guided me from the chamber to the edge of the turbulent waters. "Okay, listen up." I was overwhelmed by the reality of it all and only caught half of what he was saying. "We'll submerge quickly. Don't panic, just follow me down. Remember to take deep normal breaths, okay? I'll be right beside you. Don't worry! Look at me, Creed; I promise you'll be just fine! I've weighted the belts to drop us at the correct level. You won't have to swim just free fall. The belt will do the rest. We'll land on the first flat ridge. You can't miss the house. Keep your sinzibuckwud cubes handy and stay on the path." He led me to the edge of the rushing water. I could feel my heart beating as if I'd run a marathon. The waterfall looked more impending than it had earlier. He flung his satchel over his back. "One last thing. Try and keep quiet down there. It helps with the breathing. Besides, you never know who or what we may attract if we're too loud. Here goes nothing!"

Unfortunately, I got a chance to smell the root before I put it in my mouth. It reeked of rotten eggs. Sad to say, the flavor didn't improve my first impression. My teeth broke its stringy outer casing. A bitter lemony substance oozed from its chalky center. My first reaction was to spit it out, but somehow I managed to swallow it! He watched in amusement. "Did I forget to tell ya it has quite a pucker to it?" I waited for something intrinsic to happen. Maybe I'd sprout gills…no such luck. "Follow me!" he yelled!

He jumped in! And before I could stall for more time, he pulled me down with him!

I felt the water pass over my mouth, nose, eyes, and head! I was sinking, falling down down! I kept telling myself to remain calm. Frantically my eyes darted left and right. A dull yellow glow illuminated our surroundings. I could feel Clancey's grip on my shirt. I looked above my head as I descended into the depths. I watched the last bit of surface light fade to a pinpoint. We continued a slow free fall. Surprisingly, the water was warm. Clancy tapped me and pointed to my mouth. He could see I was holding my breath. He pointed to his face. I watched him demonstrate the breathing process. Bubbles went in and out of his nose and mouth. He didn't convulse or implode like I'd expected. The thought of breathing in water didn't go over well with me. It was against everything I'd ever heard! What happened next could only be described as downright blood curdling hysteria! I realized that I couldn't do it! I just couldn't do it! I began to feel closed in and trapped! Knowing I had little time to reach the surface, I began tearing at the weight belt that was causing me to sink. In an utter frenzy, I managed to remove one rock before I saw Burt's wide eyes staring back at me. They held an expression of disbelief. I knew it wasn't really him. I didn't appreciate him assuming my best friend's identity anyway! I'd seen what O'Keefe could shape shift into. Maybe he really wanted to drown me! Fear had swelled so much within me that I made a break for the surface! My limbs frantically began beating the water! Momentarily, I remembered a few phrases from each swim instructor I'd ever had.

"Relax; swim like a frog! Use your arms and legs like scissors. Bubbles out the nose! Bubbles out the mouth! Don't fight the water! Don't breath the water in!!"

It wasn't working!! I was sinking!!! Without hesitation and from below, Clancey did the only thing he could. He grabbed hold of both legs and down, down, we went. We were descending rapidly. I couldn't hold my breath any longer. How could I have been so stupid?! I'd been tricked! Before I could break free of him and race to the surface, my will gave way and I was forced to do the exact thing I fiercely tried to avoid… I exhaled…and cautiously inhaled. An icy sensation ran through my body. I breathed out a fizzy cloud of bubbles. The water stung my nose and gave me brain freeze! My lungs felt as though they were blocks of frozen cement. But in a split second it was over. I began to hear something. It was the sound of my own breath. It was the strangest feeling, but I was breathing quite normally. I was defying death! I was breathing under water! He saw the look of relief on my face and smiled.

"You okay?" He was speaking under water…and I could hear him!

"Yes." The shock of my own voice knocked my head back a little.

"Word of advice, don't do that again!" We continued to fall to the fathoms ridge. I tried to relax on my way down. It wasn't every day I got the chance to make the water my home. Periodic clumps of burning rocks caught my eye. They were nestled along the canyon's walls. Each outcropping gave off a bright, bubbly, yellow light which illuminated the way. Schools of neon colored fish danced among the kelp beds. The swaying of the seaweed had a calming effect. Its inhabitants passed by me like I was an everyday fixture. Brightly covered coral formed various outcroppings. My senses were at an overload. It was beautiful, but quite overwhelming. So much so that I forgot about my fear.

"Breathtaking, ain't it?" He tried to keep a straight face. Finally, we hit a sandy ridge. He handed me a rock from his belt. I inserted it back into its proper place. We began walking along an underwater pathway. I tried copying him by using my arms and legs to maneuver the trail. We walked by odd items neatly positioned at various places. For example, there was as a mailbox with its flag up, gardening tools, even a bike. None were rusted or uncared for as you might expect. On the contrary, they simply looked as though someone had been using them. Upon turning the corner I beheld the most curious little house! Setting aside the obvious, it was as if it had been plucked right off the bayou and purposefully submerged it at that very point! Welcoming lights burned brightly through each window. A fully operational waterwheel was spinning next to the flower garden! A set of steps led up to the front porch and on to the main entrance. A newspaper in a plastic bag lay on the welcome mat.

I was so engrossed with the house's uniqueness, I didn't notice the schools of fish swimming furiously past me. But I did see...*it*. Two gargantuan eyes rested at ridge level. They glowed the same mysterious vibrant yellow as the rocks! It sinisterly studied me with unrelenting intensity. At first glance it resembled a Chinese dragon with monstrous snake eyes and flaring nostrils! The beast's body was at least 15 to 20 feet long...and that didn't include the tail! Its enormous head paraded two, massive webbed fins attached to each side. With one sweep they effortlessly propelled the creature through the water! A set of fierce teeth protruded from the confines of its mouth. Strange fleshy tubules dangled from its chin. The rest of the animal's shape could be likened to that of an enormous eel. Hanging from its underbelly were powerful, jagged claws that tipped its colossal hands and feet. Sharp spines ornamented its back.

Root serpent! I thought to myself. Be calm! I looked around me. Where was Clancey? Trying not to panic, I carefully reached for the sinzibuckwud pouch. I only hoped that they tasted better than the culpie root. I saw its pupils narrow and focus on what I was doing. There was a strong glimmer of intelligence in its expression. Before I could give it my peace offering, the creature opened its humongous razor-filled jaws and let out an ear-piercing cry that rumbled the depths! What followed next was an immense volcanic wave of fire that angrily gushed from its mouth! As soon as the lava made contact with the water it exploded! The sizzling and cracking sounds were as loud as bombs! I leaped behind a large mound of earth and was showered with chunks of flaming debris. Again, the beast let out a vehement scream! In doing so, it exposed two enormous fangs, and they were barreling in my direction! Its first pass caused me to somersault backwards in a cloud of sand. I hit my head on a coral formation. I felt the back of my skull and came up with a handful of warm blood. My heart pounding, I tried to regain my bearings.

I couldn't see Clancey anywhere. Without warning, I was violently pummeled from behind! Its spiked tail furiously slammed me to the floor bed! The beast could've finished me off with ease. Instead, it was greedily enjoying the sensation of my suffering. In the blurry distance it hovered, readying itself for the next pass! Suddenly, the serpent postured itself like a bucking stallion. I braced myself behind a coral wall as it flew forward! Just as it passed, I hurled a handful of maple cubes in its jaws and tumbled out of the way! I felt myself beginning to lose consciousness. The beast was shrieking and raising a flurry of sand in every direction! Its serrated claws were ripping at an invisible enemy! My offering had not satisfied it! Our plan had failed! I knew I was going to die.

Suddenly, a figure stepped out of nowhere! "HYDRUS THANATOS!" Particles from the sandy depths began to churn and spin in a tornadic fury. Shells, rocks, coral and sand created a monumental funnel cloud! It continued to gain enormous strength until the mass swept upwards, blasting the eyes of the serpent! It reeled backwards shrieking vehemently! Clancey grabbed my arm and began pulling me toward the house. I felt the beast's powerful presence approaching from behind. Its great speed and strength caused the current to push us forward. Clancey's attack had only served to infuriate it. I tried to pull his grip away from my arm. I was slowing him down. I knew he could make it without me. The war cry of the serpent caused me to freeze in my tracks!

I straightened up. It took every ounce of courage I possessed to turn and face it! The root serpent's ominous figure was moving through the fathoms with determined speed! It was now or never! I watched my blood dissipate in the water around me. I began to recollect "the impossible" I'd witnessed in the last 24 hours, certainly not discounting the present. Thoughts and images pelted my mind one inexplicable experience after another. I'd been thinking as a Rogue…*halfway believing in only what I could see… but not daring to believe in what I couldn't…*I possessed no concrete evidence to verify I was the Son of He. Neither was I capable of manifesting anything tangible to show that I was the Apprentice. I had no proof for any of it. But that didn't matter. I just needed to believe it.

It was impossible to withhold the knowing that swelled inside of me. No doubting…No more reasoning…I released myself to believe without fear or question. It's called faith. For the first time, the Quetral stone grew warm against my skin! My thoughts became words.

"I am the Son of He. I am the Son of He… I am THE SON OF HEEEEE!!!" I stretched forth both hands toward the serpent. I embraced full command of my newfound strength. My voice thundered and echoed violently through the infinite fathoms! "HYDRUS THANATOS!!!!!" Like cannons, boulders from the cavernous walls explosively hurtled toward their target! I felt a rush of force leave my body! Sizzling balls of blue and orange electric fire shot from my mouth and fingertips! My knees buckled just as the bolts speared the serpent's head! Immediately, fluorescent pink blood spewed from its dying flesh! It screams of rage were quickly silenced. The crystal waters filled with silky pink murk. I watched its body freefall beyond the ridge toward the bottomless floor. Enticed by death, an enormous cluster of gnarled roots arose from the shadowy depths to greet it. The entangled mass flailed like a mighty leviathan! Its immense appendages gracefully fanned open in anticipation of the corpse. A school of megalodon sharks followed closely behind it.

O'Keefe began pulling me toward the entrance. Light from the creature's eyes faded leaving us in the shadows of the house. It was getting harder to breath. I relied on Clancey's strength as he dragged me up steps. He threw open the front door and thrust me inside. I took my first real breath of fresh air! Between gasps, I managed to ask, "What was that thing?" I looked around for a minute. "Why is there water out there but not in here? Why aren't we even wet?"

"One question at a time! It wasn't no root serpent, I'll tell you that, lad!" His reply was joyous. I think he was actually proud of me! "It was a Bandolix and they've been forbidden from the fathoms for centuries! I don't know how it passed through without detection!"

"It was a what?"

He acknowledged my confusion as he sat me down on the couch. "Oh, yeah, right… A Bandolix; it's kin to the Sistra…distant cousin of the Hydra." With every word he uttered, I found it harder and harder to hold my head up straight. My breathing was shallow and I could barely keep my eyes open. Something was happening … I could sense his panic. The subject was quickly changed as he hurriedly propped my feet up on the arm rest.

"Did I ever tell you 'bout the time I cast my first spell?" I barely had the strength to shake my head 'no'. "It was a simple levitation spell. I was supposed to float calming spheres. Unfortunately, I ended up floating Bogwink's wife… Anyone who knows her understands that this was no easy task! Then there was the time I was trying to impress a certain young lady…" He continued to make me chuckle with a barrage of embarrassing stories. And after a moment or two my strength slowly began to return.

"You feeling a little bit better?"

"Yeah, I think so… Just really worn out."

"That's alright. It's normal." There was a brief moment of silence. And then he burst out as if he couldn't contain his excitement. "Why, I haven't seen such craft since you battled the Acrist at Cambria!"

"Yeah, that was a fierce one! I remember father was angry because we strayed from the lake reeds! He was worried that…"

I stopped cold. For a fleeting second, images of someone else's memories ran through my mind! I came to realize those memories were mine!

Clancey was awe struck. "Creed…?"

"Don't worry, it's still me in here."

"They're…they're coming back, aren't they, lad."

It was unquestionably conclusive! Clancey had not made a mistake! I was the Apprentice… the Son of He! I was some sort of pivotal instrument, a focal point for something greater than I could imagine. I'd just faced one of my worst fears and another that I didn't even know existed!!

For the first time I realized I was capable of more than mediocrity. I just needed to believe it. My urge to find the chronicle overtook me. It was mine! It had been written for me by my father! He really did love me! And for a fleeting moment, I had remembered that love! It made me realize what I'd been missing. I was hungry for answers! "Yes, I believe they are beginning to surface, old friend." I lay back on the sofa and passed out.

CHAPTER SEVENTEEN

Tattooed at Twelve

Noisy pots and pans startled me awake. The smell of bacon permeated the air. I was starving! I sat up. No, it hadn't been a dream. The strange room and blood that dotted my pillow were quick reminders. Rightfully, I'd fallen asleep after my encounter with the Bandolix. I decided to explore the bottom floor. From the outside the house resembled a small wooden shack. It was well built however; one would've never expected what it looked like on the inside! Surprisingly, it was quite clean and had all the comforts of home. Thankfully, there was no fireplace. Curiously though, the décor was made up of retro furnishings to include a large juke box, big rectangular TV, and wall to wall shag carpeting. The sofa I'd been lying on was deep purple. It wasn't hard to miss the accompanying lime green loveseat. All around it exuded yesteryear appeal. If I didn't know better, I would've thought a car hop might pop out of the kitchen on skates! Everything in the house functioned normally, even the bathroom. Meanwhile, just outside, schools of fish swam past the front windows.

"Make yourself at home," said an unfamiliar voice.

I spun back around. "Excuse me? Hello?"

"I'm in the kitchen!" yelled Clancey. In the background I could hear more clanging, rattling, and rummaging.

"No I wasn't talking to you… I could've sworn I heard someone else."

"Oh yeah... Creed meet Fenwick, Fenwick meet Creed. He's a guest of Grapple's."

From the coat closet came a, "Nice to meet you, great sir."

I made my way over to the door. "Do you always hide in closets?" I asked.

"You would if you were me," it said.

"I'd feel much more comfortable if I could see you. I promise I won't hurt you."

The door slowly opened but still he did not come out. "Did you know you talk in your sleep great Apprentice?" And who is this Burton and why do you tell him to RUNnnnnn?!" he screamed.

"I'd be glad to tell you, but I won't do so until I can see you." There was a brief pause followed by a long sigh. Then from the dark closet came the most curious little man. He was very distinguished for his small size and dressed in fine clothing complete with royal blue pants that ended just below his knee, a ruffled white shirt, and a fancy dress coat to match. He could've easily passed for a dwarf except from the center of his forehead, and arching over each bushy eyebrow, was an external spine about the thickness of my index finger. Both protuberances were raised and covered by skin. And pending on his emotion, that particular area of skin would change color.

"Why were you in there?"

"Because I'm afraid." His secondary eyebrows turned bright yellow. I tried not to stare!

"Afraid of what?" I asked calmly.

"He's not a what, he's a who. But I must be brave even if I don't feel as such. Certainly you know of master Denegaul?" he whispered.

"I'm becoming familiar with his handiwork... yes." Fenwick appeared momentarily baffled by my reply. "Well what exactly did he do to you?"

"It's what he did to me and what I've done to him! Oh he'll turn me into toad stool as soon as look at me don't you know! He has spies everywhere! How do you think that Bandolix slipped in here? And what about those nasty little bridge trolls that greeted you?"

"Wait a minute. How did you know about that? "Oh everyone down here knows! We aren't dimwitted," he said picking bits of lint off of his coat. "But what could *you* have possibly done to Denegaul?"

He glanced around nervously. "I'm doing it now…" From his pocket he produced a tiny vial no bigger than my thumbnail. It was filled with bright, sparkling, amber liquid. "I'm to bring these to you," he reverently said. "It is filled with Cerena's tears. My people cauldron them. They're very valuable; yes very valuable…some would kill for such a prize!" He grabbed my hand, placed the bottle in the center of my palm, and gently closed my fingers over the top of it. "It will help you on your journey. Go on!" His voice was filled with such urgency that before I could even think to ask what it was for, I uncorked the container. To my surprise the liquid slithered out and calmly weaved its way through my fingers. Upon arriving mid forearm, it morphed into the shape of a rather large black and yellow spider. Its spindly legs scampered up and down my skin. I tried to remain calm. How could something so large come out of such a miniature bottle?

"Don't panic" whispered Fenwick. It will be over shortly."

"What will be over shortly? OUCH!! It bit me!"

"Well you didn't expect it to fetch the newspaper did you?"

I'd only taken my eyes off the nasty little thing for a moment and it had bitten me! "Hey, wait a minute!" Frantically, I began searching my person. Our multi-legged friend was nowhere to be found! "Oh not to worry, not to worry. She's most assuredly gone.

I promise no harm will come to you though. My people have bestowed upon you a very rare honor. It's only been bequeathed once before." We heard a loud crash in the kitchen followed by Clancey's enthusiastic rant. Fenwick scanned the room.

"Is it as they say then?" He gave me an inquisitive once over. "You know, about your memories. Are they truly gone?" I found myself nodding. What else could I do? His spider had just bitten me and now he was talking about memories? Truly, this guy was one hotcake short of a stack…But maybe if I was nice to him I'd get the anti serum...

"Tsk, tsk, tsk," he muttered. "Not even a single glint of a memory?" I just gave him a blank stare.

"Such a shame. We could certainly use your craft about now….Fiddlesticks! Never mind all that!" he added. "I'll explain quickly. I am sent from the house of Heedrin. I am not specially trained in this sort of thing you know. I am a simple potion maker by trade, an aweshushshamen. The Druix and Dorn are symbiants you see. They harvest and we cauldron fine potions for just about everything. I volunteered to bring you the tears, but mainly I come to avenge what was taken from me!" "And what exactly, was taken from you Fenwick?"

With his pinky he began drawing lines in gleaming, neon red in the air before him. A large, gold frame materialized and encompassed the images. I noticed the protuberances had changed shades. They were now a deep dark blue. Then he waved his hand over the picture and it filled with colors true to life. Next he breathed on the portrait and the images inside began moving. "This is my family great, sir. Although it seems anymore I can never get my wife's pretty smile just right…it's been a long time since I've seen it…too long." He paused. "The two small ones are my children."

He got very quiet, and subsequently chose not to speak for a short period of time. I stopped rubbing the spider bite on my forearm. The mood turned grievously somber. I was aware that something was very wrong. He removed a ring from his finger and placed it tenderly in my hand. "Put it on," he whispered. I obeyed. Instantaneously, I sensed indescribable loss, agony; suffering…The longer I wore it, the more powerful the discernment. I could see blurred images of Fenwick crying out! I had visions of his wife and children screaming! Something was preparing to attack them… I tore the ring from my finger and dropped it to the floor. The sensations stopped but I couldn't erase the emotions he'd been feeling prior to handing it to me. "I'm sorry Fenwick! I'm sorry! I just couldn't take…I just couldn't take knowing." Without question, or description, I understood his unrelenting grief. Reverently, he retrieved the band and gently placed it back on his ring finger. He forced himself to speak and as he did, he choked back the tears.

"They were executed under master Denegaul's orders. It was because we wouldn't surrender our children for the rebellion. He hunts the young ones you see… I lost everything. Nothing has been the same since his wretched greed ruined our worlds. And the signs…Yes, the signs are everywhere again…The war, it is beginning. "Watery eyed, he passed his hand over the painting and it dissolved frame and all.

"But never you mind that great one…Please excuse my digression." He wiped his eyes. The blue skin slowly reverted back to his normal tone. "Does the bite hurt?" Still somewhat dazed, I shook my head no. "Good. Good," he said patting me on the back. "Not to worry, I didn't poison you. If I would've done that, you'd have been dead five minutes ago!"

I scrunched my forehead and replied, "Point taken." He laughed softly.

"But Fenwick, if Dendura houses immortals and powerful magic then why can't you bring your family back?" He looked at me rather perplexed. "Surely you don't know? Oh yes…I see…Hasn't Clancey explained to you such things?"

"Sort of… well not really… It seems I have much to learn and never enough time to do so. I usually get a shotgun blast of information and end up with more questions than answers."

"I'm sorry to say we don't have much time either my friend. I must tell you about the gifting! You see the impartation of the knowing… " I hastily interrupted.

"Lately my whole world has been about 'not much time Fenwick.' I just fought a Bandolix for goodness sake! I don't even really know what the heck it was, except the worst thing I've ever faced in my life…well besides those Giests of course…Never mind that," I announced trying to remain focused. "My point is I've been doing nothing but barely staying alive ever since I got nailed by that stupid apple." The dwarf cocked his head sideways appearing somewhat confused.

"I can't even receive a gift without it biting me! I don't know if I'm coming or going. You can't expect a guy to keep putting his neck on the line without having reasons as to why! Besides, I don't believe there will be enough 'time' for a long time! So please. I have to learn all I can while I can… rather than when it's too late." After a second or two of contemplation he spoke.

"Well that was a mouthful wasn't it? Shall I get you a chair?" He genuinely patted my shoulder. "You must feel somewhat relieved. It's always better to get these things out in the open. Can't keep everything bottled up inside don't you know. Yes, it's much healthier this way. I suppose I can't blame you for your frustration… Okay," he said shaking his head. "But really, you ask about different subjects entirely among them: Dendura and death." He took a deep breath and chose his words carefully.

"Let's see, let's see," he said pinching the bridge of his nose with his thumb and forefinger. "Where should I begin? Aaah yes, Aaah yes...The infinity..." He loudly cleared his throat and spoke in a scholarly tone. "The Infinity is a place where time begins and stops. It hosts the magical realms where our people dwell. Dendura resides within this expanse and houses the counsel of all allianced magical worlds. Because of this, it's also considered to be the great city paramount for the embodiment of honorable magic. Dendura was of course created by your father for Genocist habitation but has since become a major force among our people. And if no one's told you, Dendura is only a microcosm within the great macrocosm. Unquestionably, there are other powerful unions which dwell peacefully alongside the Genocent's creation. Regardless, we all rely on each other to fuel our craft. It is a symbiotic relationship of sorts.

"*But,* living in such places doesn't automatically make a person immortal don't you know. Being magical doesn't involuntarily make someone immortal, I dare say. Most of us are Demigents." The dwarf put his hands behind his back and slowly strode back and forth. "It doesn't work like that, Apprentice. Anyone can live within these realms ... Semigents, Genocists, and so on. The only requirements are that residents believe in the magic and contribute positively to it. People of magic are not obligated to live within our own worlds either although it is said to be of comfort to those who prefer to be around their own kind.

"Nonetheless, make no mistake. In all our glorious knowledge and infinite wisdom, we've never discovered a true cure for death. So you see, I can't bring my precious family back. Don't be fooled either Son of He. Even immortals have their weaknesses," he added solemnly.

"If you're good and you die, you go to Heaven, not Dendura. Dendura is simply where humans of magic can exist if they so desire. The infinity accommodates all sorts of creatures, not just humans, but it does not accommodate the dead, only the living magic. After that, the classifications can be a little tricky. There are of course the wanderers, second chancers, individuals who have died missing entrance into heaven by a thread. They're given opportunities to make recompense," he whispered. Conversely, those who die forsaking the call of excellence completely will rightfully find their home within the cavernous pit of Hades, not MalDracaena, although the two are well known for doing business. Anyone can tell you that!" Both spiny processes turned a smoldering shade of black. "MalDracaena is the realm of the wicked where abominations of evil are free to practice their malicious magic," he divulged in disgust. "Nonetheless, its inhabitants are *still* considered to be among the living. In any case, pit dwellers or Dracaenians are known to be some of the foulest of all creatures and from them, choice candidates are selected to wander to and fro causing nothing but devastation and harm. But I don't think I need to tell you about that!"

"Strappin' on the feed bag in five minutes," hollered Clancey!

"But enough about those things. We need to get down to business. The Dorn will be expecting my return." He glanced at his pocket watch. "I must tell you about the great honor you have been given."

"Hey! Wait a minute!" I exclaimed. "I know that name... Did you say the Dorn? You must tell me of my friend Burton! He was taken by two guards to the ivy cottage to be treated by your people. How is he?!!"

He cut in sharply. "I'm sorry to say, I don't know of your Burton... I was sent off in a hurry you see. Oh never mind that! We are running out of time! There are many not to be trusted!" he whispered.

Just then, Clancey walked in. Fenwick became very ill at ease and quit speaking all together.

"You two getting acquainted?" I stared blankly at Fenwick. He only smiled and shrugged his shoulders. His brows gave off a subtle pulse of orange.

"Will you be traveling with us?" asked Clancey. "We could sure use someone with your medicinal capabilities," Fenwick replied with a lie.

"No. Grapple has requested some cauldroning from me. He has graciously offered for me to vacation here for as long as I need. As you can see, I am well provided for."

"What is this place anyway?" I asked.

"Upstairs is the passageway I was telling you about," replied Clancey. "It will lead us to the old smuggler's tunnels underneath the school."

"It is an entrance to the world of men...Rogues...don't you know! Nasty business if you ask me," said Fenwick. His mood brows were now a vague gray hue.

"What do you mean 'smuggling'?"

"The tunnels were secretly constructed centuries ago. Over time they've served many different purposes. As far as smuggling, you name it! People, liquor, goods...whatever was in short supply or didn't want to be found passed through those corridors...Eventually, they were turned into wine cellars and finally, they were forgotten all together."

"Then how did you come to know about them?"

He set the plates on the table with a big grin on his face. "Out of necessity, lad, necessity. Now hurry up! Let's eat! We've already wasted time with your 20 minute nap!" He helped himself to a plate of scrambled eggs and bacon.

"You too, Fenwick! I'm sure you're hungry after your journey."

"Thank you Brynth... I, I, I MEAN Clancey. Yes, uh...uh... Clancey! But...I should much rather prefer toast and kippers...Yes kippers and toast," he said nervously.

The immediate silence was stifling!! The dwarf's spines flickered bright orange and pink! I wasn't sure what just happened but the lighthearted atmosphere had been replaced with instant tension. It sounded as though Fenwick had accidentally said the wrong name, which is something I completely understood because I continually fought the urge to call Clancey, Burt. For some reason he was still parading around in Burt's likeness. Regardless, it seemed an unfortunate slip but after about a second or two things went back to normal and they were laughing like old friends.

"I saw some bread and sardines in the cupboard. Help yourself."

"Thank you Clancey." They talked drivel for a bit. I watched Clancey drown his food with hot sauce. I kept waiting for Fenwick to continue our original conversation. But he'd given me the distinct impression that he did not want O'Keefe to know anything about it!

"So I only had a 20 minute nap huh? It seemed like an hour."

"Oh clotted cream!" cried Fenwick as he rummaged through the pantry. "Wonderful!"

"Well good," he spoke between mouthfuls. "You looked like you needed it." He poured more hot sauce on his plate. I dove into my plate of eggs. They tasted delicious. Fenwick was busy preparing his meal.

"How do you like Grapple's little hideaway, Creed?" asked Clancey.

"Where's Wally and the Beav?" I replied.

"I told you, he has a collection of sorts…Just be thankful that he let us use it. You can thank him for the grub as well."

"I'm just happy nothing has tried to burn or drown me in here!" He smiled. "Our world will become familiar to you once again. You'll see."

I took the opportunity of down time to ask him a question that had been bothering me. "Clancey, why is it that you're still in Burt's form?" Fenwick dropped his fork. I noticed the dwarf would not turn to face me. The mood changed to strange again. His response was matter of fact.

"I don't know. I guess I thought it would make you feel more comfortable… You just got finished saying that our world has been somewhat of a shock to you. Besides, I can keep up with you a little better like this!" It sounded reasonable enough. And when I queried him about why Fenwick hadn't heard of Burton, he shrugged his shoulders and simply replied, "Difference in comings and goings is all. Don't worry. Burt will be fine." He changed the subject and the rest of our time at the table was spent talking about the ball.

Like all good houseguests after a meal, I helped wash and dry the dishes. I was enjoying watching two dolphins play via the kitchen window. While Clancey was clearing the table, Fenwick leaned into me over a sink full of soapy water. "The knowing doesn't work on everyone."

"What?" Fenwick looked over his shoulder.

"Now listen… The knowing, your gift, does not work on everyone, especially if they've been trained. It's better if you use a clothing item, something they've worn for at least a few days. Jewelry is good, too. Remember that time will erase the signature so you want something fresh. Above all else, tell no one you have the gift!" I found myself nodding but not fully understanding what he was trying convey. "And you best be careful of that one," he whispered.

"You mean Clancey?" I asked. He shook his head yes just as he walked in.

"We're about ready Creed. Don't forget your pack." He looked down at my feet. "Oh, I forgot about that. I think you'll be needing shoes. I'm sure we'll find something we can use upstairs."

Fenwick addressed me while drying his hands with a dish towel. "Well, here's where we part my friend."

"Will you be alright?" I asked.

"Of course! Of course! You mustn't be late for your party. We are counting on you, great sir. I know you won't let us down. DENEGUAL MUST BE STOPPED!" He was rather startled by his sudden show of exuberance and quickly covered his mouth with both hands. His eyes brimmed with tears and his brows flashed a fury of stormy colors, but it wasn't out of sadness…it was out of extreme anger.

He reached for a hug and in my ear he quietly said, "Use it wisely."

Then he spoke to Clancey. "You take care of him!"

"With my life," Clancey solemnly replied.

I followed him up the shag carpeted steps but stopped halfway. Out of the blue, I started feeling extremely dizzy and had to sit down, abruptly.

"Are you okay?"

"Yeah, just a little lightheaded."

"Oh! I almost forgot!" exclaimed Fenwick. "Now where did I put it? Ah yes!" He scurried toward the closet and retrieved an old fashion doctor's bag from inside. When he'd placed it atop the table, he touched the handles with the tip of his long dirty nail and said, "Remedicinal." The worn leather bag folded, bended, popped, and snapped into the shape of a wooden storage rack bearing hundreds of separate slots. Each compartment was filled with tiny bottles, herbs, live bugs, small tools and many things foreign to me.

"Now let me see," he said removing a black cauldron along with a small mortar and pestle. "Where did I put it? Awe yes!" He pulled out a little glass container filled with an amethyst colored fluid. "This is for you. I cauldroned it this morning. It will help with the fatigue and remnants of the spellback."

"What's a spellback?" I asked skeptically.

He turned to Clancey. "Oh dear, his recollection loss does go deep! Never mind that! Never mind that! I'm sure Clancey will explain it to you on the way, but sometimes the conjurer of a spell can receive in part, the negative effects of the very spell he intended for someone else…it bounces back so to speak if you're not careful." He happily handed it to me.

"Go on."

Considering what transpired with the last little bottle he'd handed me, I was extremely hesitant to remove the cork. Fenwick reassuringly stated, "It will make you feel better. I promise." Warily, I popped the lid and waited. Nothing happened. I exhaled. "Well come on, Creed! What are you waiting for?! It's not going to explode," insisted Clancey.

"It's not going to sprout legs or anything is it?" I murmured. Clancey gave me a strange glance while Fenwick adamantly shook his head no. "Okay, here goes nothing!" I threw my head back and prepared to empty the thick ooze into my mouth. It smelled like grape jelly which was a much better improvement over the culpie root.

"Whoa!" yelled Fenwick! "What are you doing? It does not go in your mouth, Apprentice! It must go in through the ear!" Clancey nodded furiously.

"Of course! I said cynically. "Where else would it go? What was I thinking? Bottoms up!" I toasted the air with the bottle and then poured the liquid in my ear. It was warm and tingly. These feelings went from my ears and blanketed my entire body. It felt as though I was lying in the warm sun with a cool breeze blowing over me.

Clancey picked up where Fenwick had left off. He sounded concerned. "The magic you evoked was extremely potent... It can cause problems if you're not ready to withstand the effects. To be honest you stirred up quite a ruckus back there. I'm surprised you're still sanding...You know I'd let you rest longer if I could."

"I'm good. Just needed to catch my breath." It was at that moment I realized I really was better! I didn't even feel tired let alone the pain that had been pulsating at the back of my skull! Fenwick saw my eyes brighten.

"Feeling well again?" he asked.

"Much! Thank you Fenwick! Thank you!"

"We better keep moving if we don't want to be shark bait!" quipped Clancey. Not knowing what to say, I turned back to Fenwick and gave him a solid nod. "Your sacrifice will not have been in vain. I will do my best."

"I know you will, great Apprentice. I know you will." And as he waved goodbye, his spines turned to yellow again.

I resumed my assent leaving him at the foot of the stairs. It was odd. The house appeared only to have two stories, but the stairs wound round and round, flight after flight. But what was even more strange, was the fact that as we climbed higher, the walls on either side of us would move in such a way that assorted doors and windows rolled on by. If we stopped moving, the walls stopped moving too.

"You doin' okay?" inquired Clancey.

"Yeah, better than I was."

"What do you make of Fenwick?"

"He seems like a nice enough guy. His remedy worked like a charm."

"That's because his remedy was a charm," laughed Clancey.

I was careful not to reveal my conversation with Fenwick. I still wasn't sure what his warning about my traveling mate had meant. As far as I was concerned I could trust Clancey with my life. But it certainly did make me all the more curious about him.

"Yes, he's a nice little guy...some say he's one sandwich short of a picnic...you know with his family and all." I cautiously navigated the subject away from the issue and on to something that I'd been wondering about.

"Clancey, if the Quetral stone is supposed to protect me, than why did that Bandolix throw me all around like that?"

"He was beatin' the living tar out of ya and he didn't use magic to do it! That's why! The stone can only protect you from *magic* used against you, not physical force. Besides, most of what you felt came from the catastrophic craft you released. Although I'd have to say, he got the worst end of the deal!"

"Makes sense...How about the bridge trolls? Are they as mean as they seem?

"Those sissy frilled lizards? Well usually, they don't eat human flesh but it's been a while since they've seen one... Don't let their small size fool you though. All joking aside, I once saw a Ligidor cross a bridge troll and what followed next was blood, bubbles, and b..." I cut him off.

"Never mind! I get the picture," I said laughing. "I just really wanted to say thanks, thanks for saving me from trolls as well as the police, and for standing up to that Bandolix." He seemed a little embarrassed. "Maybe I can return the favor sometime." He did nothing but smile and nod.

We finally reached the second floor. There was no landing to step up on to. The steps immediately dead ended in to a lone wooden door. As soon as the walls stopped moving Clancey opened it. Inside was a hallway with four sets of doors, one on the left and three on the right. He chose the middle door on the right. It turned out to be bedroom complete with a bed and nightstand. "Here, these should fit." He tossed me a pair of black boots from a cache in the closet. I sat on the Howdy Doody comforter and tried them on...whoever he was.

"Hey, they really fit!"

"Yeah, leave it to Grapple to see us out in style!" Outside, swarms of fish went about their business. I found myself wishing I could stay in the Druix hideaway.

"The bathroom's across the hallway. If we're heading to the ball Cinderella, we should probably try and make ourselves look somewhat respectable." His tone turned serious. "Try and hurry though. The more I think about that Bandolix, the more I'm wondering who might suspect we're here." I didn't argue.

We took turns using the facilities. I had to admit, I was shocked when I saw my reflection in the mirror. The Giest's sear and black eye had been replaced by pallor and dark circles under both eyes. I combed my hair, ran water over my face, and did my best at removing Grapple's blood from my shirt. One final glance in the mirror, and I met Clancey in the hall.

"You ready?"

"As I'll ever be!"

We walked toward the last door on the right. It was yet another small room wrought in more nostalgic décor. It contained bedroom furniture. Stacks of *Life Magazine* were neatly displayed on the nightstand. Next to the bed was a rather large chest of drawers. It loomed above both our heads. Clancey carefully removed the first drawer from the dresser. It was empty. He removed another and stacked it one on top of the first. He continued to take out each empty drawer positioning them over the next. When he was finished a tower of drawers stood eight high. He turned to me.

"Time to go. Departentrance!!" he commanded. The clanking of interlocking parts was followed by the drawers firmly seating themselves atop each other. They blended and liquefied into a solid piece of wood. Without hesitation, he swung it open as if it were a normal door. The makeshift opening exposed a secret passageway! To the natural eye it didn't make sense. It was an absolute one dimensional wonder. I peered around the rear of the doorway…nothing but the backs of old drawers. Returning to the front side, and looking past the portal's threshold, I observed a completely new realm! It looked very dark in there. A rush of cold air hit my face as we stepped on through.

CHAPTER EIGHTEEN
A Blind Eye View

Silently we walked down a series of earthen corridors lined with cobblestone floors and black lamp posts. At one time, the iron giants had lit up the darkness but now their glass tops were filled with dirt, cob webs, and decaying wicks. The passageways showed signs of previous human habitation. In one hallway we found old books, lanterns, and barrels. In another we discovered bedding, a pot belly stove, and outdated clothing. Each new passageway was filled with articles from the past, many of which were fit for a historical museum. Some, I didn't recognize. In several areas it was evident that these tunnels had served as people's homes. I knelt down to pick up a dusty wooden toy but in the process, almost fell over. "Are you sure you're okay? Let's have a look at your head. Does it hurt?" I flinched a little while he examined the cut.

"Really, I'm good. I just lost my balance. Fenwick's potion did wonders. I only wish we had more."

"Overall, I think you fared pretty well." I couldn't argue with him there. "It doesn't look bad. Just a minor cut really. Your hair covers it up." He studied my face for a moment, and then slapped me on the back.

"What was that?" I asked. He cast a glance upward. I could hear faint voices and movement.

"We're under Devonshire."

"You're serious?"

"As a man could be," he exclaimed. "I'll bring us up in one of the side corridors first. We can monitor the guests or unwanteds from various locations per these tunnels. There are many entrances down here that lead to different parts of the school…and other places. We'll use as many as possible until we find her. Chances are when she sees you, she'll know not to bring attention to the matter. I know my plan leaves some room for error, but we'll handle that when it comes." He reached inside his knapsack. "Here, complements of Grapple!" He tossed a small linen bag at me.

"What's this?" I untied the bag's drawstring. It contained a black mask. Someone had taken the time to intricately engrave gold scrolling on its surface. A design had been etched around the eye, mouth and nose holes to make them appear as if they belonged to a winged serpent. "Did you get one, too?" He dug in his pack and pulled out a mask similar to mine.

"Want to trade?" he joked.

I was getting nervous. I was starting to gain an understanding of what lay ahead. "So, our main goal is to find my mom and learn where the chronicle is." He made a quick downward motion with his head. "Then what?" The sides of his mouth turned upward.

"We'll be headin' to Dendura, of course!"

"You mean I can actually go there?"

"Go there?" he said sarcastically! "You will maintain its existence!"

"But how will we get there?"

"You ask too many questions. We have a different mission ahead of us right now. We need to concentrate on *it*!" He spoke quickly out the side of his mouth. "There is a gateway down here. It will put us on the road to Dendura."

"You mean like a portal?"

"Yes, only a trained eye can spot them," he boasted. "Now ready your mask. It's time!"

I removed Grapple's handiwork from the cloth sack and hung it around my neck. We went a little further down the cobblestone walkway. The sound of my stomach growling filled the tunnels. I was still hungry! I guess a few near-death experiences had really increased my appetite! We stopped in an area filled with rows of vacant wine shelves. They were worn with age and garnished with countless cobwebs. "Wait here." I turned away only for a moment to adjust the strap on my mask. As I spun back around, the wine rack he was standing in front of was no longer empty. It was completely filled with colorful and ornate glass containers! He was careful to pull out particular bottles only part way. Others were removed entirely from their resting places. They floated in mid-air waiting patiently to be re-shelved. Some he pushed in or turned counter-clockwise. He continued to manipulate the bottles like a locker combination. Finally, the rack gave way and opened as though it was a sliding glass door. It exposed nothing but a solid brick wall. He turned to me, smiled, and preceded to stick his hand straight through the stone barrier! It disappeared somewhere on the other side!

"This will take us up into the kitchen. We can get a feel for the party by listening in on the hireds. If we're lucky, at some point your mom will conference with the caterers in there."

A terrible thought crossed my mind. "What if she never makes it to the kitchen?"

He put on his mask and replied, "Then we'll have to go looking for her or try another tunnel. But I doubt that very much." He adjusted his satchel. "Once we're in, it's a pretty tight fit. We'll have to crawl a ways before we get there." He turned back to the wall and managed to step halfway through. Before I could think to ask any more questions, he was violently thrust back out! An empty wine rack broke his fall! The floating bottles came crashing down! Pure black fury swung from the depths of the camouflaged passageway! Savagely, it began slashing at him! His screams echoed through the wine cellar! The Giest's serrated claw lacerated the flesh on his thigh! My face was spattered with his blood. The warm droplets trickled down my cheek and neck. He grabbed for the wound as blood began to gush freely. He was trying to yell something, but agony prevented him from clear speech. The hellish figure danced excitedly around him! Its sickle-shaped talons made the sound I'd come to fear. CLICK CLICK CLICK CLICK …Both weapons were highly decorated in waves of gold and black tally marks. They glistened and sparkled all the while displaying their evil history.

I aimed both hands toward it. "HYDROUS THANATOS!!!!" Its twisted gelatinous hand swatted the air overhead as though I were a pesky insect. "VECTH LORE AVIATIAN!!!" Its many voices blended together to form a chorus of deranged laughter. I couldn't keep guessing. I was losing precious time. Two imprisoned souls were allowed temporary freedom. But why had they been set free? They took up position on either side of Clancey. It was then the Giest stood firmly fixed ready to disembowel him with its bloody talon! The triad attack! Both henchmen greedily waited, ready to capture his soul once set loose. It was at that moment I realized any craft I'd summoned came from copying or repeating what I had seen *Clancey* do!!! I did the only thing I could. I resorted to hitting the cloaked demon with old bottles, cans…anything I could throw! The projectiles entered its body and bounced back like they'd been shot from a giant sling shot! The two minions hid behind a shelf!

I'd succeeded in distracting it long enough for Clancey to slide himself out of the way. He aimed a bloody hand in the direction of the beast and screamed, "DEMI NOCT...*something*!" I couldn't make it out! He'd generated enough craft to send the Giest sailing backwards! I saw the look of astonishment on the creature's face as it slammed into the very rack protecting its two accomplices! Souls imprisoned within the hellish being sloshed back and forth similar to fish inside an unsteady tank! The serpent's huge tongue shot out of the Giest's mouth and seized the hiding collaborators! They were drug inside the creature's body kicking and screaming! After sizing me up, the creature turned its back to me.

Once again, the Quetral stone radiated heat. From within the inner recesses of its vaporous cape materialized a person I knew very well. It was Isabelle! She was in the same clothes she'd been wearing the day of our fight. Her hair was matted and she looked like she hadn't slept. She was walking toward me, crying hysterically. Two souls for one... Two souls for one... Immediately, I recognized the foul stench of decay! The noxious fumes were radiating from her!

"Isabelle?"

Her voiced deepened to an almost growl. "Yes! Yes! It's Isabelle..." I took a step backward, wiping the blood from my face and neck. In the process, my hand was shocked as it passed over my father's stone. I looked down and saw the talisman radiating silver light. I knew what to do! "Yes, it is Isabelle! Please help me, Creed! It's horrible! You must save me!" I looked at the stone and then her. She trembled. "Please Creed! No...No!!! STOOoopppp!!!"

I grabbed the stone in one hand and raised the other. I was to serve as a transformer for its magical powers! The craft I'd summoned generated such intensity, I was afraid to continue my assault! I could feel it flowing through every part of my being! Its magnitude was so immense I could barely restrain it! It frightened and exhilarated me all at the same time! Isabelle's imposter received the brunt of my initial attack. Waves of cobblestone ripped themselves from the floor with explosive force! Her footsteps were blocked by hurtling blocks of rock. She froze and started screaming wildly. The bricks began encasing her within a concrete sarcophagus! Simultaneously, the Giest reeled backwards sensing her impending defeat! The brick coffin was nearing completion. It encompassed her from the neck down. I watched in awe as her face started to distort and her head became pinched. The ghastly beast morbidly transformed, turning from body to spirit. It flew around the room like a balloon losing air, all the while escaping eternal interment.

The hideous spirit was reabsorbed by the cape, screaming and cursing. I held tightly to the talisman and redirected the next blow. Without much forethought, the remainder of the spell flowed from my lips freely. "DEMI NOCT TOTALIS GISHT!" Raw kinetic bolts of energy violently burst from my mouth, eyes and fingertips. They struck the Giest with staggering force! I fell to my knees! In horror, the Giest watched its own plasmatic body zipper open. The soul-filled innards expelled like a flood! The serpent's tongue flailed in vain, hissing and thrashing! The escaping spirits blew furiously past me. They disappeared within the recesses of the smugglers' tunnels, giddy and laughing maniacally!

Instinctively I turned, ready for more battle, but the Giest lay curiously still. Before my eyes its horrific disguise washed away revealing a human boy draped in a black velvet cloak! Cautiously, I poked his leg with my foot, but no reaction came of it. He lay slain on the cold brick floor. I was stunned, but grateful. Immediately, I became overpowered by exhaustion. Without warning I fell to the ground but only because I could no longer see! "CLANCEY!!!" I screamed in terror.

His voice was weak. "You're okay, lad…talk to me. What's going on?"

"I CAN'T SEE ANYTHING CLANCEY!!! I'VE BEEN BLINDED! I CAN'T SEE!!!!"

"Creed! Creed! Get a hold of yourself boy! It's the spellback! It will go away in a minute or two! I PROMISE! Calm yourself! They're all gone. I want you to concentrate on slowing your breathing down! Do as I say! NOW!" I tried not to panic but my mind's eye kept replaying the attack. Frantically, I fumbled for anything I could use as a weapon. During my chaotic display, Clancey did something completely absurd…he began telling me jokes!

"Why did the student eat his homework? Because his teacher told him it was a piece of cake!" It was so stupid and out of place, we both ended up laughing! He told me more. "When do doctors get angry? When they run out of patients!" More laughter! "This one gets me every time... Why was the tomato blushing? Because he saw the salad dressing!"

Within a few seconds and after a lot of laughter, things came into a hazy focus and slowly back to normal. I was able to see again! Burt's muddled outline turned clear! He was smiling. "You okay?"

I nodded. "I guess now's a good a time as any to teach you about the spellback… Just as we are taught how to mask our powers, we are also taught how to diffuse the consequences they can produce against the very person who summoned them. I've taken it for granted until now. But to get straight to the point, the secret is pure laughter. It deflects the harmful effects of a spell…"

I hadn't heard too much of what he'd said. I'd realized the full immensity of what I'd done. A glimpse of the boy's lifeless body brought things back into a harsh perspective. One bloody talon rested in solace next to each of his feet. I understood this to be only a sampling of what was to come. I followed the trail of red drippings back over to Clancey. It became immediately clear he'd lost a good amount blood. It was puddling underneath him! "Are you okay? Please be okay!" He had his eyes closed and was gripping the injured thigh.

His response was rather winded. "I'm good, lad."

"Are you sure?"

"I'll be fine. I've been in feistier scrapes! It looks worse than it is."

"What was that thing?"

"Tis a Giest, of course! They return to their original state when defeated." He looked over at the slumped figure. "Twas Buchenwald."

"You know him?"

"Aye…very well. He was a good kid before Denegaul vexed him."

"But he's a human…a boy!!"

"Why are you so surprised, Son of He? The Giest ranks are a mixture of souls drawn from a multitude of origins. Evil comes in all ages, shapes, and sizes. Never mind what the outer shell looks like. Hand me my satchel, will ya?" I searched out his bag among the wreckage. I found the pack and gave it to him. He began to bandage his leg by ripping material from my old shirt. "Most were traitors of Dendura; others were rallied from the forbidden realms. You see, Denegaul favored the collection of children from every race, faith, and walk of life for his purpose…promising them immortality, love, power, fame, wealth… whatever he could in exchange for their everlasting servitude." He took a laborious breath and expressed his next statement in an ominous tone. "Oh tis a special kind of evil when a young one goes bad... Over a long span, the wicked one convinced many a young one to do his bidding. As you can see, he doesn't keep his end of the bargain too well."

"You mean he killed perfectly innocent people?"

"In a way, yes. It's my understanding that he needed to establish a formidable army in order to create any sort of threat toward the Genocent. At first he recruited from within. But as time passed, it became clear that humans, more specifically human children, were the quickest and most plentiful source. Denegaul believes a child's allegiance insures absolute loyalty, not to mention a lifetime to work his evil through. It's a lengthy story, but that's part of the reason we're not to do magic around Rogues in general. Even though most would be blind to it...no pun intended," he added. "It's just that we can't be sure if they can be trusted again. Our belief is that they are easily swayed. And if it's to the wrong side... well you've already experienced what they're capable of." He finished securing his bandage as best as he could and dusted himself off.

"No one ever suspected the deceitful lord's dark intentions! It happened right under our noses! When Holgraham finally did discover the plot of overthrow, Denegaul and his followers were made Demigent." "You mean semi mortal?" I interjected. "Yes. And then they were banished! Now all of the signs are the same as before." He bowed his head. "We believe he's collecting children again and in the process found the one he'd been searching for: you." He looked toward Buchenwald and sighed. "It didn't quite work out as he'd planned." I began trying to make sense of it all.

"Do you mean those kids that have been disappearing lately?" He nodded. "What about Isabelle?"

His reply was most confident. "I think her abduction served a dual purpose, to add another soul to Denegaul's ranks and to frame you." He threw me a piece of cloth.

"What's this for?"

"You've got some of my blood on you."

As I was wiping it off I couldn't resist asking. "And what about you? You're bleeding."

"Well, you didn't think I'd spout green blood, did ya? I am what you call a Semigent, half human mixed with something else. Genocists are all human, and Intelligents are all animal. Of course there are others but for now, those are the main three you need to know about."

"So you're a Demigent Semigent?"

"Very good Creed. As I told you, most of us are Demigent, but that only refers to our extended longevity, not our heritage. When a Semigent changes form, we literally respond like whatever we shifted to would. When I take the form of a human, I am susceptible to their pains weaknesses. And I'll confess, I don't miss it one bit! When I am hit, I feel the pain. When I am cut, I bleed just as any human would. Now, gather up our stuff, lad! We've got to rethink our infiltration! Will you hand me those?" He was pointing at the bloody talons.

"Sure," I said, sounding somewhat grossed out.

They were surprisingly warm and solid. The elaborate detailing was amazing consisting of thousands upon thousands of tiny black and gold tally marks. The etchings were as intricate as in scrimshaw work. Upon further inspection it was clear that each mark contributed to a final picture. There were four images one on each side. I didn't recognize the first three, but the fourth depiction was astonishing. "Hey that's my picture! He put my picture on his killing claws!" It was crazy to think that my face might've been the last thing his victims ever saw!

It was at that moment I discerned...I knew! While holding the talons in my hand, Buchenwald's explosive hatred surged through me...his rage...and utter abhorrence toward me. I'd never experienced such consuming hatred in all my life! I could feel his obsession to slaughter me in the most painful way possible! He wanted me to suffer...I was momentarily given access to his mind, his way of thinking, his memories! In a split second my mind's eye was flooded with glimpses of violent kills he'd made in the past! I was a witness to each and every horrific act! I understood his disbelief in the last moments of life...I tried to hide my monumental shock but at the same time rid myself of his abominable thought invasion. Hastily I handed the claws over to Clancey. I watched and waited for some sort of shocking reaction. However, he acted as though it was business as usual. I could tell he'd sensed nothing at all. Is that what Fenwick meant by the 'knowing?' This was no gift. It was a nightmare!

I made sure to conceal my disturbing discovery by keeping up with the conversation. "Why would he do something like this? Why would he put my face on these?"

Clancey just smiled at me and shoved the talons in his satchel. "Each Giest personalizes his or her talons a lot like humans personalize their license plates or cell phone rings. It's a status thing. They're a much sought-after souvenir! Yes, highly prized and rare at that! Tis not every day one can walk away from a Giest free and clear!"

"Who are the other three?

"His parents and brother. T'was a sinister thing to do if you ask me, but that was Buchenwald's way. His family was good people though..." He cleared his throat.

"By the way, thanks for savin' me life."

An awkward silence filled the cavern. I searched for something normal to say. "Uhh, I guess we're even then?"

"That we would be, lad! That we would be!" He finished tying the bandage around his thigh. "There! Good as new!"

I gathered my belongings and collected our masks among the shambles. I couldn't erase the flashes of Buchenwald's violent life… his seething emotions. They'd stained my thoughts. If it were possible, I would've washed my brain right then and there. His way of thinking was unbearable. The depths of his deceit clearly showed in his twisted beliefs. It was methodical madness followed by an insatiable urge to perpetuate hate and evil. Buchenwald enjoyed it. If this was the gift I'd been bestowed, I respectfully wanted to return it. Realizing I couldn't afford prolonged distractions, I tried refocusing. The Giest's attack had left me exhausted. It felt like I'd run a marathon. I ached everywhere.

"Clancey?" He was still fiddling with his satchel.

"Hmm?"

"Why does Denegaul want to kill my father? I mean what started it all? I understand he was made Demigent…but it was he who plotted the overthrow."

He paused for a little bit. His eyes searched the piles of cobblestone left then right. "Tis a good question, but a lengthy story. For the most part, I'd have to say it was due to a mixture of arrogance and lust for power. But, mostly for power. Tis something that all beings crave. However for some, it is an insatiable thirst. Unfortunately, in the wrong hands it is a catalyst for destruction. I think you can understand that now more than ever." I wiped the blood from Grapple's mask and handed it over. "Congratulations," he said.

"Thanks, but I don't feel right celebrating my victory at someone else's expense." I looked over at Buchenwald. He had completely vanished, cape and all! "Hey! Where'd he go?"

Clancey's head made a motion toward my hand. "No Creed, congratulations on your Trist!"

"Huh?" I looked down. Whatever it was, when I first laid eyes on it, I wanted to give it back!

"Your Trist… Come here! Come here! Tis a mark of honor! It is the sign of only the most powerful magic! It's what I've been telling you about!"

Nervously I asked, "Does it come off?"

"Does it come off?" he replied excitedly! "Why no! Of course not! Only you, the Son of He, can attain such an iconic mark! Of course your father has his, but no one other than his bloodline is honored in this way! No one! Tis a glorious one to behold at that!" He grabbed both arms for a closer look. "What a wonderful gift! All who witness it will know you are mighty! It's happening slowly, but at least it's happening!" he declared.

I tried to respond humbly, but I didn't know how I would ever explain it… to my mom…Burton…anyone! I was twelve years old and the proud owner of my first tattoo. And not just any tattoo. Peering out from beneath my left sleeve were intricate waves of black scrolling made up of tiny ornamental designs. They stung something fierce! The markings encircled my wrist like a thick watchband. I had to blink twice! What was it with these people and their gifts?!!

This was no ordinary tattoo! It was alive! The scrolls and ink patterns floated freely as if they were tiny living organisms. I kept waiting for them to wriggle up my arm, however they did not leave the boundaries of the band they'd created. Thankfully, just a small portion of it could be seen outside of my sleeve. After careful inspection, I realized only one arm had received the branding. My right arm was free and clear. Studying the tattoo in more detail, I recognized at times the animate symbols would combine together to give the impression of one larger picture. I found the image of some sort of doorway on the inside of my wrist. But those daunting marks… I watched them squiggle and pulse within my skin. I'd seen them before…but where?

"What does this mean and why are they moving?"

"It means I will have my old friend back in no time! This is just the beginning! You'll see. Can you remember anything new?" he asked excitedly. I searched my memories for something different or out of place but there wasn't anything. I didn't think I should tell him about Buchenwald. For some reason Fenwick had warned me to keep the knowing quiet. Besides, those memories were his not mine. Somehow I didn't think the Trist had anything to do with that. I simply shook my head "no".

"Do we still need to find the chronicle?"

He let out a raucous laugh! I knew that was his answer. He stood up slowly and brushed himself off. The blood stains blended into his black clothing. "They move because they are feeding off of the magic inside of you. As time passes they will grow stronger and so will your memory. Come, we need to get moving. We can only hope that we haven't signaled the wrong side…I believe the safest way in will be through there. It's not good to stay here much longer." He pointed at the very door the Giest attacked from.

"Are you crazy? What do you mean go back in there?"

"I think we can safely say we've secured this passage. I'm sure if we were to try any other, they'd be waiting to seal our fate." He made a good point. I graciously conceded.

"I'm in!" He gave a half grin.

"This way! We have no time to waste!"

CHAPTER NINETEEN

To Walk Among Body Hijackers

The tunnel was small and suffocating. Initially, there wasn't enough room to stand so we started out crawling. At one point, we had to take off our packs and slide them ahead of us. I prayed nothing would attack from behind! Subtle light creeping past the floor boards overhead dimly lit the way. I followed him through the twists and turns of the passageway. Voices and commotion from the masquerade ball were getting louder. I could hear laughing and the resonating sounds of dinnerware. I continued to crawl until I ran into the back of Clancey. He'd made an abrupt stop. I realized the tunnel ahead had opened up. There was enough room for both of us to stand. It was a small outlet no bigger than a coat closet with built-in benches on either side. I was thankful to be able to stretch. At the back base of the closet was a set of small rectangular wood panels. He raised a finger to his lips and pointed over head to a floor grate. Quietly, we began listening in. The sound of people chopping food and preparing entrees filled our ears. Vibrant chatter and excitement radiated from the ball's ambiance. I recognized Chef DeBonairte's voice instantly. It sounded as though he'd been drinking again. He was happily singing in a mixture of French and broken English. Every other word was "Sophia…..Sophia…!" Her name was followed by his imitation of a growling tiger. "My leettal baguette, I neverrr forget my Sophia…Grrreeow!" More obnoxious sound effects followed with periodic interjections that boldly proclaimed his manhood.

"He's singing about my mother! That creep!" Clancey elbowed me in the ribs shaking his head and laughing.

"That corny little culinary Casanova still has a thing for your mum hey?"

"I'd like to wipe his memory!" I hissed.

People were constantly entering and exiting the room. It was hard to zero in on just one conversation. Someone was panicked because the supply of hors d'oeuvres was running low. One of the waiters sounded giddy because he'd attended to a diplomat from Morocco. I could still hear, "Sophia, Sophia..." Busy sounds and delectable smells permeated the small chamber. I knew we were in the heart of Devonshire's cookery. Another chef bellowed something about dinner being served in one hour. Although I hadn't seen a clock for a while, this was the first indication of time. I calculated it was probably five to six o'clock. I tried imagining my mother's itinerary.

The noise of clanking dishes and clattering trays echoed all around us! Fortunately, everyone was talking above the clamor. With the help of a little more eavesdropping, we found out that Professor Loremont intentionally left a fake display for Professor Howelgood to pillage. Therefore, when Howelgood destroyed the display, he'd really only demolished a decoy and not the real thing! Loremont won the trophy! "That little cheater! Did I tell you that Burt and I saw him stealing the science department's entry supplies?"

And then I heard them... "Murderous wretch he is! Why, I bet he killed her and buried her in the woods! Poor little thing; they still haven't found her body! And thanks to that ingrate, the police are all over this place! I was glad to hear Packwood finally put his foot down! At least the police are not allowed inside! Why, it makes Devonshire look like a reform school! I can only imagine what the parents must think! I mean really! Twisted little low life! Him and that grubby sidekick probably did away with poor Fiona Talbert…And maybe Timothy Holderman knew something about it so they got rid of him, too!" On and on she went. I recognized that escalating voice the instant I heard it. It was Ms. Stillwell and I knew she was talking about me!

A strange voice chimed in. "Yeah, and that mudder uf is… She walk round dis place like nuthin wrong! She hidin da boy! That why polis here! But she parade erself in dat king get up like she ist one!" They had a hearty laugh.

Clancey put his hand on my shoulder. I knew he could sense my fury. He carefully pushed me away from the grate. "Well lad, I think we've found out three important things. The police are not allowed to patrol inside, dinner is in an hour, and your mom is dressed as a king."

I added one last detail. "And Stillwell is a vicious lying wench!"

He stopped himself from giggling. "I can't argue with you there, Creed! She is quite the bitty! Did you know she doesn't have any teeth?"

I couldn't help but chuckle. "What did you say?"

His response was entirely serious. "I'm not kidding, Creed! Found 'em in a cup while cleanin' her office one day! Gave me a bit of scare they did! She's as toothless as a coon skinnin' hillbilly! But thankfully, she is irrelevant to our situation." I took a deep breath. He'd made a good point.

"Where do we go from here?" He motioned for silence once more then knelt down and carefully removed a section of the wood paneling. I saw another panel behind it. He removed the next panel with caution. To my surprise, I recognized the internal view of a cupboard and it was overflowing with snacks! We'd hit the jackpot!

He grabbed a tin of cookies, boxed drinks, chocolate candies, and passed them back.

"Here have some chips, too." I was so hungry, I didn't hesitate tearing them open. Happily, we filled our stomachs until he suggested stopping. He added, "...in case we have to run or something." I shoved all I could in my backpack and brushed off the crumbs. We gave each other a once over. "Well, I guess we look presentable." We put on our masks and waited for the kitchen to calm. It gave me time to quietly study my new tattoo.

"That's it!" I yelled!

Clancey glared at me. "Keep it down! Do you want them to know we're here?"

"No! Listen! These markings... I knew I'd seen them before! My mother got a letter the day that Isabelle went missing! It caught fire as soon as I tried reading it! At first I thought it was some sort of joke. I didn't understand any of it except for the part where my name was written in plain English! The letters... they're the same as this," I said, pointing at my wrist! "What does this mean? Can you read it?"

He looked at me as if I were delirious. "Creed," he said, grabbing my forearm, "Tis a mighty mark, no doubt, but what are you talking about? I don't see any letters. I see a fierce dragon with flames shooting from his mouth! It's true he has motion... but there are no letters! Maybe we should find you some more food?"

Of course I knew I'd never once saw the dragon he spoke of. The only picture apparent to me was that of a doorway, and even it appeared at random. The symbols moved about my wrist with no noticeable destination! Whenever they felt like it, the individual marks would join together to form an image of the doorway which appeared on the underside of my wrist. "Why don't you believe me? Is it because *you* don't see them? All this time you've been lecturing me about believing!" I began transcribing the markings from my arm onto the earthen floor. I didn't understand why he couldn't see past the tattoo. The strange letters were as clear as day.

It was Clancey who stood up. He was livid! "How do you know this?" He was staring down at floor, then back at me. "How? How do you know this? Did Fenwick say something?" Somehow, I'd made him angry. "I'm sorry! What did I write? I only copied what I saw!" There was no time for discussion! He popped a piece of candy in his mouth and chewed vigorously. His head lifted and his eyes closed. "Do you hear that?" Instantly, we were interrupted by the sound of orchestra music.

I could hear the deep melodic tone of the cello followed by a rush of violin strings. It seemed odd that they would start playing before dinner. Every year I'd attended, dancing came after dinner, never before. My mother always followed such a strict schedule. Clancey was well versed in Andromeda etiquette. In fact, he had attended many more than I. He couldn't hide his curiosity. "I thought that chef said dinner wouldn't be ready for an hour?" We studied each other's facial expression for half a second before we came up with the same conclusion.

"It's a signal!" I yelled!

"Shush! You'll give us away! Of course it's a signal! Your mum's no fool! She's calling to us!"

I gave a wide-eyed nod. "She must be trying to get our attention!" I was hoping we wouldn't have to leave our hiding spot, but it looks like that plan was annihilated back in the tunnels.

"Hold on and let me get a bird's eye." I looked on as he finished removing the entire contents of the cupboard. I grabbed a few more snacks and shoved them in my pack. I wasn't sure what lay ahead, but at least I had food for the journey. He positioned himself halfway within the boundaries of the cabinet. He was listening for an opportune time to take a quick peek at our surroundings.

After a few minutes he looked back at me and nodded. The kitchen had quieted down some. The servers must've refilled their trays and left. They were most likely wandering among the guests with fresh offerings. He painstakingly opened the cabinet's most outer doors. I watched his head go up, down, left and right. Slowly, he closed them back up. "What did you see?"

"We're in good shape, lad! We're in the back pantry!" I knew exactly what he meant. All students attending Devonshire got a tour of kitchen duty, at least those of us who got in trouble any way. The pantry was located in the very back of the kitchen. It was within its own hallway and slightly out of view from the central body. To the right was a door that led to our main destination, to the left the belly of the kitchen and another service entry. "Here's the deal. It looks fairly empty right now. From what I can see, the chefs are busy staging the main entrees. There was no sign of servers inbound or out. They must be on the floor with the last of the hors d'oeuvres. We move now! We'll exit quickly and to the right. Before we set foot in the great hall, we have three wings to traverse: Kendall, Crosswaithe, and Wilverton. And, I don't have to tell you that each wing has a number of hallways and corridors. I'll do my best to take the safest route. Bring your pack. We'll stash them as soon as we're able.

He put his mask on. I did the same. "I've got to tell you one last thing. I know I'm putting a lot on you. I was hoping we wouldn't have to actually mingle amongst the guests. So before we head out there, you need to know about Gheddons." I felt for my stone. "They are the possessors… a cunning lot if you will. Their high priest is Nakht. He is a vial and nasty being! He really enjoys the pain he inflicts and that kind of stuff." He continued to speak as if we were having normal table talk. "The Gheddons are body hijackers. They infect most hosts with ease. The hijacked become puppets for whatever evil scheme is devised…murder, robbery, you get the picture! Only the strong-minded can resist them. I'm not worried about you or I, lad. It's the guests that pose a serious problem."

"When you say hijacked, do you mean like possessed? But how can they do such a thing?"

"It's quite simple really. Gheddons enter through acceptance of something from them to you."

"I don't get it. What do you mean, like a gift?"

"No, it's far less complicated than that. It can be a handshake, a compliment or even a blessing after you sneeze! They've been known to be quite tricky. Acceptance of anything from them by you allows a Gheddon free entry. Once inside, a Gheddon functions to overtake your will through conscience suggestion…sort of like an alter conscience. If they succeed, the host loses his ability to discern right and wrong. His will gives way to the Gheddon's. They've been hijacked. They are quite subtle spirits, but very overpowering. When the Gheddon's fun is over, it finds a new life to destroy. The old host is left picking up the pieces of whatever mess the Gheddon created for him or her."

"So what you're saying is not to talk to anyone…not to accept anything from anyone…not to shake anyone's hand?"

"Now you're getting the hang of it," he whispered!

"But what happens if I make a mistake?"

"Then you'll know it, won't you!"

I could feel my heart pounding. Clancey was the first one to crawl out. He quickly looked back and nodded for me to follow. I didn't even look left. I could hear the sound of sizzling food and rapid chopping. I went from a crawling position to an upright stride. We passed quickly through the pantry and out the side door. Finally, we stood amidst the guests of the Andromeda Ball. The Kendall wing was jam-packed with wall to wall masqueraders. We managed to drop our packs behind an antique wall chair and proceeded to nonchalantly blend in. Laughter and excitement resonated through the crowded hallways. Brilliant stars hung from the ceiling. They sparked with an array of colored fiber-optic lights. A series of fog machines would occasionally erupt, filling the room with a cloudy mist. It produced a mystical atmosphere.

Distant melodic sounds from the orchestra fueled the mood. This year's turnout must've exceeded all expectations. I'd never seen so many guests attend the ball before. Waiters and waitresses walked among the huddled groups offering delectable appetizers. Exquisite costumes flooded the room as far as my eyes could see. Each lady's gown was a designer's masterpiece exhibiting only the utmost propriety for such an upscale event. Their dresses sparkled and shimmered with flowing movement. The men accompanying such glamorous women appeared distinguished and refined. They modeled renaissance disguises of prestige and honor. Masks were unique to each costume and just as detailed. Guests gracefully held to character as we brushed by. The room exuded of wealth and power. Oh, the gossip going on and the tall tales being uttered! Devonshire was sure to pick up more enrollees from the party's outcome.

I wasn't so much interested in what people were wearing, or saying, but who or what hid behind those masks. I knew somewhere in the midst of this party were remorseless creatures that craved my capture. I felt for my Quetral stone. I kept my wits about me as we continued walking toward the great hall. Every so often, I would sniff the air in search of Giests. So far, the aromas had been pleasant. After passing a crowd of people in the corridor, Clancey asked me, "How are your limbs? Do ya feel any tingling?" He was of course searching for Fallons.

"No, I'm good!" He gave a half smile and continued walking toward the great hall.

"I love your costume."

"Excuse me?"

"I love your costume." The voice was speaking to me. "It is so authentic! Who was your designer?" I looked back at Clancey. He was carefully inspecting our female intruder. Her identity was partially hidden by the sequined and feathered facial covering she wore. I didn't recognize her as one of my classmates. "And your masks... Are they hand forged?" I nodded. "My compliments to the artist!"

I was quick not to accept the compliment just in case. I shrugged my shoulders and said, "I really think they could've done a better job." I could feel Clancey tugging my sleeve.

"My name is Faraday, Faraday Evanston. My parents own Evanston Industries." She glanced back at them. Her father raised his cup in our direction. I didn't acknowledge it. Avoiding Gheddons might be harder than I first thought. "They want me to attend this stuffy place! I'm trying to talk them out of it. Most of my friends are enrolled at Pemberton Academy. But after tonight's gala, I think it will be a little difficult to persuade them otherwise. Do you guys attend Devonshire?"

"Yes, we do. It's not so bad."

She smiled. The waiter came from behind her and offered us canapés. As delicious as they looked, it was obvious I could not accept one. "So are the rumors true about the student who killed his girlfriend? Is that why the police are here? That could provide a whole new angle for not enrolling." She kept talking and talking.

I could tell I'd have to be rude in order to get away. The Quetral stone grew warm against my skin. That was never a good sign. Without warning, I turned to leave, but sudden weaknesses in my legs prevented me from doing so. It felt like I was in one of those bad dreams where you're being attacked, but incapable of fighting back. I knew better than to think this was a dream! My body wasn't responding to my commands. A cold, tingling, sensation started in my feet and made its way toward my calves. My hands were losing functionality also. I tried to make small fists, but the movements were extremely slow. I could feel an icy numbness creeping up my arms. I looked over at Clancey. He looked down at his hands and feet in dismay. We had been easily trapped!

My talisman radiated heat. I searched the room for Fallon. I saw nothing. Everyone was absorbed in their own little cliques. When I was done scanning, the only eyes staring back at me was the waiter who'd just offered appetizers. He was dressed as a barkeep and wore a half mask that covered most of his facial features. For a split second, I could've sworn his eyes went stark white. He flashed an arrogant smile. His teeth were brilliant white and perfectly straight. He looked fairly normal, but somewhat conceited. His hair had been combed to perfection and I smelled a strong hint of aftershave radiating from his person. I'd seen a few ladies eyeing him earlier. Upon further dissection, I found the clue I'd been looking for. He was wearing white serving gloves. The one on his right bore a hole at the tip of the index finger. Just barely peeking through the opening was a dirty, razor-sharp, conical-shaped nail. It must've punctured its way through!

I didn't panic. I didn't have time to. Before I could react, he turned and offered more appetizers to other guests. He looked like he was actually enjoying himself! Clancey whispered, "I said they were cruel, not intelligent! This place is probably crawling with them!" I could feel the blood starting to circulate in my extremities once more. Meanwhile, Faraday had maintained an ongoing conversation with herself. She was stomping her foot. At first I thought it was to get my attention, but I realized it was to keep it from falling asleep.

I caught up to her at the point of, "...so what do you guys think?"

Clancey finally interrupted. "You know, it's been a pleasure conversing with you, but we shouldn't keep our dates waiting."

She looked at me with disappointment. "Oh! Yes, of course! I'm sorry. Well, I hope to see you again... What were your names?" I was trying to think fast on my feet, but in looking back it was the stupidest thing I could've ever done. I wasn't about to tell her our real names, so I introduced myself as Thaddeus Wilton, the wealthiest boy at Devonshire. I made Clancey, Lowell Briggs, the second wealthiest boy at Devonshire. What could it have hurt? I'd never actually met either one of them! I'd seen them in passing once or twice around the school. Mostly, I'd heard incredible stories about their lives. Thaddeus' parents were wealthy oil tycoons. Lowell's family were real estate magnates. All of a sudden she was giddy. She forcefully grabbed my hand and started leading me over to meet her parents! I looked back at Clancey. He was making big eyes and shaking his head.

"Mom, Dad, I'd like to introduce you to Thaddeus Wilton!" She was cooing all over me.

Mr. Evanston put out his hand. "Pleased to meet you, son."

What could I do? I had been instructed not to accept anything, not even a handshake! There was an awkward split second when her father realized I wasn't going to shake his hand. But before he could say anything, we were pummeled by Ella Travers, the society columnist from *Dazzle*! Her photographer followed close behind.

"Thaddeus! Oh Thaddeus! We must talk!"

I felt a strong kick to the back of my calf. I didn't have to guess who it was from. I heard Clancey whisper, "Lose her now!"

It had come to my attention that we had drawn quite a large crowd. They were acting as if I was some sort of rock star! "Hello Ms. Travers."

"Oh, please Thaddeus! Call me Ella! It's good to see you again! Love the mask!"

I cut her off at the pass. "Have you met Mr. Evanston and his lovely wife?" I could tell all was forgiven. Mr. Evanston was thankful for the gracious introduction to the press.

"And, of course, we must not forget their charming daughter, Faraday!" She giggled. "From our experience, Faraday could talk the bark off of a tree." I hoped her introduction would aid in our escape. While the family posed for a society picture, Clancey and I tried to make a sly exit. "Really Thaddeus! Did you think you could get away that quickly?"

"Well, we'd like to get back to our dates."

"Excellent!" she said, slapping her photographer on the back. "We'll accompany you! Is there a prospective Mrs. Wilton you'd like for us to meet?" I rolled my eyes. Frankly, this woman was harder to get rid of than gum on a shoe! I could tell there would be no shaking her. I tried to think fast.

"Certainly, I'd love to introduce you! Ella, if you would wait for a moment, I need to make a quick stop in the men's room. I won't be but a minute!"

"Oh wonderful," she exclaimed! "We'll be waiting with bells on, love!"

She didn't waste much time. Before we'd entered the men's bathroom, she was mingling with the other guests. "A most obnoxious woman!" grumbled Clancey! We carefully searched the bathroom for any signs of occupants, but none were found. "What do you think you're doing, lad? Do you want to get us both killed?" It wasn't hard to tell he was angry. Not a good sign. On instinct, I offered him a piece of candy I'd taken from the hidden cupboard. I'd noticed his habit of popping candy when he was getting upset. He grabbed it from my hand and tossed it in his mouth without even so much as looking at it! The creases in his brow relaxed. It worked! Instantly, he became soothed by the happy taste of sugar. *Mental note: always keep candy handy.* "Really lad! We've got to be more careful."

"I know…I know! I wasn't sure what name to say. His was the only one I could think of! It just came out!"

He looked toward a window in the bathroom. "We can crawl out of here!" I gazed hopefully toward it. "But," he added, "we might easily run into a policeman patrolling the grounds. We need to get rid of that woman! We're drawing too much attention!"

"I'm sorry, it's my fault!"

He steadily drummed his fingers on top of the marble sink. "Let me think… Let me think… I've got it! Tell that greedy vulture you'll give her an exclusive interview! But first, you want to let your date freshen up. Tell her your girlfriend would never forgive you if you let her picture be taken without forewarning! Tell Ms. Travers you will meet her at the marble entry at 8:00 sharp!" It sounded like a credible plan. "At least it will buy us enough time to get to yur mum."

I watched him splash water on his face, then carefully unwrap his bandage. I'd almost forgotten he'd been wounded by Buchenwald.

"Are you okay?"

"I'm good, lad, just light housekeeping. I need to keep this clean. Fallons are capable of honing in on trace amounts of blood!" He cleansed the wound lightly with paper towels.

"I must admit this isn't going as well as I'd hoped. The plan has changed so many times; I feel we might need a little assistance."

"Can we do that?" I blurted out.

"Of course we can. But as I told you before, it always adds the risk of being discovered and the probability that Rogues will be hurt. Our adversaries have little regard for anyone but themselves!" He finished securing his bandage. Next, he drew a small key from his pocket. "If we get separated..."

"What do you mean separated?!!"

"Calm yourself! As I was saying, if somehow we get separated, you know the plan. You need to find your mother at all costs. I've seen to it that should the situation arise, you'll be well taken care of."

"Wait a minute, "I protested.

"No time for discussion, Creed. I need silence for just a minute."

With his hands stretched flat, he began searching the air in front of him. He looked like a mime trapped behind glass. A big grin stretched across his face. Although I could see nothing, it was clear he had found what he was looking for. He polished the key with his shirt tail and then slipped it into an invisible lock suspended in front of him. It held its mid-air position long after he removed his hand. He rubbed his palms together, then turned it to the right. I heard a clicking sound. The door had been opened. I watched his arm disappear and come out with a small, brilliant blue, pocket watch. The outer encasement was ornately gilded.

There was no time to ask questions. Someone else had entered the men's bathroom. I tried not to look conspicuous. The sound of the key falling echoed loudly. I started washing my hands. Clancey had disappeared into one of the stalls. He was muttering something about tasteless hors d'oeuvres. He flushed the toilet. Our visitor was politely going about his business in another stall. Clancey came out and washed his hands. His head tipped in the direction of the door. "Your press awaits, Thaddeus."

CRAPTER TWENTY

My WayMaker is a What?

s we exited the bathroom, we were immediately met by Ella Travers. "Why hello, Thaddeus. I have someone I'm dying for you to meet."

I put our plan into action. "Why Ella… if you give me a just a moment, I can afford my date the courtesy of freshening up also. We can meet you at the marble entry for an exclusive say…around 8:00?" There was a cynical look on her face.

"That sounds grand, love, but I've got someone I'd like to introduce you to first." There was no chance of pulling away. We had been encircled by guest goers on all sides. I could see Faraday. She'd taken her mask off. Her face bore a hurt expression.

A boy dressed in astute renaissance garb joined us in the middle of the circle. "Why, hello Thaddeus," he said.

I humbly answered, "Hello. To whom do I have the pleasure of meeting?"

His shrill screaming caused several guests to jump. "This is preposterous! This boy is an imposter! I am Thaddeus Wilton!!! I want this violator thrown out!!!"

Something in my gut told me to maintain all manner of calmness and etiquette. I kept my response orderly and civil. The words smoothly rolled off my tongue as if his threat had no impact. "Is this some kind of joke?" I could hear doubt and murmuring rumble through the onlookers. I continued as calmly as I could. "Surely you don't believe this scoundrel." The crowd became silent. "I can't believe what I'm seeing in the midst of my fellow brethren. Do you not know one of your own? Look at his manner. Just look at him! Very uncouth…yes very uncouth. Certainly no man with a proper upbringing would resort to such an unruly and slanderous outburst. You must see this."

I could hear people debating amongst themselves. One woman commented loudly. "Why, he's right!"

"Such a young gentleman," said another!

A man patted me on the back. I was quick to pull forward for fear of Gheddons. "Well done, Thaddeus!"

Our audience had been amazingly swayed by my argument. "Father has always taught me that everything can be solved diplomatically." I couldn't believe it, but the crowd went wild. My statements were applauded. I saw one woman dab her eyes with a handkerchief. "No, no I cannot accept your applause or appreciation for such a simple act of common decency."

Clancey nudged me. "Could you have possibly laid it on any thicker?" Ms. Travers was vigorously writing on her notepad. The photographer was snapping photos, one after the other.

"Diplomacy!" he screamed. "You, tell me about diplomacy… You ignorant little rat!!! Why I ought to…" During the commotion, someone had gotten a police officer. He looked as though he was happy to see two rich brats about to throw blows.

I took another glance at the policeman. I recognized him from somewhere…of course I did. How could I not? It was Officer Farnsworth! But instead of escorting me out, he grabbed the real Thaddeus Wilton by the arm. "Let's do some cooling off outside, son."

He tried to break free of his grip without success. "If you're the real Thaddeus Wilton, remove your mask!" The crowd quieted down. I put both hands on my hips wondering how I would smooth talk my way out of this one. But before I could come up with anything, the situation was handled for me. Thaddeus made such a violent motion to remove his mask that Farnsworth wrestled him to the ground. He never got the chance to unveil his identity. He was escorted from the corridor kicking and screaming. People were stunned. It was time for us to make our exit. Ella followed closely behind.

"Thaddeus... Oh Thaddeus, I hope we can still be friends after this little mix-up." She continued to grovel at two paces behind us until I couldn't take her anymore. I decided to get rid of her once and for all.

"Ms. Travers!"

"Yes?" Her smile was a plasticated one.

"Goodnight!" My voice was firm and unwavering.

"Oh, yes. I see. Well, my apologies for making you late for your dates."

"No apologies needed. Please leave us."

"Yes, I'll do that then." She turned and didn't have the nerve to look back.

The crowd had long since dissipated. The real Thaddeus was probably somewhere in the back of a cop car. We left Kendall Hall and made our escape into the corridors of Crosswaithe. It, too, was crowded. I could hear the rhythms of the orchestra drawing closer. People were talking and laughing. We walked past several groups just trying to lose ourselves in the crowd. Then, out of nowhere, I spotted her! I took a second glance. It was her! It really was her! She was disguised as a king just like we'd overheard! If my history served me well, I believed she was masquerading as King Francois. It made sense. That must've been the costume she intended for me. She stood eloquently poised as if she had not a care in the world. She was diligently entertaining a small group of guests! They were laughing at her amusing story. I nudged Clancey. "It's my mom!" I started to move toward her, but Clancey stopped me.

"Wait! We've got to be careful, Creed! I'm sure they are watching every move she makes!" I took a deep breath. We surveyed the room for mysterious eyes or conspicuous actions. We found nothing. Before we could come up with a good plan, she turned around. She was most definitely a he…The person dressed as the king was a complete stranger. He must've been in attendance from a foreign country. From beneath his mask swelled a large braided beard. His skin was very dark and he spoke with a deep accent. He caught us staring at him and responded by lifting his mask and brandishing an amused expression.

"False alarm," whispered Clancey. He patted me on the back. "Don't worry, lad, we'll find her." We resumed our travels through Crosswaithe, making our way past the small clusters of guests. Clancey broke the silence. "You know, it won't be long before that cop discovers he has the real Thaddeus cuffed in the back of his car." I knew he was right.

"What about the back-up? Did you have time to summon them? Will they be here soon?"

"*They* is a *he* and his name is Progerious. He is a WayMaker. One of the best if you ask me!"

"A what maker?"

"A Way…." Clancey's explanation was swiftly interrupted.

"Excuse me, you dropped this." Someone tapped Clancey on the shoulder. "Excuse me, sir, you dropped this." In his palm rested the talon from the dead Giest! I knew full well, Clancey could not accept anything from the hand of a stranger.

"What kind of claw is this?" he exclaimed.

"It looks like an authentic Velociraptor claw to me. Only this specimen is ivory and seems to be in perfect condition! You must tell me where you got this! Are you a collector, too?"

I watched Clancey stare longingly at his prized possession. "I'm afraid you've got the wrong guy. Whatever it is, that thing isn't mine."

"But," the mysterious man replied, "Not only did I see it fall from your pocket as you left the men's bathroom, but it has *his* picture on it" he said turning toward me. "I think it accidentally cut its way out. It is rather sharp."

I could feel my Quetral stone starting to get hot. How he knew what I looked like was beyond me. My mask covered my face completely. It was very apparent something wasn't right. Clancey sensed it, too. "No, really, it's not mine. You can keep it, uh uh…What is your name?"

The stranger spoke coldly. "I think you already know my name."

Clancey continued to remain cool. "I'm sorry, sir, I've never seen you before in my life!"

"Well," said the intruder, "I'll tell you a little joke and maybe you can figure it out. Nakht Nakht…." We both froze. He said, "This is the part where one of you boys is supposed to say, 'Who's there?'"

We both looked at each other. Of course I'd just made the acquaintance of Nakht, the high Gheddon Priest. From the look of it, he had taken over the body of a male guest. "Okay," he hissed! "we can do this calmly or we can create a scene! Rogues will be hurt. I can start with the one I'm occupying if you'd like!" Clancey said nothing. "Honestly, you didn't really think you could just waltz in here completely undetected! This is a war we're fighting…and one you've lost, I might add!"

The lights began to flicker. My mind raced for ways to escape. The scuttling of approaching Giest feet flooded my mind with terror. Their over-powering stench solidified my fears. I knew they were eager to repay us for the loss of Buchenwald. The fog machines continued to belt out white mist. Through the intermittent lights I could see a parade of possessed party goers joining Nakht. They stared hungrily through zombie eyes. Subtle tingling in my limbs commenced. It immediately became difficult to execute quick movements. I knew Fallon were near. A heavy breeze blew overhead. Casting a glance upward, at first I thought the fiber-optic stars were falling. Soon, I recognized what was making them sway. Human shapes swirling like bats beneath the starry ceiling... Each one glided and spun like a corkscrew. Their faces contorted with hideous smiles. Together they formed a bizarre aerial race track. Unsuspecting guests clapped and pointed, thinking it was all a part of the festivities. "Looks like the Fallons have taken flight," murmured Clancey.

"You didn't tell me they could do that!" I whispered. We were severely outnumbered. Without warning, there was a loud popping sound followed by the room turning completely dark! Drinking glasses clanked. A man yelled something about a blown fuse. The room filled with soft grumblings. The putrid odor of Giests flooded my nostrils. No longer could I hear their clicking footsteps. I knew they surrounded us. It was impossible to make sudden movements...too many eyes...too many Fallon... One wrong move and we were done for! Either that or they would start hurting innocent people.

Nakht laughed. "Do you surrender?" I couldn't believe what I heard next.

Clancey replied, "Yes." He felt me starting to reach for my stone, but stopped me. "Wait," he said.

What was I supposed to do? They'll kill me, I thought. *They'll kill everyone if I try and escape.* Suddenly, I felt a set of claws scale my leg, my side, and came to rest at the back of my neck. "Be absolutely quiet," it said. "I am Progerious, your WayMaker. Do as I say." I remembered to breath. Two strong sets of arms forcefully grabbed me from both sides. I could feel their conical nails ready to pierce my skin. We were being carefully escorted to an unknown destination in pitch darkness. I lost Clancey's whereabouts. Guests started to realize the lights weren't coming back on any time soon. Progerious spoke almost inaudibly. He was so close to my ear, I could feel his whiskers tickling me. "Listen carefully. I will take you to your mother. On the count of three, I want you to pull forward with all of your might and run to the orchestra pit in the Great Hall.

ONE..."

Then someone started yelling. "OH FOR THE LUV OF... What's going on here? Where is he? The little shyster! Imposter! I'll teach him to make a fool out of me!" I recognized the voice! It was Officer Farnsworth!

"TWO..." The Fallon's grip tightened. Several flashlight beams flooded the room. People parted the way. He was accompanied by more uniformed reinforcements.

In the darkness I heard Nakht speak. "Officers... Officers... I think we have the individual you're looking for." It was just as Clancey predicted! I was being turned over to the police for safekeeping.

I felt Progerious crawl to the middle of my back. "THREE!!!!" both Fallon captors screamed. I broke free of their grip! I ran limply toward the Great Hall with everything in me! Clancey was not at my side. Progerious was clawing onto my pant leg for dear life! The further I distanced myself from the Fallon, the easier it was to move. I reached down in mid-stride and grabbed a handful of fur. He felt strange. I didn't care. Whatever he was I owed him my life! He was furry, lightweight and I think he had four legs. Whatever he was, I set him atop my shoulder.

I heard him say, "Much obliged." The low rumble from the guests grew louder. The lights were still out. Glow in the dark ceiling stars faithfully lit the path in front of me. Many people were curious about the commotion coming from behind rather than why I was running past. I could hear police sirens.

"Where is Clancey?" I whispered.

"Clancey can take care of himself."

CHAPTER
TWENTY-ONE
Never Cheat a Time Bender

"**W**ilverton up ahead!" yelled Progerious. I made a sharp turn. His claws gripped my shoulder. Surprisingly, the hall was empty and eerily silent. I slowed down a little. Curious masqueraders must've left to investigate the goings on. A series of black lights fluoresced the fog and anything white in the room. This wing had been reserved for the science exhibits. A few scattered presentations dotted the vicinity, but there was no mind-boggling display from Howelgood as I'd seen in years past. A pre-programmed laser light show was performing its tricks for a disappearing audience. Colorful images of constellations splashed across the walls and ceiling.

"They must have a backup generator in here."

"Yes," replied the WayMaker, "but don't turn on the lights quite yet. We don't need to give our position away so freely." We passed a number of empty experiment booths. Abandoned plates and cups were everywhere. They told a story of their own. Progerious switched shoulders. I felt his tail hit my face.

"Do you know any shortcut through these halls?" he asked.

"I know this school like the back of my hand, but I have to admit I know it better when I can see it!" There was a brief hesitation and then I was compelled to ask a rather presumptuous question. "If you don't mind me inquiring, what are you?"

A second or two passed. I'd hoped I hadn't offended him. "Didn't Clancey tell you?"

"As you can see, we didn't have much time for talking."

"Oh, then pardon my lack of introduction. I am Progerious Hoptonotess, WayMaker and friend at your service! I am extremely knowledgeable in portal transference. Go over there," he said. He directed me to an all-white couch. It was heavily fluoresced by the lighting. He leaped into the center of it so I could get a better look.

"You're a, you're a, you're a ferret?" He had an all-white face except around his eyes; it was the color of night. It looked as though he was wearing a mask! The rest of his body was silken ivory and black. Around his middle he wore a belt with a tiny pouch tied to it. The bag's contents were unknown but it jingled with movement.

His answer was cynical. "Perhaps you were expecting a bunny rabbit?" He spun around rather sharply and shoved both hands down the couch cushions! "What are you doing?" Swiftly, his hand snapped open signaling for me to be silent. When he was done fishing, he'd come up with some loose change and a button, of which he happily placed in his satchel.

I regained my composure and decided I'd better not attempt to ask... He scaled my leg and claimed my shoulder once more. "No, I just didn't know what I expected."

"Well, of course I'm a ferret! A black-footed one at that! Like my father, and his father, and his father before him! We are all WayMakers. I was trained in the art at a very young age by my great, great, great, great grandfather!"

"I had a hamster once… He wasn't as cute as …"

"How dare you Sir!!" His tail stood straight up like an exclamation point! "Don't you EVER insult me by calling me *that* word again! I am a fierce warrior like my father, his father, his father and his father before him!"

"All right, don't get your tail in a knot," I said restraining laughter. "I didn't mean to offend you. I'm very sorry." The forced sincerity in my voice caused his fur to unruffle.

"Apology accepted."

I proceeded to pick up the pace again. "But why....?"

He finished my sentence. "Why would I be helping you? Clancey was right. Your memory really was expunged wasn't it? Do you think that humans have the only stake in magic? Or do you believe animals can attain the same status?" In a sly way he was asking me if I thought humans were superior to animals.

My reply was an honest one. "I guess I haven't given that a lot of thought, but I'm sure animals are every bit as crucial to this cause as Genocists." "You've got that right my friend!" he scoffed. "So you're what they call Intelligent, an animal that possesses magical powers? Is that correct?"

"I see Clancey has schooled you a little," he snapped! "If Denegaul and his accomplices get that chronicle, all animals are done for! He thinks we're nothing but mindless slaves...something to be trampled underfoot! Oh, some of us have joined his armies, but many that still believe in the old ways! You must understand our communal synergy. All good Semigents, Intelligents, Genocists and so on contribute to the same pool of magic. We rely on each other as a source of craft. Our powers are interconnected in one way or another. If one fails, the other will most surely fail, too. We're here," he whispered!

I stopped abruptly outside the entrance to the Great Hall. The massive double doors had been purposefully shut. Surely anyone inside would know we were entering. Was this a trap? I couldn't hear the orchestra anymore, not one peep! I smelled the air...nothing. I felt my stone. It rested snug against my neck. My limbs were normal. "What do you think?" I could feel him slide from shoulder to shoulder. He stood up and carefully listened, then sniffed the darkness.

"I think you will be okay to go in. Do not take too long! We must be on our way! There is still great danger here! Do you understand?"

I said yes, not fully appreciating his directions. I walked toward the hand-carved entrance. Carefully, I turned the knob. There was so much I wanted to say to her. So much I wanted to ask. The room felt hollow. It was completely cavernous and dark. I was fortunate to know its layout well. All students were required to attend graduations and school productions, most of which were held in this very room. I imagined the rows and rows of empty tables stretched out across the vastness of the building, each set with the most ornate and delicate details. I envisioned the colossal 16th century candlelit chandelier meant for such an occasion. I couldn't help but feel bad for my mother. She'd done so much work and it had gone to waste on account of me.

"You're almost there," Progerious exclaimed!

I headed toward the front. I remembered there was an enormous dance stage with beautifully patterned wooden floors. Beneath it, an orchestra pit used for musical and theatrical performances. I'd made it within a few feet of the pit when the lights began to flicker on and off. Its effects were similar to that of a massive strobe light. At first my eyes had trouble focusing. Progerious perched himself on my shoulder, trying to see amidst the strange flashes. After my eyes had adjusted, I tried using the intermittent lighting to my advantage. I scanned the room for any sign of disturbances. In doing so, I saw her! She was standing at the center of the pit dressed much like the gentleman we'd mistaken her for earlier. She was waving me over! I ran to her. Unsure, I stopped a few feet shy.

"It's okay, Creed. It's me!" I ran to her and gave her the biggest hug I could! I didn't know when I would get to do that again.

"Mom! Mom!"

"I know, Creed," she said calmly. "I know about all about it. From the Bandolix to the Giest! I should have told you! But, I was always afraid I would say too much…everything would come back to you…they would try and capture you again…"

"But it's happening anyway."

"I'm so sorry. I'm so very sorry. I've tried my best to protect you!" Tears were streaming down her face.

Progerious made himself known. "Excuse me, She great woman of He, but there is danger!"

She nodded. She gripped both my shoulders. "I will be quick to details, Creed." Without warning, the lights came back on in full. We ducked down in the pit for cover. I watched her feel her Quetral stone and listen to the empty air around us. "They're coming," she said! Without hesitation, a massive crowd of people began to flood the hall!

"They're here," yelled Progerious! "Quickly! Tell him!" We could hear hoards of people moving up and down the table aisles calling my name.

"Creed? Creed?" Officer Farnsworth and his reinforcements were extremely vocal. "Creed! Creed Griffon! We know you're in here! Ms. Sophia Griffon! Word has it that you are in here, too. We have serious laws against aiding and abetting!" His voice was getting closer. I began to hear talons. I knew the Fallons and Gheddons were close at hand.

"What do I do, Mom?"

She looked at me, clenched her stone, and stood up. She was about to do something very wrong… until I stood up, too. I gripped her hand. "That is not the way, Mom. I'll be okay. We'll find a way."

Farnsworth caught site of me. "There he is!!!! Capture the little killer!!!" I did not run. I did not make a move. Progerious had hidden himself somewhere within the orchestra pit. "Grab him!" I was swarmed by uniformed officers and guest goers alike. They shoved me to the floor face first. I heard my mother's sobs. It was Farnsworth who put the cuffs on me. "Thought you could get away from us, did ya?" His boot smashed my foot into the floor. It wasn't an accident. From a kneeling position I was able to stand. Another officer read me my rights. I saw Progerious peaking out of a backpack. He leapt from its confines with a small blue pocket watch in his mouth. I recognized Nakht among the crowd. He was standing next to Professor Stillwell. They both started applauding. The rest of the two hundred or so guests filtered in to witness my capture. They were overjoyed "the killer" had been caught.

I looked over at my mother. She was speaking to a female police officer. I saw Progerious hidden nearby her. I scanned the crowd for Clancey, but he was nowhere to be seen. I had been caught, but I knew I had friends. They would not rest until I was set free. My capture was only temporary. At least that's what sounded good anyway. I was roughly escorted from the pit. Guest goers parted the way like I had some sort of contagious disease. Of course I was used to this treatment. I'd never fit into this school or with these people. I was always considered not up to par...a bad seed... I had become what they believed me to be, but what had changed was I no longer believed it.

They paraded me through the Great Hall. Oh the comments I was pelted with! "Nasty little murderer!" "I hope he gets the electric chair! "Hope you like prison food throwback!!!" On and on they went.

When I was finally within range of Ms. Stillwell, I couldn't resist popping off with a comment of my own. I cleared my throat, and calmly screamed, "YOU GLUED YOUR TEETH IN CROOKED!!" You could've heard a pin drop! …Oh the satisfaction….Immediately, she reached for her mouth, darted out of the room, blubbering, and in tears! "Well, that felt good!"

I happened to pass by Ella Travers. Her photographer was relentlessly snapping photos of my situation. I heard her utter, "Typical low-class trash." Everyone laughed.

And then I heard the laughter turned to a low murmur. A lady screamed! I picked my head up to see what the fuss was about. There she stood. Dirty, wet and sobbing. Isabelle Polanski had entered the Great Hall!!! Her clothes were muddy. Her brown hair was wet and mashed against the sides of her head. I recognized a fellow school mate in the crowd. She tore off her mask and ran toward Isabelle screaming her name! Three cops left my side and sprinted to meet the girl. I could hear extraneous words like, "It's her??" "It's really her!!!" Next, subtle whispers filled the room. They grew louder and louder. "She says he's not the one!" "HE'S NOT THE ONE?" "HE'S NOT THE ONE!"

Immediately, the police ran toward me. I thought I'd be pummeled for sure! But instead, they unlocked my handcuffs and set me free. The crowd parted. Isabelle was walking straight toward me. She embraced me and began to cry. "It's all right," I heard myself say. "You're going to be okay."

She whispered in my ear, "The Druix and some type of Minotaur thing saved me. They've told me what to do and say. And Creed, I know who you are now…" Before I could ask her any more, the police hurriedly brought her a blanket and something warm to drink. I knew they were very interested in her story. An officer released me from the restraints. People, who were once ready to stone me, began shaking my hand. They patted me on the shoulder. It was all good until I remembered that doing such things were enticements for Gheddons. I turned my attention back to my mother. She was waiting in the pit. She had a huge smile on her face. I started walking toward her and just happened to pass by Isabelle. She was giving the police her story. Nearby stood Ella Travers. She was poised like a vulture, notepad in hand. I decided to get a little satisfaction.

I interrupted the policeman in the middle of taking Isabelle's statement. My voice was calm. "Isabelle?"

She wiped both eyes. "Yes."

"Can you do me a favor?"

"Sure Creed, anything."

I turned toward the columnist. "Don't give a word of your story to this piece of trash right here! She's not worth it!" Isabelle nodded most solemnly. Two officers asked Ella to remove herself from the perimeter. I didn't look back. I could hear Ms. Travers having the most unladylike fit. I ran to meet my mom! She hugged me so hard I couldn't breathe.

"We must be quick! It's not over." She spoke with such urgency, I knew not to waste time with useless questions. I felt claws scale my leg. "Progerious will show you the way from here. You can trust him with your life! And I have arranged for a guest to accompany you on your journey." I felt a tap on my shoulder. I turned quickly. It was Burt! He was standing in front of me in plain street clothes! My eyes grew big.

"What's the password?"

"What? Oh, of course it's Whydah, stupid! And have I got a ton to tell you!"

"Burton!" I screamed! "I'm so glad it's really you!"

My mom's motherly tone quelled our excitement. "Burton," she said, "remember what we've discussed." He nodded. "I will make sure your mom is well protected. You won't be missed!" She grabbed a set of satchels I recognized instantly. They were the very packs Grapple had given Clancy and me. "Go quickly! There is no time to waste! You have what you need."

I just stood there in a state of confusion. "But what about the chronicle?" I blurted out. "What about you? Who will take care of you?"

She calmly repeated herself. "You must go, Creed. You have what you need. You've always had what you needed! I can't say anymore. There are too many eyes…too many ears. Take your bags and go now!" I could feel the Quetral stone starting to warm.

"But I don't understand!" I was startled by a loud roar! Guests began to scream. Some took cover underneath the tables. Others tried to run out, but were stopped by possessed guests blocking the exits. They thrashed violently at anyone who tried to escape! Fallons had taken flight. They looked so odd against the domed mosaic ceiling. Policemen had flipped over some tables and were using them as cover. The Giests had not shape shifted! They remained purposefully visible in their natural state. It was obvious that they were not masquerading. Ella Travers' photographer was snapping pictures of the entire event!

My mother looked toward the sky and began rummaging through her pockets for something. She came up with a small blue pocket watch. It was the one I'd seen Clancey pull from his invisible safe…the one I'd seen Progerious carrying! Anticipating her next move, the Fallons went wild! They began swooping and tearing at her! She tried to hide, but they wouldn't let up! They were swarming her, trying to lift her off the ground! It was sheer pandemonium!

Suddenly, I heard a wild battle cry! "YI YI YI YI YI YI YI!!!!" Chef DeBonairte?? He was running, butcher knife in each hand, as fast as his little legs could carry him! "AWAY YOU DEMONS! I WILL SAVE YOU MY SOPHIA!" He sprinted to her viciously wielding his blades. Upon his swift arrival, he proceeded to take fierce swipes at her assailants! His valiant efforts bought enough time to put her plan in motion.

"CREED! CREED!" she screamed. I spun around just as she hurled the clock at me. It landed underneath a chair in the orchestra pit. "BREAK IT!" she yelled. "BREAK IT!!!!!"

Both Burton and I dove for the time piece. A pair of Fallon and Giest watched the throw intensely. They, too, raced for the clock as if we were playing some sort of deadly football game. I dove over two sets of chairs and crashed into a set of music stands! I managed to reach it first. Burton was close behind. I did as commanded and smashed it under foot, but it wouldn't break! I threw it to the floor, but nothing happened.

Burton screamed, "THEY'RE COMING! THEY'RE COMING! BREAK IT!"

I caught a glimpse of the pursuing Giest rip its claw within inches of his stomach. He picked up a chair and threw it at his attacker while the other Giest came to aid in the fight. The Fallon were flying toward me, nails out and poised for destruction! I shoved the clock underneath the leg of a chair and pressed with all my might! I heard a CRACK!!…and then it was all over… It turned completely and utterly silent! The screaming stopped. The yelling, everything, had stopped!! The chaos had stopped! I looked around. Nothing moved, nothing breathed…not Guest, Gheddon, Genocist, Fallon or Giest! Even my mother had been frozen amid the Fallon assault. Her hand clenched around the Quetral stone and the other outstretched protecting her from the assailants. The wicked creatures hung motionless in the air above her with teeth barred and knife like nails inches from her flesh! Nearby, Francois DeBonairte was positioned like a maniacal mannequin, butcher knives brandished, defending the woman he loved. I'd never been so touched and repulsed at the same time! Countless masqueraders including the police were statue stiff! Their expressions embodied fear and confusion. Burt too was absolutely stationary. He was suspended in a mid-air dive position, arms reaching out for the time piece!

What had I done? I turned to witness the arrival of a massive wooden pirate ship! Its considerable size took up half of the auditorium. Bilge water steadily dripped from her starboard side. A modestly carved mermaid crested its bow. The vessel floated just below the ceiling all the while navigating toward the dance floor. It delicately squeezed by the enormous 16th century chandelier and in doing so, spontaneously lit the vast tiers of candles! Mightily moaning and groaning, she docked her barnacle covered hull. Cannons were peering out the blast doors, prepared to fire. The sails were unfurled and flailing in a nonexistent wind. A blue flag hung from its indomitable mast. I was startled by a booming voice! "Yous summoned?"

I swung around ready to fight! "What's happening here?" I stammered.

"Why, yous called the time benders, yous did!" He was dressed as a pirate…an honest to goodness in the flesh buccaneer! I peered past his shoulder and saw more shipmates exiting the boat. "Gevoricht is the name!" He thrust his hand out for a shake.

"What do I do?"

He stared at his hand and back at me. "Blyme! You shake it!"

"No, no," I said in frustration. "I mean, what do I do?"

His face scrunched up. "Why, YOUS called us! Our time clocks ain't come by cheap!" He turned to his crew to urge laughter.

"I'm serious. How does this work?"

He sensed urgency in my tone. Right then! "Yous got any Drexel?" he said gruffly.

"Drexel? What are they?" Explosive laughter erupted from his shipmates.

"Yous mean you don't know?" I just stood there waiting for him to continue. "Why money, of course. Where yous been? What's your name?" he hissed.

"Creed…Creed Griffon." I watched the old pirate stiffen up a bit.

"Do yous mean…I mean…well… You're He…Son of He…The Apprentice? Are yous? I mean… Well, of course," he said, looking down at the Trist. His eyebrows rose and he cleared his throat. "Uhh…well, I'm sorry for the outburst there. Yous look a little different from what I's remember…It's been a long time since you's been on my watch though…Special assignment you's were." A few of his crew gathered round. I saw one pirate draw the attention of another to my tattoo. "You see… Well, everyone, no not everyone… Most knows time benders…and how weez operates. Do yous knows what I mean? Well, ah no, I guess yous don't. I see. Okay, here's how it goes. We don't choose sides. Theys sort of chosen for us. Since yous the one that called, yous gets to choose which adversary to awaken."

"Then what?"

He looked back at his men and rolled his eyes. "Why, then yous barter for our services."

"I see. You want to be paid for your, your expertise."

That made him smile. "Now yous get it! Our 'services' ain't go cheap! Theys go to the highest bidder! For yous, we can restore everythings to the way it was. We can set time back before any of this happens."

"Will they remember anything?"

He looked insulted. "Of course theys won't remember nothing! We ain't a bunch of rookies!"

"What about my mom?"

"Yous mum? Well taken care of!"

"And her," I said, pointing to Isabelle. He gave me a sly smile while raising his eyebrows up and down.

"It's not what you think! I feel responsible for what happened to her!"

"We'll be sure she makes her grand entrance at the right time. Yous name will be cleared. I'll even throw in the photographer's camera as a parting gift!" I started to laugh until I noticed a few pirates wandering amongst the guest eyeing jewelry. One of the thieves took a ring right off a lady's finger! She stood immobile and oblivious while he removed the band and slipped it into his pocket! Another stole a watch off of a man's watch chain!

"I'm really not sure which adversary to wake up. I've only met one. Actually, he introduced himself. And I'm not too fond of seeing him again. Do I really have to wake Nakht? Things seem to be so much better when…"

Gevoricht came unglued! He burst out yelling! I took a step back. "Where is he that low down, no good, welcher!!! I'll make sure he rues the day he ever crossed Gevoricht! Why, he owes me ♌25 Drexel! Says he'll pay me come soon. But he never pays! I've been wantin' to get even with that low-down body snatcher!" He put both hands on his hips and lectured me on the evils of crossing a time bender. I looked around the room and just happened to notice a few more pirates slipping silverware and crystal into their bags. I feared if this situation were to take any longer, they would rob everyone blind! "Here's what weez gonna do," he said, slapping me on the shoulder. "I'll do yas a favor this time because…well, yous can understand. Forget Nakht! You can choose two companions to take with yas. Everyone one else will be set back to the time before yous entered Kendall Hall."

"How do you know all of this?" I asked. "I mean, how you do know where I've been, or anyone else for that matter?"

He burst out laughing! "All in a day's work, Creed. Yes, all in a day's work! Although I have to admit theys kept you pretty well hidden…Well then," he said wiping his eyes, "I understand yous have a journey to begin." What did he mean "journey to begin"? I'd done nothing but "journey" since I left Burton's house!

"I'll take Burt and my mom."

Gevoricht shook his head. "No boy! We've been instructed that she must stay here!"

"By whom?" I said harshly.

There was a challenge in his tone. I knew better than to push my luck. "Choose someone else!"

Of course, my next choice was Progerious. Although, I'd never tell that I'd chosen my mother and Burt over him, but I knew he'd understand. "I'll take Progerious."

"Good then, weez set!"

"Hey, wait a minute!" He turned sharply. "Can you tell me where Clancey is?"

He flashed mischievous smile. "That ole scalawag!? I'm confident you'll cross paths again! Look here, we must be about our work! I've broken enough rules for tonight!"

"What about your payment?" I asked.

"It looks like my men will find enough here to cover that."

"Wait!" I ran toward Clancey's satchel. "I'm sure he wouldn't mind." After a little bit of rummaging I sparked the old pirate's curiosity. "Will this do?" I held out the remaining Giest talon. His eyes became as huge as saucers! Speechless, he looked at me, then down at the talon.

"Fer me? Why, I couldn't! Yous just want a give it to me? Twas you that rid us of Buchenwald! And if I might say so, we're all the better for it! But, tis a rare and fine trophy...no...no...tis something yous earned." He seemed satisfied with his reasoning.

I wiped Clancey's blood off the tip. "Here," I said. "I'd like for you to have it." The room went completely silent! I could've sworn I saw a glint of tears in his eyes.

He gingerly removed it from my palm, then turned quickly! "All right, listens up! Puts everythings back yous stole! If I find one gem or even one gold tooth from this night, you'll be scraping barnacles off the hull for eternity! Catch!" In return he threw me a very small cloth bag. It felt like it contained a mixture of sand and cotton.

"What's this?"

"Secret family recipe." he whispered. "Tis filth of bunny!"

"What?!"

"You's know, small clumps of filth from under furnitures and in corners that ain't cleaned regular. Really boy, yous gotta gets out more!"

"So you're serious. This is filled with dust bunnies?"

"Of course I am! It's a combination of dirt, dead skin, lint, debris...Tis very valuable stuff! Sprinkle it on your traveling mates' heads and they'll wake right up from a time freeze! But that'll be our little secret." I nodded. "Now be quick! Yous must prepare for your journey!" He turned back to his men. "Okay, ya lot of dimwitted sea slugs, weez got work to do!!!!" I couldn't help but survey the scene. It was amazing! Sets of unmanned lifeboats were jettisoned from the main ship; they floated across the dance floor with oars rowing. What were they for? Then it hit me! How would my mom know I was safe? Quickly, I dug in my satchel for something to write with. Nothing! I scoured the ground and came upon an old pencil and sheet of music paper. I wish I could've written more, but under the circumstances I knew it was better if I didn't.

Mom,

I love you. Will be okay. Am with Progerious and Burton.

Creed

"What's takin yous so long, ya land lover?" Gevoricht startled me.

"Oh, I was just making sure I have everything for the journey."

"Then wake your friends! Yous must go. Yous seen enough!"

"Gevoricht?" I said hesitantly.

"Yez"

"Can you do me one last favor?"

"I'm listenin."

"Can you and your men arrange it so Professor Howelgood wins the trophy this year? I know Loremont cheated."

"Now him I knows about! Weez been watchin' that one for a long time! Bamboozler!! That's what that one is! Do yous want explosions or what?"

"You're serious? Yeah I guess you are. No, no, nothing like that...just please make sure Howelgood wins!" I said laughing.

The pirate removed his hat and thrust his hand out once more. I looked him in the eye and gave it a hearty shake. Then he hopped in a lifeboat and stood at the bow bellowing orders. I could see the talon hanging from a leather cord around his neck.

Thankfully, Progerious had been frozen next to my mother. His sharp teeth were exposed, ready to defend her from the Fallon attackers. Before I reached him, I slipped the note and pencil in her pocket, sprinkled the powder on him and waited.

His first words were, "Oh great! Not these bandits again!"

"Progerious, be quiet and help me wake Burt! We've got to go!"

"But they're holding the guests for ransom! Look at them! They've got everyone rounded up in the lifeboats! This is an outrage! I shall inform the Council of Methods and Procedures at once! Then it's off to the shadow lands or worse for the lot of them!"

"No, no, no, Progerious! They haven't stolen one thing! I promise! They're just putting everyone back to where they were an hour or two ago! I'll tell you later, but right now they don't want us around."

"Yeah, I bet," he muttered. I grabbed the bags and ran for Burt. There wasn't much dust left. As I touched him, he floated ever so slightly. His weightless body allowed me to put him back in the upright position. I turned the pouch upside down over his head. He woke instantly with a loud sneeze!

"What's happening? Why do I smell dirty socks?" His eyes panned the room from left to right. "Do you know we're being attacked by pirates?"

"Actually, they're on our side, buddy."

"Really? Can we stay and ask them some questions? This is a dream come true! I'd really like to…"

"No time for treasure hunting tips. They've asked us to leave. Grab your pack. It's time to go." I could feel Progerious' claws scale my leg and back. He perched himself atop my shoulder. "Progerious, meet my best friend, Burton Woods. Burton Woods, meet Progerious, our WayMaker. He is our friend and guide through the portals."

CHAPTER
TWENTY-TWO

Libraries are a Real Trip

"**S**o you're saying Clancey was me?"

"Yes! The night Mallanot and Vesh took you away, he shape shifted!" Burton looked overwhelmed...and a little violated.

"You know I heard about the Bandolix and the Giest! Way to go with the water phobia," he whispered. Of course being my best friend he didn't want to embarrass me in front of Progerious."

"Hey, how did they heal the Borraye bite anyway?" Suddenly, we found ourselves being severely reprimanded!

"Really you two! Would you like me to set out a picnic blanket with tea and cakes? Keep moving! We have no time to get reacquainted. We're being hunted! Remember? The time benders will be done shortly. It won't take 'our friends' too long to figure out what's happened. They are well acquainted with the work of time reversal. Most likely, they have scouts further out than what the pirates set their time restraints for!"

Burt leaned into me and spoke softly out of the side of his mouth, "He reminds me of your hamster. Except your hamster wasn't as..." I gave him a wide-eyed look and furiously shook my head no!

"He wasn't a warrior like Progerious!" I added loudly. Burt looked at me funny.

"Once those scouts realize they've had no contact with the spies on the inside, we're done for! There, turn left there!" yelled the ferret.

"Where are we going?" I asked.

"To Hollingsworth Library," he said.

"Do you think the chronicle is hidden in there?" I asked.

He sounded insulted. "Why no! Of course not! It holds a gateway. I don't know where your chronicle is! Never you mind that. First things first! We must get to the portal!"

We ran by several of Gevoricht's men. They were hard at work. Guests stood motionless inside floating row boats. His crew was carefully placing each one into posed positions like props. They were being put back to wherever they'd been two or more hours ago. We had a steady stride going until Burton skidded to a complete stop. "Creed?"

"Yeah Burt?"

"When did you get a tattoo?" He grabbed my arm and pulled up the sleeve. "Whoa!!! Cool!!! It moves!!!!"

"THAT'S IT!" Progerious yelled. "I've had it with the lot of ya! No more memory lane! No more extraneous chatter until we've made it to the gateway! Got it?"

He whipped around and in doing so flicked his tail in my face twice. Burt started laughing, but stopped abruptly once Progerious gave him the eye. I likened our ferret friend to a pint-sized Napoleon, but with a kind heart. Not that he'd admit any such thing. He was a little bossy, but he came highly recommended...and he had in fact, saved my life! Faithfully, he guided us through the twists and turns until we reached the Anvil wing. "I see the library!" exclaimed Burton! He ran to the door. Locked! Wait a minute! I began digging through the packs. I remembered seeing our special key ring at the bottom of one of them.

"There's no time," announced Progerious! "Take me to the doors!" I stopped what I was doing. "Kneel down," he yelled. I did as commanded. It placed him eye level with the door lock. He used his nail to fish inside the key hole for a second or two. Then he picked the lock clean open! "No time to congratulate me," he muttered. "Go!"

Cautiously, we stepped inside the vastness of the library. Diffuse moonlight filtered through the glass dome ceiling panels. I felt quite uneasy. "I encountered a Giest welcoming committee the last time I was here!" I announced. Burt was looking around, too.

"Don't turn on any lights," ordered Progerious! "I need you both to listen very carefully!" He jumped on top of the librarian's sixteenth-century writing desk. He would've suffered certain death had she seen him. The ferret paced back and forth until bumping into Mrs. Murtaugh's paperclip pot. His whiskers rapidly twitched while removing a few of the metal fasteners, along with a couple of pens, and pencils. He hurriedly shoved them in his pouch. Burt gave me a questioning stare. I slowly shook my head no and whispered, "Don't ask." "The gateway will open once we've secured the proper sequence. I need both of you to follow my directions to the letter! Remove that piece of cloth!" He pointed to a massive, intricately stitched, throw rug. It had been there as long as I could remember, purely for ornamental reasons, or so I'd thought. No one ever dared to walk across it except Mrs. Murtaugh. Everyone else just went around it. We did not question his directions. Burt and I followed orders. We claimed the same side of the carpet and started rolling it in the shape of a tube. Beneath it was the same intricate inlaid square patterns as the rest of the flooring. "You, over there," said Progerious! Burt ran to the square tile and stood. "You there!" I stood facing Burt on a separate row of tiles. "On the count of three I need you both to jump two tiles up! Do you understand?"

Burt and I looked at each other and responded, "Yes."

"You must land on your square at the same time! In doing so, you cannot touch any other tile! Are you ready?" We nodded. "Okay," said Progerious "ONE...TWO...THREE..." We jumped in unison! "So far so good. Now listen carefully," ordered Progerious! "Your next jumps will be done separately. Creed, you go first. Jump one space to the right." I did as instructed. "Burton two spaces to the left...or is it two spaces right," he mumbled. "No, no, I'm right," argued Progerious. "Burton, two spaces to the left." As soon as his feet hit the correct square, the tiles started to slowly move. They maneuvered up, down, side to side, just like a real tile puzzle! I held out my arms for balance. "Hold steady, men," commanded Progerious! He jumped from atop Mrs. Murtaugh's desk and landed between us. "You boys don't get seasick, do ya?"

Just as he finished his sentence, the tiles ceased to move. Instead, the walls which consisted of enormous archways began to rotate around us! It felt like I was standing fixed in the middle of a whirlwind! Not one book fell from their shelves! No mess was made! The structures continued to swirl at a steady pace. I managed to look down. The inlaid tiles had formed a picture of an open door beneath our feet. I remember thinking, *How did that get there*? I'd seen this doorway before, but where? I looked up just in time to realize the walls ceased to move. Everything appeared normal except for one massive archway. It no longer contained books from floor to ceiling. It was now a doorway that opened up to the outside. I glanced upward at the library's stained glass windows. Moonlight barely shined through them. I looked back at the archway... The gateway emitted bright daylight! But how could it be night and day in the same place? "Quickly," said Progerious! "Through the port door!" We grabbed our packs. I took one last look at the library. All was dark and quiet.

CHAPTER TWENTY-THREE

One Last Surprise

O ur journey began on a long dirt road. The sun shined brightly. The air was cold and crisp. Trees that lined the path were covered in red, gold, and orange leaves. We walked a long ways, but remained silent. It gave me time to ponder things. I finally placed the image of the library portal to that of the doorway picture on the underside of my wrist… However the image was now gone. I watched and waited for it to re-appear but, it did not. Progerious caught me examining my Trist a few times. So much had transpired; it was hard to know where to begin. Burt broke the silence. "Where are we anyways?"

"How many times must I tell you? We are on the road to Dendura," replied the ferret.

Burt sounded confused. "But it doesn't look much different from where we come from!"

Progerious jumped down from my shoulder and started walking upright on the path ahead of us. Vigilantly, he began sniffing the air from left to right as though he were searching for something. "That's because, in so many words, we have not left your world, my friend. We must travel through different gateways before the entrance to the great city is opened to us. Much like Hollingsworth archways spin, so does time and the different worlds that are bound by it. Gateways are doors in time…always opening and closing. We will ride the safest portals available to us.

Burt tried to interject. "Can't we just…"

"AND before we go playing twenty questions, once a gateway is closed, it cannot be accessed again until ready. But be patient, eventually another door will show itself available. You just have to know how to spot them."

"So we're not there?" I said incredulously! "I fought Fallons, Gheddons and Giests, not to mention a Bandolix, and we're not there?! It's like we're following some crazy bus schedule!"

"I swear, Apprentice!" spat the ferret. "Think tactics! We can't just ride the gateway any ole way we want! Our enemies will be searching for us via the obvious ports first. We'll have to take the back roads so to speak. We'll have less chance of getting caught this way. We may have a few stops here and there but rest assured, this will be safer than the direct route!" We watched as he gathered a small clump of dirt and leaves, molded them into a ball, then sniffed it. "Odd," he mumbled.

"Why did you choose this place then?" I asked.

"Frankly speaking, it wasn't my first choice" he said sounding somewhat concerned. "We hopped the closest opening available to us.

"But *you* just finished telling us we can't ride any ole port!" exclaimed Burt. "First of all, the port we used is not well known and I'd like to keep it that way! I'm hoping it closed up immediately after we transported! Actually, I had different door picked out entirely. But given the circumstances, it became painfully evident that we needed to escape Devonshire…Or were you unaware of that?! He raised his eyebrows in a condescending manner. "…So, we landed here, not necessarily the place of my choosing but I know it to be a rather inconspicuous platform. What I can't figure out is why our landing terminal didn't quite look as I remember, and it smells different too," he added curiously. "But we'll find our way around well enough." Suddenly, Progerious turned and faced us. "Shush!" His eyes searched the air. "I hear someone coming! Hurry! Over here!"

We jumped into a thicket of trees. The noise was getting louder. *Clip clop, clip clop, clip clop…* A horse-drawn carriage came into sight. I had never really seen such an authentic looking one except in my father's book collection. The old-fashioned carriage housed three male occupants, a driver and two passengers. But what was even more unique was their style of dress. They wore long-tailed shirt coats and big top hats.

"Where are we?" asked Burton.

"When are we?" I added. "It looks like they robbed Abraham Lincoln's wardrobe."

Progerious brushed the leaves from his tail. "I don't like this," he muttered. "Experience tells me we need to follow that carriage, but at a secure distance until we've figured out what's going on. If I'm not mistaken, we've landed far from where we're supposed to."

We readied our packs and carefully followed the sound of the horses. The dirt road seemed to go on forever. I was thankful it was flat. The trees continued to shroud the path. They provided a quick cover should anyone come from behind. The sound of the carriage ceased. We took refuge in yet another patch of foliage. Progerious was confident that the travelers had reached their destination. Cautiously, we emerged from our hideout and proceeded to walk the remainder of the way. We came upon a rather large brick wall that gated some sort of establishment. Its height obscured most of our view except for a wrought iron opening which had allowed the men passage. The carriage was stopped in front of a steep row of steps. They led to a set of ornate double doors. Other than the entrance, the brick wall masked the ground level view. However, it could not contain the turrets that reached high above them. They were beautiful and yet somehow cold and barren. Burton kept saying my name. "Creed…" I ignored him. Something was bothering me. "Creed…" This place, this castle. It was so new…and yet… "Creed!"

"What Burt?!"

"This is Devonshire Academy!!!!" It clicked. The annoying feeling of déjà vu left me. He was right! We were standing at the gates of Devonshire. However, this was not the 400-year-old version. Everything was new! The trees, the brick, the house…everything looked like it had recently been built! "It can't be," whispered the WayMaker. "That portal is not set for this location!"

Suddenly, a man in a black coat with tails and top hat exited the castle. He carried a gold-tipped cane over his shoulder. He said something to the driver before he got into the cab. They passed through the gates. Burton, Progerious and I dashed behind a cluster of trees. I saw another man on the path walking toward the carriage. He had a rifle slung over one shoulder and a dead rabbit in the other hand. The carriage stopped and the passenger got out to greet the hunter. I recognized the passenger instantly! I had memorized that face. I had stolen his picture from my mother's special album! There was no mistaking it….he was my father!

But how? Why? The gateway…Yes, it was the gateway! It had chosen to reunite us! I heard him laughing at something the hunter said. It struck me as funny. That was the first time I'd ever heard my father laugh. It was a warm laugh and I relished it. I was so thankful to find him…to see him! Would he recognize me? Would he understand? In the middle of their conversation, I emerged from my hiding place. Verbal warnings were flying out of Progerious' mouth. As I stepped on to the path, he caught sight of me. He stopped mid-laugh and canted his head. There was no denying the look of astonishment on his face. He said something to the hunter, who didn't look back. Instead, he immediately got inside the carriage. The horse was then prompted resulting in the coach being drawn back toward the house. My father stood on the path in front of me, waiting. He looked so young, robust, and full of life! It was all surreal. His eyes filled with tears. The astonished look was replaced by the most sincere expression. He removed his top hat and pressed it against his chest. I was drawn to him. I was home!

"Creed, my son?" I ran full speed and crashed into him! His hug was strong. His hug was safe. He hiccupped in between sobs. He had not wanted to cry in front of the hunter.

"Yes! It's me, Father…it's me!" He wiped the tears from his face. He looked so much like his picture…handsome with the world at his fingertips!

"You must tell me of your journey, my child! Did you bring friends, belongings, with you?" I nodded. "Well, go and get them! You shall stay with me! We shall have a most glorious celebration!" I turned and ran to get our satchels. Burt and Progerious stood awestruck on the path. I waved them in.

"Come on! Come on! We're okay!!" In the midst of running toward them, I heard a loud vehement string of indistinguishable words. I watched curiously as both my friends dove off the path. Without hesitation, earth shattering pillars of liquefied fire thundered all around me! I was knocked head first into the ground! Everywhere trees were engulfed in flames! I looked around confused. The bright sky turned grey. The dust began to settle. The only one left standing on the path was him.

"Why did you come here?" he screamed.

This must be a mistake, I thought! He thrust his hand toward me! I froze, unable to move! His power paralyzed me! I could feel intense pressure around my neck and chest. He was suffocating me! It was deliberate, sure, and unrelenting! I sensed the fury that swelled within him! It drove him...it empowered him! Fingers flared, palm up, he sharply snapped his wrist inward. Immediately, I felt an intense twisting pressure around my head and neck. I fought fiercely trying to counter my body's awkward contortions. Again he made the same forceful gesture. I knew he was going to break my neck. It was then that Progerious appeared out of nowhere! He flung a pile of burning leaf ash into the Genocent's eyes! I heard my father's screams of rage! Momentarily, I regained freedom of movement and gasped for air. I did the only thing I could during the diversion. I ran and hid behind a mound of dirt. Warm blood bubbled from my forehead. My neck felt as though I narrowly escaped the gallows. Why was he doing this? My mind raced! *What's going on? I don't understand?* But then, his bellowing voice erupted, maliciously taunting me to respond. Surely this could not be my father! My father loved me! He was a great man!

"Why did you come here, Creed?! You should never have come, unwanted spawn! Miscreant! I should've killed you, but she begged me! She begged me! And I gave in to her!" he shrieked.

Suddenly, Grapple... I remembered Grapple...the vision... the sobbing...I'd seen the past...she was begging for my life. Grapple tried to warn me! My father is to be my cause of death! "You will find no answers with me," he yelled! He spat each word with intense hatred. "But you, my precious son, have done me one small favor. Now I can simply dispose of you without having to search the world over!" My death warrant had been signed. *But why?* The ground beneath me trembled at his command!

I reached for the Quetral stone, wondering how come I'd not felt its warning of impending attack. Instead, the apple that hung from the snake's mouth produced a small glow of red light. Suddenly, turbulent gusts of wind began passing over me. I clung to anything I could for fear of being plucked right off of the ground. From my hiding place I snuck a quick peek. I witnessed the Genocent doing something very bizarre… He was stirring the air with his hand. And as he made this movement, a robust whirlwind of burning leaves rose up from the ground and began spinning in the same circular motion.

Subsequently, he breathed into the center of the flaming foliage. The revolutions became more chaotic and rapid as the funnel rose higher and higher. Unexpectedly the fiery fury began to take shape! And what travailed from its center was the most hellish creature I'd laid eyes on yet! It had the body of a muscular man wrapped in a ragged loin cloth. His skin was the color of clay soil and a matching scorpion's tail adorned his backside. Its face resembled that of a human but with long, boney, distorted features and an elongated chin. His eyes were like the eyes of a goat, piercing and evil. On top of his head were a set of scorpion claws that thrashed wildly whenever he roared. I ducked back down; I could hear slow footsteps drawing closer. "Did you really think your daddy missed you?" His laughter curdled my blood! "I should've killed you when I had the chance!" My mother's words ran through my brain: *I had all that I needed*. What did she mean?

The chronicle was nowhere! Would it really matter? It was my only defense against his malicious magic. And then I remembered her words in the pit, "You've ALWAYS had what you needed." That's it! I grabbed a rock.

"Creed!!!" Burton's screams were horrific! "Don't come out! He'll kill you!" I tore the stone from my neck and ran to meet them on the path. Burton was being held upside down by the monstrous beast. His fanged teeth gnashed inches from Burt's flesh! I saw no sign of Progerious.

"Let him go!" I shouted. Hologram stood stone-faced. He had actually put his top hat back on!

"I do not think you are in a position to barter." I looked down at my Trist, then back at him. I saw a glimmer of fear in those eyes. He searched for my other hand, but it clenched the rock in my pocket. "It is possible that I've underestimated your powers, son…I am not afraid of you," he added calmly. Proudly, he removed his coat and set it aside neatly. He unbuttoned his shirt being careful not to take his eyes off me. I watched him reveal a most extraordinary Trist. He displayed each arm for me as though he were some sort of magician. "Nothing up my sleeves!" he said menacingly. The purple scrolling saturated both arms front and back. It encompassed his neck, chest, and torso. Every mark, every symbol, every hint of the tattoo squirmed and squiggled. He stood completely still but his skin didn't. It was unnerving to look at. I got past the motility of the overall branding and began to look at it in more detail. I was struck by horrific scenes of ghastly creatures hidden amidst the distinctive designs. They lay buried within the artistry of the picture. It was like staring at optical illusion art at the mall…until you finally discover the picture within the picture!

I caught a glimpse of something moving along the back of his arm but couldn't be sure. As it rounded the front side my suspicions were confirmed. Its massive girth grew to three times the size of his extremity. Its grisly form was olive green overlaid with black splotches. Eerily the snake's thick rubbery body weaved its way upwards. *But where had it come from?* The Genocent remained totally calm as the beast ritualistically encircled his neck twice. The head and tail came to rest on the collar bone closest to each. Just before laying its head down, the demon buried its monstrous fangs deep in his chest. The Genocent did not flinch. He closed his eyes and breathed in slowly. After comfortably positioning itself upon its throne, the hideous reptile transformed from a living creature into a mere image. It simply melted into his skin and became nothing more than a drawing in his ghastly tattoo! He waited for my reaction. I gave none. Quickly, he bent his arm at the elbow. I made a slight flinch. I took notice that even his fingers were saturated with marks. With a flick of the wrist, he spoke these words: "TEVENDORE ABBADINOT!" The grotesque scorpion ogre instantaneously disappeared. Burton fell to the ground with a thud! I knew not to make any sudden moves. I tried to buy time.

"Why are you doing this? We can be a powerful team!"

"I do not need your power," he hissed! "Do you not have eyes?! I need my chronicle! But it is obvious to me that you've already gotten to it!"

"You don't need it anymore!"

"Where did you hide it? I knew she'd stolen it! The little liar! I've been searching EVERYWHERE and all this time YOU had it!!"

"If I show you, will you let us go?"

His expression lightened and his voice turned sweet. "Of course, my son!" His response was cool and insincere. I knew he was lying, but this was my only chance.

"It is in my backpack over there."

Without words, he simply looked in the direction of my satchel and it flew to his hands. I eyed Burton. Progerious stood carefully fixed behind Holgraham. While he was intently searching the bag, I dropped the Quetral stone to the ground. With one powerful blow, I fell to my knees and struck the talisman with the rock. A burst of red light exploded from the pendant. The molten fragments pierced my arm and shoulder. I could hear Holgraham's screams of rage! "NOOoooooo!!!"

My surroundings were gone! No Genocent, Burton, Way-Maker or school…No ground, no trees, or sky…. I was encircled by a flaming whirlwind of blinding white fire! Spontaneously it detonated crackling and popping upwards! It began revolving around me with an angry ferocity. A tornadic force tore me from the ground and held me captive mid air, arms outstretched body dangling. Furiously, I tried pulling my arms down to my sides but they would not budge! A small, thick, brown book appeared. It was somewhat worn, and its spine lightly tattered. *This is the chronicle?* I thought to myself.

Unfortunately, there was no time to consider the possibility. The cover flung open and pages began madly ripping themselves from the binding. Thunder cracked and snarled announcing the escaping sheets' freedom! The first few took the shape of cylindrical instruments. They twisted and rolled forming a long thin body with a "v" shaped tip. Other pages folded themselves into bizarre looking spiders, birds, trees, snakes... whatever could be summoned was. Upon their completion, I realized that each creature or object broke the barriers of the firewall and disappeared to the world outside. I was overcome by fear! It was a set up!!! "Burton! Progerious! Look out!" I screamed. "They're coming!!!!"

Again I was alone with the chronicle! No more creatures, just a rotating wall of flames and relentless winds. A resonating hissing sound filled my ears. It was accompanied by a flapping noise that stirred the already active storm. From the outside world, passing through the blazing wall came a winged serpent poised to strike! It shot through the inferno, pupils narrowed, spiny wings thrashing! Effortlessly, it metamorphosized from a simple paper reptile to a real live, in the flesh snake! It was vibrantly embellished with red and yellow markings layered atop a black winged body. I couldn't believe my eyes! Fearlessly the snake barreled toward me! Scales glistening, it slithered rapidly through the havoc.

I was petrified but fully aware that I was the intended target! It raced toward me fueled by the pinions of hell's fury. Its sinewy body landed then clutched and coiled the length of my arm! Purposefully, it paused and looked up at me… then sunk its fiery fangs into my arm! Head convulsing, tail wriggling, and wings flapping against my skin…I howled in tortuous agony! The serpent's black eyes glowed then fluttered dramatically losing itself in blissful splendor. I couldn't contain my screams! Excruciating pain!!! It was as if a thousand icy razors were being injected into my flesh! Within seconds the snake seizured backwards, and then disintegrated leaving behind two small puncture wounds! Seeping out of the two holes was a sea of black venom. It puddled, pooled, and trickled, waiting to waft into the depths of my skin.

Without hesitation and through the scorching barricade shot a pint sized paper dragon. Its crimson color was magnificently ornamented with elaborate black pigment outlining layers upon layers of fleshy scales. Instantly, the creature took to the air above me all the while brandishing an array of miniature spiked armor that adorned its back and tail. With one deafening shriek, its inanimate shape gave way to living breathing flesh! With each pass the demon grew bigger and bigger. Its stealthy musculature moved and glided like a well oiled machine. Instinctively, I began yanking wildly against the invisible restraints! Meanwhile the dragon's gargantuan body struggled to stay inside the confines of the barricade! In disbelief I realized, it was flying menacingly closer. The fierce talons that tipped both hands and feet were not easily missed. After the third loop it plummeted unexpectedly, intentionally finding itself within a few yards of my situation. Such an ominous presence commanded nothing but fear and trepidation. The demon's agile wings beat proudly against its broad chest. Smoke rising from the nostrils buried in its massive head produced steady plumes.

No!!! This is unbelievable! I didn't make it this far to have it end like this! Sinister red eyes actively studied me from beneath a set of spiked horns. Its pupils narrowed forming thin slits. With a keen sense of understanding, the beast carefully observed my disposition at bay. Regardless, and in spite of my relentless attempts, it knew as well as I that there would be no escaping. I hung helpless suspended in the crucifix position unable to reach the ground. Without provocation the creature sprung open its razor filled jaws! I was given no choice but to stare down its pink fleshy gullet. Saliva drippings beaded and fell from the roof of its mouth! I knew I was destined for a painful death.

Frantically I tried recalling what little magic I knew. But it was too late! Shell shocked and confused, the words did not come… I held my head high and gazed into the dragon's face…but instead of the unthinkable, it did something completely unexpected… Savagely its head snapped to the side. Cylindrical instruments were flooding the area. Each spindly body produced a primitive pen donning a quill. Two by two they flew points in and plumes out. In doing so they constituted a makeshift set of wings. Quick as a flash the dragon took flight! Bursts of fire exploded and crackled all around me! Its gnashing teeth gleaned the air while its mouth spewed volcanic flames! Pieces of its victims…feathers and ashes fell to the ground. The demon was preventing them from reaching me!!! *But why?* It didn't take long to figure out.

Regardless of the beast's fierce efforts, legions of new recruits broke the barrier and saturated the enclosure. There were just too many! Thoroughly enraged the monster continued its erratic flight. But it couldn't kill them all. Those that managed to evade annihilation hurriedly dipped themselves in the puddling snake venom! They absorbed various strands of the poison twirling and teasing it around their tips like strings of spaghetti. In return, each venom filled instrument struck my arm with sharp slashing movements inscribing me with their sacred ink. But it wasn't over!

The pages kept coming forming new beings, hungry to give up their secrets. Miraculously, all transformed from paper into living breathing creatures. One after the other, dwellers of the air and earth broke through the molten barrier prepared to elude an evil outcome.

Carefully, the beast hovered and waited ready to devour anything that came near me! Those that evaded such a fate frantically blindsided me trying desperately to impart their knowledge. I could feel myself ready to pass out from the pain. I was bitten, stung, struck, and tattooed by those whom the predator failed to slay. And then…all was abnormally quiet…peacefully quiet…Opening my eyes, I discovered that I was alone with the chronicle again, and I was afraid. The dragon had disappeared! The book's inhabitants were nowhere to be found! Were they hiding on the other side of the barrier? I didn't know…The flaming whirlwind continued to maintain its rapid speeds. Immediately, I tried determining if anything was broken. It was at that moment, I caught sight of something else emerging from the chronicle's pages. It was neither flesh nor paper. Gracefully it maneuvered through the air without form. As it drew near, I realized it was a small body of crystal blue water. The liquid tranquilly rolled and glided its way toward me. It was strange to see water floating! I'd determined there was nothing inside just a few bubbles and kelp. When it was within arms' reach it began to swirl and sway. A funnel formed from its center. Gracefully the water peaked higher and higher until it molded into the shape of a girl about my age. She was not of flesh and bone but completely comprised of transparent sapphire water! She was mysteriously beautiful. Her long emerald lochs were made of kelp. They flowed and tussled around her face and body. Instead of legs, she was held upright by a pillar formed from the remaining liquid. Her movements were slow and serene as though she were still under water.

"Is it…is it over?" I asked. But she did not answer. She simply gazed upon me in a most soothing fashion. "Can you talk?" Slowly, she shook her head no. "Well then please, can you help me get down from here?" Once again I received the same response. Something was wrong. I remembered a similar conversation I'd had with a mer-girl in Grapple's room. I also recalled his warning.

"Well if you can't get me down, can you tell me…?" I stopped short when noticing that her delicate features were shifting. Her transparent eyes turned stark white while piranha type teeth burst out of her mouth! Her long soft hair had been replaced by a swarm of horrific yellow eels! They viciously snapped and lunged at me! She wasted no time and darted over to my tightly bound arm. I could do nothing but watch! Her mouth greedily opened preparing to inflict a generous amount of pain. But before she could think to take her first bite, the eels began awkwardly flailing about her face. It appeared as though they were trying to yank her backwards with their awkward movements. The hag's eyes ominously rolled upward. Her expression was one of fear as she withdrew from the intended assault.

Unexpectedly, the fierce winds and fiery barricade began to churn and rotate in reverse. Something worse was about to happen! The fire was snuffed out and the barrier turned dark grey. Its winds continued to accelerate and emit a loud hissing sound. Swiftly, the funnel cloud including all of the devastation it had produced began to liquefy creating a tumultuous wall of water. Powerless, the sea hag somersaulted backwards melting into water vapor as she went. She violently swirled and spun around me! Inevitably, she joined the blurred images of the chronicle's creations both paper and flesh, as they too were prisoners of the water's tidal wave force! From within the spiraling chaos, a colossal figure began to take shape. Slowly the water wound round and round closing in tighter and tighter. "Why does it have to be water?" I moaned. I knew I had no culpie root to save me. It continued encircling and slithering providing subtle hints as to its deceptive masquerade. I saw the creature's eye's first. They were icy cold ruby red slits glaring down from on high. The sides of its neck abruptly flared in a cobra like manner as its liquid coils suddenly stood on end! Without hesitation the beast furiously lurched forward preparing to strike! Its body undulated up and down gaining momentum with each motion. I scrunched my eyes tight! Deafening detonations and sonic blasts filled the air! Then all at once, it was utterly silent! Not a sound was heard except the beating of my heart. I peeked just as the wall of water exploded upward... And before I could capture my breath everything vanished!

Chards of memories shattered my conscious thought! They drowned me in merciless confusion! It felt like I was somehow waking up for the very first time! The memories... they were coming at supersonic speeds! It was impossible to make sense of them all at once! In my mind's eye, I was watching fragments of my life on a hyper drive fast forward screen... Everything I'd ever thought....wasn't... but was...Bits and pieces of trivial information, snapshots from a forgotten past pasted themselves amongst my current memories....faces...places...words...Oh I saw Egypt...in all of its glorious splendor! I saw flashes of myself going about daily Egyptian life. It seemed so common place that it would've been boring except for my current situation. I caught a glimpse of myself playing a game of Senet with another boy by the Nile River. I didn't even know I knew what Senet was until that moment! Despite the shock, it was definitely me. I looked so strange in Egyptian garb. But the other me didn't seem to care. At the same time, I could remember my present life! It was as though I had two people living within me and each set of memories were struggling for dominance over their counterparts. Which recollections do I believe? Which person am I supposed to be? The more revelations I tried to acknowledge, the more intense it became. Without warning, the invisible restraints released me. I fell to the ground and lay there. The feelings were overwhelming. They were maddening! But they still kept coming.

And then, amidst the disheveled memories, I heard a voice. I did not see who it belonged to. I already knew... I saw the temple where she'd been searching for him. It was my mother... and she was calling his name, "Denegaul? Denegaul? Denegaul? Where are you? It's time to come home son."

I cried out with legendary force..."LEAVE ME ALONE! GO AWAY! GO AWAY! YOU LIE!!!! YOU LIAR!!!!!!" Burt's wails of panic somehow comforted me.

"CREED!!!!" Burton screamed. "Hold on! CREED!!!! It will be okay! Give it time! Do you hear me?"

Progerious shouted, "Don't touch him!" And then it was over.

I lay on the ground clutching the Quetral stone. I was throbbing everywhere. "Did they hurt you?" I said gasping for air. "Are you both okay?" My left arm felt like it was on fire! My chest stung so bad I could barely speak! The whirlwind was gone. The colorful leaves came into focus. They blew softly in the breeze untouched in the aftermath. I hurt everywhere.

Burton and Progerious knelt next to me. Burt lifted my head from the ground. "We're both okay...He's gone, Creed! When you broke the stone, he was thrown back about two hundred yards! And then he vanished! Call me crazy... I know there was a lot going on, but I think he drew a door and disappeared inside of it!" Progerious pulled something from my pack and brought it over to me.

"Drink, Son of He."

I rebuffed that name. "I am not his son!"

"Control your tongue!" spat the ferret. "First of all, that most certainly was NOT your father! Surely it was a shape shifting imposter, sent to fool the unsuspecting. Didn't you see the color of his markings not to mention his horrific actions? And you!" he said glaring at Burt. "Do you realize what you're saying?! Intentional portal tampering is not only illegal, it is next to impossible! You can't just arbitrarily pick any spot and open your own gateway! Get your eyes checked! Everyone must use the approved transportation system! That way no one gets hurt!" He was so fired up that he briskly spun himself around to face me. I was ready for him.

"But Clancey and I did just that down in the fathoms!"

"No you didn't!" argued the Ferret! "Are you telling me, a WayMaker from kithood, that Clancey just zippered open a doorway and interfered with port transference? No! He engaged a known portal that has been mapped and in use for thousands upon thousands of years! Let me guess…Upstairs bedroom, dresser drawer stack up. Right?

"Get a hold of yourselves! Don't fall prey to any of their tricks! The Genocent would never be involved with heinous acts such as these! Do you hear me?" He looked down at my arm quizzically. My shirt was shredded. No longer was the tattoo bound by my wrist. It climbed past my cuff, up my arm, and crossed over my heart and collar bone.

"That's strange," muttered the ferret. "I've seen the real Genocent's markings and they cover so much more …!"

"Never mind all that," Burton said harshly! "Can't you see he needs rest?!"

"Huh? Oh yes, of course. You're right. It's just that….Well, never mind. I know of just the place, but we will have to wait a bit before gaining entrance." replied the WayMaker. "For now, we must move him to a safer spot."

I put an arm around Burt's shoulder. He helped me to stand, and then walk. They listened intensely as I recalled my amazing yet painful experience. I told them of the inscription process. I spoke of the dragon and how it had tried to prevent me from receiving the knowledge.

"Obviously sent by that wicked shape shifting demon!" interjected the ferret. I was about to inform them of who's voice I'd heard calling for Denegaul when Progerious began yelling.

"Blasphemy, lies, lies, lies, planted by that unscrupulous imposter! I will not listen to such dark lies! And you best not listen to them either!!!! Know this, Apprentice, neither your father nor your mother would ever do anything to harm you!!!..." And he stormed off ahead of us fur ruffled and tail at attention. As soon as he was out of earshot Burton spoke up. "If no one was tampering with the portals, then how does he explain us landing in this place?" "I don't know," I said solemnly. I agreed about the lies… And yes the portal tampering, and the fact that the ritual had been sabotaged, but in my heart of hearts I was certain that I'd been attacked by my father and no one else. I felt his limitless power. And nothing thus far had even come close to it. I was positive that it *was* him. I think Burt was, too. But trying to convince Progerious of this fact would've been like trying to describe the color blue to a blind person…you simply can't find the right words.

CHAPTER
TWENTY-FOUR

Do Unto Others

We were able to hide in the woods outside of Devonshire. The Genocent's attack had been brutal. I wiped the blood from my forehead. If it weren't for his beloved talisman...I would've died. His own magic had protected me! Progerious and Burt kept watch while I lay still gazing up at the sky. It offered me no peace. I was very weak and sore all over. I rotated the Quetral stone between my fingers. The red apple that once hung from the snake's mouth was gone. The mark I'd received from it no longer confined itself to my wrist. Upon contact with the chronicle, my left arm and part of my upper torso were saturated with endless strings of elaborate markings.

I studied the tattoo in detail. It resembled a living, fluid kaleidoscope. Each pattern *amoebically* motored below my skin sometimes completely disappearing and resurfacing a short distance later. A sharp pain whisked me back to reality. The tattoo continued to throb and sting with great force. At times the pain would peak and leave me feeling nauseous. My mind was in turmoil. Holgraham's tattoo encompassed so much of his body... As of yet, I saw no images in my tattoo, just symbols with unknown meanings. I was thankful that they didn't create horrific depictions like I'd seen in the Genocent's branding. Even so, I found no comfort in their cryptic appearance.

Could I remember my first past? The fact that I was sure I had more than one was a breakthrough. But truthfully, the majority of memories were slurried with shreds of insignificant details, heavily fragmented, and for the most part, hazy. Overall I'd regained short clips, recollections of inexplicable events, words, mysterious faces, and places. But where does one begin to know how to put it all together? What pieces do you choose to finish a picture from a puzzle you've never seen before? I didn't want to think about it and talking about it only fueled controversy.

I was willing to accept that *not* everything restored to my memory was factual. I knew my mother would have nothing to do with Denegaul. It was the Genocent who had sent the dragon and the sea hag in after me. He had done so in a last ditch effort to prevent me from receiving the full knowledge…hence my partial Trist. If he had gone to all that trouble, then why wouldn't he add lies to my memories? Why not help splinter my trust in those I cared about? But what other lies had been implanted? Which ones were real and which ones weren't? Regardless, the monumental let down was that I still remained a mystery to me… There were no solid answers, only more questions.

I knew it wasn't over. I tried to shake my thoughts. Survival mode was where I needed to stay. But my mind wouldn't leave it alone. And what about Clancey? Things didn't turn out the way he'd explained. Fueled by a mixture of anger, resentment, and mental chaos, I was unable to rest. I thought the chronicle was supposed to enlighten me not make things worse! Clancey had warned me to be afraid of Denegaul and his henchman, not my own flesh and blood! Why hadn't my own mother cautioned me?! I fumbled with the talisman in my pocket. All these years I thought he was dead! I thought I was missing something because I didn't have a dad! And the moment I discover he's alive, he's willing to kill me for a stupid stone! What a cruel joke!

While the sun fell below the horizon two men emerged from the house. They stepped inside a waiting carriage. Suddenly, the maid came running down the steps! "Sir Wingate, Sir Wingate!" She was holding his scarf in her hand. He accepted the gesture graciously. It was Sir Wingate Devonshire in the flesh! I knew of him only through school lore and a few old oil portraits I'd seen. I felt sorry for him. Eventually, the love of his life would shun him. He'd turn to his work for satisfaction and wind up a lonely recluse in the confines of the castle. Progerious began gathering the packs. "I think we're safe to go now."

Burton braced me as we walked. "Where are we headed?" I asked.

"To the tunnels below the school…I mean house… You know what I mean! You men will find much needed respite there. I'll make sure to secure food."

Carefully, we walked the trail that led to the front entrance of Devonshire. The lights of the Great Hall scarcely lit the grounds. It was beautiful, but very strange and empty. Its newness fascinated me. At the same time, it took my mind off the betrayal I felt. I was so angry! I was standing at the crossroads of love and hate, a pathway often hindered by head versus heart. As we carefully walked the grounds it was clear that some of the out buildings hadn't even been constructed yet. Our guide led us hastily toward what was yet to be Mendel Greenhouse. The further we strayed from the main house, the darker it became. We arrived at a small potting shed. Progerious stood ready to usher us inside. "There's an entrance that leads to the tunnels in here. Come, Apprentice, you have lost blood! You need rest!"

"You okay, Buddy?" I couldn't hide my anger from my best

friend. I think he knew what I was feeling and in some small way, he could relate. For whatever it was worth that brought me consolation. I paused briefly, trying to make sense of it all, but my reply ended up coming out all wrong.

"I thought things would be so different! I'm sorry you got involved in this mess! I almost got you killed…I took you away from your mom! And for what? So you could watch my father turn on me? It's no good! I can't go back. It's too late for me. But if you'd like to return home, to your real home, then I'll have Progerious guide your way. I don't want anyone getting hurt because of me."

"And what will you do?" asked Burton.

My answer was swift. "I'm going to find the man that calls himself the Genocent and do unto him, before he does unto me."

Burt spoke without hesitation. "I'm in man, let's go."

CPSIA information can be obtained at www.ICGtesting.com
Printed in the USA
LVOW080551051212

309942LV00001B/9/P